THE LEGEND of SLEEPY HOLLOW and OTHER TALES

The Legend of Sleepy Hollow and Other Tales

Washington Irving

Illustrations by Arthur Rackham
Afterword by Haskell Springer

THE WORLD'S BEST READING

The Reader's Digest Association, Inc.
Pleasantville, N.Y. • Montreal

The Legend of Sleepy Hollow and Other Tales

Color illustrations by Arthur Rackham courtesy of Images Colour
Library Ltd., England.

Story openers, a detail from a line drawing by Arthur Rackham: pages 13, 49,
61, 83, 87, 171, 173, 178, 190, 195, 204, 210, 218, 226, 251.

Line drawings by Arthur Rackham: pages 14, 21, 28–29, 31, 36, 46, 47, 81,
86 (detail), 177, 189 (detail), 194, 209, 225 (detail), 250 (detail).

Line drawings by Lars and Lois Hokanson: pages 54, 59, 64–65, 71, 95, 104,
121, 140, 168, 172, 203, 217.

Library of Congress Catalog Card Number 86-62660
ISBN 0-89577-255-8

Printed in the United States of America

Reader's Digest Fund for the Blind is publisher of
the Large-Type Edition of *Reader's Digest*. For
subscription information about this magazine,
please contact Reader's Digest Fund for the
Blind, Inc., Dept. 250, Pleasantville, N.Y. 10570.

Contents

Illustrations

The Legend of Sleepy Hollow

FOUND AMONG THE PAPERS OF THE LATE DIEDRICH KNICKERBOCKER

A pleasing land of drowsy head it was,
Of dreams that wave before the half-shut eye;
And of gay castles in the clouds that pass,
For ever flushing round a summer sky.
— CASTLE OF INDOLENCE

In the bosom of one of those spacious coves which indent the eastern shore of the Hudson, at that broad expansion of the river denominated by the ancient Dutch navigators the Tappan Zee, and where they always prudently shortened sail, and implored the protection of St. Nicholas when they crossed, there lies a small market-town or rural port, which by some is called Greensburgh, but which is more generally and properly known by the name of Tarry Town. This name was given, we are told, in former days, by the good housewives of the adjacent country, from the inveterate propensity of their husbands to linger about the village tavern on market-days. Be that as it may, I do not vouch for the fact, but merely advert to it for the sake of being precise and authentic. Not far from this village, perhaps about two miles, there is a little valley, or rather lap of land, among high hills, which is one of the quietest places in the whole world. A small brook glides through it, with just murmur enough to lull one to repose; and the occasional whistle of a quail, or tapping of a woodpecker, is almost the only sound that ever breaks in upon the uniform tranquillity.

I recollect that, when a stripling, my first exploit in squirrel-shooting was in a grove of tall walnut-trees that shades one side of the valley. I had wandered into it at noon-time, when all nature is particularly quiet, and was startled by the roar of my own gun, as it broke the Sabbath stillness around, and was prolonged and reverberated by the angry echoes. If ever I should wish for a retreat, whither I might steal from the world and its distractions, and dream quietly away the remnant of a troubled life, I know of none more promising than this little valley.

From the listless repose of the place, and the peculiar character of its inhabitants, who are descendants from the original Dutch settlers, this sequestered glen has long been known by the name of SLEEPY HOLLOW, and its rustic lads are called the Sleepy Hollow Boys throughout all the neighboring country. A drowsy, dreamy influence seems to hang over the land, and to pervade the very atmosphere. Some say that the place was bewitched by a high German doctor, during the early days of the settlement; others, that an old Indian chief, the prophet or wizard of his tribe, held his pow-wows there before the country was discovered by Master Hendrick Hudson. Certain it is, the place still continues under the sway of some bewitching power, that holds a spell over the minds of the good people, causing them to walk in a continual reverie. They are given to all kinds of marvellous beliefs; are subject to trances and visions; and frequently see strange sights, and hear music and voices in the air. The whole neighborhood abounds with local tales, haunted spots, and twilight superstitions; stars shoot and meteors glare oftener across the valley than in any other part of the country, and the nightmare, with her whole ninefold, seems to make it the favorite scene of her gambols.

The dominant spirit, however, that haunts this enchanted region, and seems to be commander-in-chief of all the powers of the air, is the apparition of a figure on horseback without a head. It is said by some to be the ghost of a Hessian trooper, whose head had been carried away by a cannon-ball, in some nameless battle during the Revolutionary War, and who is ever and anon seen by the country folk, hurrying along in the gloom of night, as if on the wings of the wind. His haunts are not confined to the valley, but extend at times to the adjacent roads, and especially to the vicinity of a church at no great distance. Indeed, certain of the most authentic historians of those parts, who have been careful in collecting and collating the floating facts concerning this spectre, allege that the body of the trooper, having been buried in the churchyard, the ghost rides forth to the scene of battle in nightly quest of his head; and that the rushing speed with which he sometimes passes along the

Hollow, like a midnight blast, is owing to his being belated, and in a hurry to get back to the churchyard before day-break.

Such is the general purport of this legendary superstition, which has furnished materials for many a wild story in that region of shadows; and the spectre is known, at all the country firesides, by the name of the Headless Horseman of Sleepy Hollow.

It is remarkable that the visionary propensity I have mentioned is not confined to the native inhabitants of the valley, but is unconsciously imbibed by every one who resides there for a time. However wide awake they may have been before they entered that sleepy region, they are sure, in a little time, to inhale the witching influence of the air, and begin to grow imaginative, to dream dreams, and see apparitions.

I mention this peaceful spot with all possible laud; for it is in such little retired Dutch valleys, found here and there embosomed in the great State of New York, that population, manners, and customs remain fixed; while the great torrent of migration and improvement, which is making such incessant changes in other parts of this restless country, sweeps by them unobserved. They are like those little nooks of still water which border a rapid stream; where we may see the straw and bubble riding quietly at anchor, or slowly revolving in their mimic harbor, undisturbed by the rush of the passing current. Though many years have elapsed since I trod the drowsy shades of Sleepy Hollow, yet I question whether I should not still find the same trees and the same families vegetating in its sheltered bosom.

In this by-place of nature, there abode, in a remote period of American history, that is to say, some thirty years since, a worthy wight of the name of Ichabod Crane; who sojourned, or, as he expressed it, "tarried," in Sleepy Hollow, for the purpose of instructing the children of the vicinity. He was a native of Connecticut, a State which supplies the Union with pioneers for the mind as well as for the forest, and sends forth yearly its legions of frontier woodsmen and country schoolmasters. The cognomen of Crane was not inapplicable to his person. He was tall, but exceedingly lank, with narrow shoulders, long arms and legs, hands that dangled a mile out of his sleeves, feet that might have served for shovels, and his whole frame most loosely hung together. His head was small, and flat at top, with huge ears, large green glassy eyes, and a long snipe nose, so that it looked like a weathercock perched upon his spindle neck, to tell which way the wind blew. To see him striding along the profile of a hill on a windy day, with his clothes bagging and fluttering about him, one might have mistaken him for the genius of famine descending upon the earth, or some scarecrow eloped from a corn-field.

His school-house was a low building of one large room, rudely constructed of logs; the windows partly glazed, and partly patched with leaves of old copy-books. It was most ingeniously secured at vacant hours by a withe twisted in the handle of the door, and stakes set against the window-shutters; so that, though a thief might get in with perfect ease, he would find some embarrassment in getting out: an idea most probably borrowed by the architect, Yost Van Houten, from the mystery of an eel-pot. The school-house stood in a rather lonely but pleasant situation, just at the foot of a woody hill, with a brook running close by, and a formidable birch-tree growing at one end of it. From hence the low murmur of his pupils' voices, conning over their lessons, might be heard on a drowsy summer's day, like the hum of a bee-hive; interrupted now and then by the authoritative voice of the master, in the tone of menace or command; or, peradventure, by the appalling sound of the birch, as he urged some tardy loiterer along the flowery path of knowledge. Truth to say, he was a conscientious man, and ever bore in mind the golden maxim, "Spare the rod and spoil the child."—Ichabod Crane's scholars certainly were not spoiled.

I would not have it imagined, however, that he was one of those cruel

potentates of the school, who joy in the smart of their subjects; on the contrary, he administered justice with discrimination rather than severity, taking the burden off the backs of the weak, and laying it on those of the strong. Your mere puny stripling, that winced at the least flourish of the rod, was passed by with indulgence; but the claims of justice were satisfied by inflicting a double portion on some little, tough, wrong-headed, broad-skirted Dutch urchin, who sulked and swelled and grew dogged and sullen beneath the birch. All this he called "doing his duty" by their parents; and he never inflicted a chastisement without following it by the assurance, so consolatory to the smarting urchin, that "he would remember it, and thank him for it the longest day he had to live."

When school-hours were over, he was even the companion and play-mate of the larger boys; and on holiday afternoons would convoy some of the smaller ones home, who happened to have pretty sisters, or good housewives for mothers, noted for the comforts of the cupboard. Indeed it behooved him to keep on good terms with his pupils. The revenue arising from his school was small, and would have been scarcely sufficient to furnish him with daily bread, for he was a huge feeder, and, though lank, had the dilating powers of an anaconda; but to help out his maintenance, he was, according to country custom in those parts, boarded and lodged at the houses of the farmers, whose children he instructed. With these he lived successively a week at a time; thus going the rounds of the neighborhood, with all his worldly effects tied up in a cotton handkerchief.

That all this might not be too onerous on the purses of his rustic patrons, who are apt to consider the costs of schooling a grievous burden, and schoolmasters as mere drones, he had various ways of rendering himself both useful and agreeable. He assisted the farmers occasionally in the lighter labors of their farms; helped to make hay; mended the fences; took the horses to water; drove the cows from pasture; and cut wood for the winter fire. He laid aside, too, all the dominant dignity and absolute sway with which he lorded it in his little empire, the school, and became wonderfully gentle and ingratiating. He found favor in the eyes of the mothers, by petting the children, particularly the youngest; and like the lion bold, which whilom so magnanimously the lamb did hold, he would sit with a child on one knee, and rock a cradle with his foot for whole hours together.

In addition to his other vocations, he was the singing-master of the neighborhood, and picked up many bright shillings by instructing the young folks in psalmody. It was a matter of no little vanity to him, on Sundays, to take his station in front of the church-gallery, with a band of chosen singers; where, in his own mind, he completely carried away the palm from the parson. Certain it is, his voice resounded far above all the rest of the congregation; and there are peculiar quavers still to be heard in that church, and which may even be heard half a mile off, quite to the opposite side of the mill-pond, on a still Sunday morning, which are said to be legitimately descended from the nose of Ichabod Crane. Thus, by divers little makeshifts in that ingenious way which is commonly denominated "by hook and by crook," the worthy pedagogue got on tolerably enough, and was thought, by all who understood nothing of the labor of headwork, to have a wonderfully easy life of it.

The schoolmaster is generally a man of some importance in the female circle of a rural neighborhood; being considered a kind of idle, gentleman-like personage, of vastly superior taste and accomplishments to the rough country swains, and, indeed, inferior in learning only to the parson. His appearance, therefore, is apt to occasion some little stir at the tea-table of a farm-house, and the addition of a supernumerary dish of cakes or sweet-meats, or, peradventure, the parade of a silver tea-pot. Our man of letters, therefore, was peculiarly happy in the smiles of all the country damsels. How he would figure among them in the church-yard, between services on Sundays! gathering grapes for them from the wild vines that overrun the surrounding trees; reciting for their amusement all the epitaphs on the tombstones; or sauntering, with a whole bevy of them, along the banks of the adjacent mill-pond; while the more bashful country bumpkins hung sheepishly back, envying his superior elegance and address.

From his half-itinerant life, also, he was a kind of travelling gazette, carrying the whole budget of local gossip from house to house: so that his appearance was always greeted with satisfaction. He was, moreover, esteemed by the women as a man of great erudition, for he had read several books quite through, and was a perfect master of Cotton Math-

er's *History of New England Witchcraft*, in which, by the way, he most firmly and potently believed.

He was, in fact, an odd mixture of small shrewdness and simple credulity. His appetite for the marvellous, and his powers of digesting it, were equally extraordinary; and both had been increased by his residence in this spellbound region. No tale was too gross or monstrous for his capacious swallow. It was often his delight, after his school was dismissed in the afternoon, to stretch himself on the rich bed of clover bordering the little brook that whimpered by his school-house, and there con over old Mather's direful tales, until the gathering dusk of the evening made the printed page a mere mist before his eyes. Then, as he wended his way, by swamp and stream, and awful woodland, to the farm-house where he happened to be quartered, every sound of nature, at that witching hour, fluttered his excited imagination; the moan of the whippoorwill† from the hill-side, the boding cry of the tree-toad, that harbinger of storm; the dreary hooting of the screech-owl, or the sudden rustling in the thicket of birds frightened from their roost. The fire-flies, too, which sparkled most vividly in the darkest places, now and then startled him, as one of uncommon brightness would stream across his path; and if, by chance, a huge blockhead of a beetle came winging his blundering flight against him, the poor varlet was ready to give up the ghost, with the idea that he was struck with a witch's token. His only resource on such occasions, either to drown thought or drive away evil spirits, was to sing psalm-tunes; and the good people of Sleepy Hollow, as they sat by their doors of an evening, were often filled with awe, at hearing his nasal melody, "in linkèd sweetness long drawn out," floating from the distant hill, or along the dusky road.

Another of his sources of fearful pleasure was, to pass long winter evenings with the old Dutch wives, as they sat spinning by the fire, with a row of apples roasting and spluttering along the hearth, and listen to their marvellous tales of ghosts and goblins, and haunted fields, and haunted brooks, and haunted bridges, and haunted houses, and particularly of the headless horseman, or Galloping Hessian of the Hollow, as they sometimes called him. He would delight them equally by his anecdotes of witchcraft, and the direful omens and portentous sights and

†The whippoorwill is a bird which is only heard at night. It receives its name from its note, which is thought to resemble those words.

sounds in the air, which prevailed in the earlier times of Connecticut; and would frighten them woefully with speculations upon comets and shooting-stars, and with the alarming fact that the world did absolutely turn round, and that they were half the time topsy-turvy!

But if there was a pleasure in all this, while snugly cuddling in the

chimney-corner of a chamber that was all of a ruddy glow from the crackling wood-fire, and where, of course, no spectre dared to show his face, it was dearly purchased by the terrors of his subsequent walk homewards. What fearful shapes and shadows beset his path amidst the dim and ghastly glare of a snowy night!—With what wistful look did he eye every trembling ray of light streaming across the waste fields from some distant window!—How often was he appalled by some shrub covered with snow, which, like a sheeted spectre, beset his very path!—How often did he shrink with curdling awe at the sound of his own steps on a frosty crust beneath his feet; and dread to look over his shoulder, lest he should behold some uncouth being tramping close behind him!—and how often was he thrown into complete dismay by some rushing blast, howling among the trees, in the idea that it was the Galloping Hessian on one of his nightly scourings!

All these, however, were mere terrors of the night, phantoms of the mind that walk in darkness; and though he had seen many spectres in his time, and been more than once beset by Satan in divers shapes, in his lonely perambulations, yet daylight put an end to all these evils; and he would have passed a pleasant life of it, in despite of the devil and all his works, if his path had not been crossed by a being that causes more perplexity to mortal man than ghosts, goblins, and the whole race of witches put together, and that was—a woman.

Among the musical disciples who assembled, one evening in each week, to receive his instructions in psalmody, was Katrina Van Tassel, the daughter and only child of a substantial Dutch farmer. She was a blooming lass of fresh eighteen; plump as a partridge; ripe and melting and rosy-cheeked as one of her father's peaches, and universally famed, not merely for her beauty, but her vast expectations. She was withal a little of a coquette, as might be perceived even in her dress, which was a mixture of ancient and modern fashions, as most suited to set off her charms. She wore the ornaments of pure yellow gold, which her great-great-grandmother had brought over from Saardam; the tempting stomacher of the olden time; and withal a provokingly short petticoat, to display the prettiest foot and ankle in the country round.

Ichabod Crane had a soft and foolish heart towards the sex; and it is not to be wondered at that so tempting a morsel soon found favor in his eyes; more especially after he had visited her in her paternal mansion. Old Baltus Van Tassel was a perfect picture of a thriving, contented, liberal-hearted farmer. He seldom, it is true, sent either his eyes or his thoughts beyond the boundaries of his own farm; but within those everything was snug, happy, and well-conditioned. He was satisfied with his wealth, but not proud of it; and piqued himself upon the hearty abundance rather than the style in which he lived. His strong-hold was situated on the banks of the Hudson, in one of those green, sheltered, fertile nooks in which the Dutch farmers are so fond of nestling. A great elm-tree spread its broad branches over it; at the foot of which bubbled up a spring of the softest and sweetest water, in a little well, formed of a barrel; and then stole sparkling away through the grass, to a neighboring brook, that bubbled along among alders and dwarf willows. Hard by the farm-house was a vast barn, that might have served for a church; every window and crevice of which seemed bursting forth with the treasures of the farm; the flail was busily resounding within it from morning till night; swallows and martins skimmed twittering about the eaves; and rows of pigeons, some with one eye turned up, as if watching the weather, some with their heads under their wings, or buried in their bosoms, and others swelling, and cooing, and bowing about their dames, were enjoying the sunshine on the roof. Sleek unwieldy porkers were grunting in the repose and abundance of their pens; whence sallied forth, now and then, troops of sucking pigs, as if to snuff the air. A stately squadron of snowy geese were riding in an adjoining pond, convoying whole fleets of ducks; regiments of turkeys were gobbling through the farm-yard, and guinea fowls fretting about it, like ill-tempered housewives, with their peevish discontented cry. Before the barn-door strutted the gallant cock, that pattern of a husband, a warrior, and a fine gentleman, clapping his burnished wings, and crowing in the pride and gladness of his heart—sometimes tearing up the earth with his feet, and then generously calling his ever-hungry family of wives and children to enjoy the rich morsel which he had discovered.

The pedagogue's mouth watered, as he looked upon this sumptuous promise of luxurious winter fare. In his devouring mind's eye he pictured to himself every roasting-pig running about with a pudding in his belly, and an apple in his mouth; the pigeons were snugly put to bed in a comfortable pie, and tucked in with a coverlet of crust; the geese were swimming in their own gravy; and the ducks pairing cosily in dishes, like snug married couples, with a decent competency of onion-sauce. In the porkers he saw carved out the future sleek side of bacon, and juicy relishing ham; not a turkey but he beheld daintily trussed up, with its gizzard under its wing, and, peradventure, a necklace of savory sausages; and even bright chanticleer himself lay sprawling on his back, in a side-dish, with uplifted claws, as if craving that quarter which his chivalrous spirit disdained to ask while living.

As the enraptured Ichabod fancied all this, and as he rolled his great green eyes over the fat meadow-lands, the rich fields of wheat, of rye, of buckwheat, and Indian corn, and the orchard burdened with ruddy fruit, which surrounded the warm tenement of Van Tassel, his heart yearned after the damsel who was to inherit these domains, and his imagination expanded with the idea how they might be readily turned into cash, and the money invested in immense tracts of wild land, and shingle palaces in the wilderness. Nay, his busy fancy already realized his hopes, and presented to him the blooming Katrina, with a whole family of children, mounted on the top of a wagon loaded with household trumpery, with pots and kettles dangling beneath; and he beheld himself bestriding a pacing mare, with a colt at her heels, setting out for Kentucky, Tennessee, or the Lord knows where.

When he entered the house, the conquest of his heart was complete. It was one of those spacious farm-houses, with high-ridged, but lowly-sloping roofs, built in the style handed down from the first Dutch settlers; the low projecting eaves forming a piazza along the front, capable of being closed up in bad weather. Under this were hung flails, harness, various utensils of husbandry, and nets for fishing in the neighboring river. Benches were built along the sides for summer use; and a great spinning-wheel at one end, and a churn at the other, showed the various uses to which this important porch might be devoted. From this piazza the wandering Ichabod entered the hall, which formed the centre of the mansion and the place of usual residence. Here, rows of resplendent pewter, ranged on a long dresser, dazzled his eyes. In one corner stood a huge bag of wool ready to be spun; in another a quantity of linsey-woolsey just from the loom; ears of Indian corn, and strings of dried apples and peaches, hung in gay festoons along the walls, mingled with the gaud of red peppers; and a door left ajar gave him a peep into the best parlor, where the claw-footed chairs and dark mahogany tables shone like mirrors; and irons, with their accompanying shovel and tongs, glistened from their covert of asparagus tops; mock-oranges and conch-shells decorated the mantel-piece; strings of various colored birds' eggs were suspended above it, a great ostrich egg was hung from the centre of the room, and a corner-cupboard, knowingly left open, displayed immense treasures of old silver and well-mended china.

From the moment Ichabod laid his eyes upon these regions of delight, the peace of his mind was at an end, and his only study was how to gain the affections of the peerless daughter of Van Tassel. In this enterprise, however, he had more real difficulties than generally fell to the lot of a knight-errant of yore, who seldom had anything but giants, enchanters, fiery dragons, and such like easily conquered adversaries, to contend with; and had to make his way merely through gates of iron and brass, and walls of adamant, to the castle-keep, where the lady of his heart was confined; all which he achieved as easily as a man would carve his way to the centre of a Christmas pie; and then the lady gave him her hand as a matter of course. Ichabod, on the contrary, had to win his way to the heart of a country coquette, beset with a labyrinth of whims and caprices, which were forever presenting new difficulties and impediments; and he had to encounter a host of fearful adversaries of real flesh and blood, the numerous rustic admirers, who beset every portal to her heart; keeping a watchful and angry eye upon each other, but ready to fly out in the common cause against any new competitor.

Among these the most formidable was a burly, roaring, roistering blade, of the name of Abraham, or, according to the Dutch abbreviation, Brom Van Brunt, the hero of the country round, which rang with his feats of strength and hardihood. He was broad-shouldered and double-jointed, with short, curly black hair, and a bluff but not unpleasant countenance, having a mingled air of fun and arrogance. From his Herculean frame and great powers of limb, he had received the nickname of BROM BONES, by which he was universally known. He was famed for great knowledge and skill in horsemanship, being as dexterous on horseback as a Tartar. He was foremost at all races and cockfights; and, with the ascendency which bodily strength acquires in rustic life, was the umpire in all disputes, setting his hat on one side, and giving his decisions with an air and tone admitting of no gainsay or appeal. He was always ready for either a fight or a frolic; but had more mischief than ill-will in his composition; and, with all his over-bearing roughness, there was a strong dash of waggish good-humor at the bottom. He had three or four boon companions, who regarded him as their model, and at the head of whom he scoured the country, attending every scene of feud or merriment for miles round. In cold weather he was distinguished by a fur cap, surmounted with a flaunting fox's tail; and when the folks at a country gathering descried this well-known crest at a distance, whisking about among a squad of hard riders, they always stood by for a squall.

Sometimes his crew would be heard dashing along past the farm-houses at midnight, with whoop and halloo, like a troop of Don Cossacks; and the old dames, startled out of their sleep, would listen for a moment till the hurry-scurry had clattered by, and then exclaim, "Ay, there goes Brom Bones and his gang!" The neighbors looked upon him with a mixture of awe, admiration, and good-will; and when any madcap prank, or rustic brawl, occurred in the vicinity, always shook their heads, and warranted Brom Bones was at the bottom of it.

This rantipole hero had for some time singled out the blooming Katrina for the object of his uncouth gallantries; and though his amorous toyings were something like the gentle caresses and endearments of a bear, yet it was whispered that she did not altogether discourage his hopes. Certain it is, his advances were signals for rival candidates to retire, who felt no inclination to cross a line in his amours; insomuch, that, when his horse was seen tied to Van Tassel's paling on a Sunday night, a sure sign that his master was courting, or, as it is termed, "sparking," within, all other suitors passed by in despair, and carried the war into other quarters.

Such was the formidable rival with whom Ichabod Crane had to contend, and, considering all things, a stouter man than he would have shrunk from the competition, and a wiser man would have despaired. He had, however, a happy mixture of pliability and perseverance in his nature; he was in form and spirit like a supple-jack—yielding, but tough; though he bent, he never broke; and though he bowed beneath the slightest pressure yet, the moment it was away—jerk! he was as erect, and carried his head as high as ever.

To have taken the field openly against his rival would have been madness; for he was not a man to be thwarted in his amours, any more than that stormy lover, Achilles. Ichabod, therefore, made his advances in a quiet and gently insinuating manner. Under cover of his character of singing-master, he had made frequent visits at the farm-house; not that he had anything to apprehend from the meddlesome interference of parents, which is so often a stumbling-block in the path of lovers. Balt Van Tassel was an easy, indulgent soul; he loved his daughter better even than his pipe, and, like a reasonable man and an excellent father, let her have her way in everything. His notable little wife, too, had enough to do to attend to her housekeeping and manage her poultry; for, as she sagely observed, ducks and geese are foolish things, and must be looked after, but girls can take care of themselves. Thus while the busy dame bustled about the house, or plied her spinning-wheel at one end of the piazza, honest Balt would sit smoking his evening pipe at the other, watching the achievements of a little wooden warrior, who, armed with a sword in each hand, was most valiantly fighting the wind on the pinnacle of the barn. In the meantime, Ichabod would carry on his suit with the daughter by the side of the spring under the great elm, or sauntering along in the twilight—that hour so favorable to the lover's eloquence.

I profess not to know how women's hearts are wooed and won. To me they have always been matters of riddle and admiration. Some seem to have but one vulnerable point or door of access, while others have a thousand avenues, and may be captured in a thousand different ways. It is a great triumph of skill to gain the former, but a still greater proof of generalship to maintain possession of the latter, for the man must battle for his fortress at every door and window. He who wins a thousand common hearts is therefore entitled to some renown; but he who keeps undisputed sway over the heart of a coquette, is indeed a hero. Certain it is, this was not the case with the redoubtable Brom Bones; and from the moment Ichabod Crane made his advances, the interests of the former evidently declined; his horse was no longer seen tied at the palings on Sunday nights, and a deadly feud gradually arose between him and the preceptor of Sleepy Hollow.

Brom, who had a degree of rough chivalry in his nature, would fain have carried matters to open warfare, and have settled their pretensions to the lady according to the mode of those most concise and simple reasoners, the knights-errant of yore—by single combat; but Ichabod was too conscious of the superior might of his adversary to enter the lists against him: he had overheard a boast of Bones, that he would "double the schoolmaster up, and lay him on a shelf of his own school-house;" and he was too wary to give him an opportunity. There was something extremely provoking in this obstinately pacific system; it left Brom no alternative but to draw upon the funds of rustic waggery in his disposition, and to play off boorish practical jokes upon his rival. Ichabod became the object of whimsical persecution to Bones and his gang of rough riders. They harried his hitherto peaceful domains; smoked out his singing-school, by stopping up the chimney; broke into the school-house at night, in spite of its formidable fastenings of withe and window-stakes, and turned everything topsy-turvy: so that the poor schoolmaster began to think all the witches in the country held their meetings there. But what was still more annoying, Brom took opportunities of turning him into ridicule in presence of his mistress, and had a scoundrel dog whom he taught to whine in the most ludicrous manner, and introduced as a rival of Ichabod's to instruct her in psalmody.

In this way matters went on for some time, without producing any material effect on the relative situation of the contending powers. On a fine autumnal afternoon, Ichabod, in pensive mood, sat enthroned on the lofty stool whence he usually watched all the concerns of his little

literary realm. In his hand he swayed a ferule, that sceptre of despotic power; the birch of justice reposed on three nails, behind the throne, a constant terror to evil-doers; while on the desk before him might be seen sundry contraband articles and prohibited weapons, detected upon the persons of idle urchins; such as half-munched apples, pop-guns, whirli-gigs, fly-cages, and whole legions of rampant little paper game-cocks. Apparently there had been some appalling act of justice recently inflict-ed, for his scholars were all busily intent upon their books, or slyly whispering behind them with one eye kept upon the master; and a kind of buzzing stillness reigned throughout the school-room. It was suddenly interrupted by the appearance of a Negro, in tow-cloth jacket and trousers, a round-crowned fragment of a hat, like the cap of Mercury, and mounted on the back of a ragged, wild, half-broken colt, which he managed with a rope by way of halter. He came clattering up to the

school-door with an invitation to Ichabod to attend a merry-making or "quilting frolic," to be held that evening at Mynheer Van Tassel's; and having delivered his message with that air of importance, and effort at fine language, which a Negro is apt to display on petty embassies of the kind, he dashed over the brook, and was seen scampering away up the Hollow, full of the importance and hurry of his mission.

All was now bustle and hubbub in the late quiet school-room. The scholars were hurried through their lessons, without stopping at trifles; those who were nimble skipped over half with impunity, and those who were tardy had a smart application now and then in the rear, to quicken their speed, or help them over a tall word. Books were flung aside without being put away on the shelves, inkstands were overturned, benches thrown down, and the whole school was turned loose an hour before the usual time, bursting forth like a legion of young imps, yelping and racketing about the green, in joy at their early emancipation.

The gallant Ichabod now spent at least an extra half-hour at his toilet, brushing and furbishing up his best and indeed only suit of rusty black, and arranging his locks by a bit of broken looking-glass, that hung up in the school-house. That he might make his appearance before his mistress in the true style of a cavalier, he borrowed a horse from the farmer with whom he was domiciliated, a choleric old Dutchman, of the name of Hans Van Ripper, and, thus gallantly mounted, issued forth, like a knight-errant in quest of adventures. But it is meet I should, in the true spirit of romantic story, give some account of the looks and equipments of my hero and his steed. The animal he bestrode was a broken-down plough-horse, that had outlived almost everything but his viciousness. He was gaunt and shagged, with a ewe neck and a head like a hammer; his rusty mane and tail were tangled and knotted with burrs; one eye had lost its pupil, and was glaring and spectral; but the other had the gleam of a genuine devil in it. Still he must have had fire and mettle in his day, if we may judge from the name he bore of Gunpowder. He had, in fact, been a favorite steed of his master's, the choleric Van Ripper, who was a furious rider, and had infused, very probably, some of his own spirit into the animal; for, old and broken-down as he looked, there was more of the lurking devil in him than in any young filly in the country.

Ichabod was a suitable figure for such a steed. He rode with short

stirrups, which brought his knees nearly up to the pommel of the saddle; his sharp elbows stuck out like grasshoppers'; he carried his whip perpendicularly in his hand, like a sceptre, and, as his horse jogged on, the motion of his arms was not unlike the flapping of a pair of wings. A small wool hat rested on the top of his nose, for so his scanty strip of forehead might be called; and the skirts of his black coat fluttered out almost to the horse's tail. Such was the appearance of Ichabod and his steed, as they shambled out of the gate of Hans Van Ripper, and it was altogether such an apparition as is seldom to be met with in broad daylight.

It was, as I have said, a fine autumnal day, the sky was clear and nature wore that rich and golden livery which we always associate with the idea of abundance. The forests had put on their sober brown and yellow, while some trees of the tenderer kind had been nipped by the frosts into brilliant dyes of orange, purple, and scarlet. Streaming files of wild ducks began to make their appearance high in the air; the bark of the squirrel might be heard from the groves of beech and hickory nuts, and the pensive whistle of the quail at intervals from the neighboring stubble-field.

The small birds were taking their farewell banquets. In the fulness of their revelry, they fluttered, chirping and frolicking, from bush to bush, and tree to tree, capricious from the very profusion and variety around them. There was the honest cockrobin, the favorite game of stripling sportsmen, with its loud querulous notes; and the twittering blackbirds flying in sable clouds; and the golden-winged woodpecker, with his crimson crest, his broad black gorget, and splendid plumage; and the cedar-bird, with its red-tipt wings and yellow-tipt tail, and its little monteiro cap of feathers; and the blue jay, that noisy coxcomb, in his gay light-blue coat and white under-clothes, screaming and chattering, nodding and bobbing and bowing, and pretending to be on good terms with every songster of the grove.

As Ichabod jogged slowly on his way, his eye, ever open to every symptom of culinary abundance, ranged with delight over the treasures of jolly autumn. On all sides he beheld a vast store of apples; some hanging in oppressive opulence on the trees; some gathered into baskets and barrels for the market; others heaped up in rich piles for the cider-press. Farther on he beheld great fields of Indian corn, with its golden ears peeping from their leafy coverts, and holding out the promise of cakes and hasty-pudding; and the yellow pumpkins lying beneath them, turning up their fair round bellies to the sun, and giving ample prospects of the most luxurious of pies; and anon he passed the fragrant buck-wheat fields, breathing the odor of the bee-hive, and as he beheld them, soft anticipations stole over his mind of dainty slapjacks, well buttered, and garnished with honey or treacle, by the delicate little dimpled hand of Katrina Van Tassel.

Thus feeding his mind with many sweet thoughts and "sugared suppositions," he journeyed along the sides of a range of hills which look out upon some of the goodliest scenes of the mighty Hudson. The sun gradually wheeled his broad disk down into the west. The wide bosom of the Tappan Zee lay motionless and glossy, excepting that here and there a gentle undulation waved and prolonged the blue shadow of the distant mountain. A few amber clouds floated in the sky, without a breath of air to move them. The horizon was of a fine golden tint, changing gradually into a pure apple-green, and from that into the deep blue of the mid-heaven. A slanting ray lingered on the woody crests of the precipices that overhung some parts of the river, giving greater depth to the dark-gray and purple of their rocky sides. A sloop was loitering in the distance, dropping slowly down with the tide, her sail hanging uselessly against the mast; and as the reflection of the sky gleamed along the still water, it seemed as if the vessel was suspended in the air.

It was toward evening that Ichabod arrived at the castle of the Heer Van Tassel, which he found thronged with the pride and flower of the adjacent country. Old farmers, a spare leathern-faced race, in homespun coats and breeches, blue stockings, huge shoes, and magnificent pewter buckles. Their brisk withered little dames, in close crimped caps, long-waisted shortgowns, homespun petticoats, with scissors and pin-cushions, and gay calico pockets hanging on the outside. Buxom lasses, almost as antiquated as their mothers, excepting where a straw hat, a fine ribbon, or perhaps a white frock, gave symptoms of city innovation. The sons, in short square-skirted coats with rows of stupendous brass buttons, and their hair generally queued in the fashion of the times, especially if they could procure an eel-skin for the purpose, it being esteemed, throughout the country, as a potent nourisher and strengthener of the hair.

Brom Bones, however, was the hero of the scene, having come to the gathering on his favorite steed, Daredevil, a creature, like himself, full of mettle and mischief, and which no one but himself could manage. He was, in fact, noted for preferring vicious animals, given to all kinds of tricks, which kept the rider in constant risk of his neck, for he held a tractable well-broken horse as unworthy of a lad of spirit.

Fain would I pause to dwell upon the world of charms that burst upon the enraptured gaze of my hero, as he entered the state parlor of Van Tassel's mansion. Not those of the bevy of buxom lasses, with their luxurious display of red and white; but the ample charms of a genuine Dutch country tea-table, in the sumptuous time of autumn. Such heaped-up platters of cakes of various and almost indescribable kinds, known only to experienced Dutch housewives! There was the doughty doughnut, the tenderer oly koek, and the crisp and crumbling cruller; sweet cakes and short cakes, ginger cakes and honey cakes, and the whole family of cakes. And then there were apple-pies and peach-pies and pumpkin-pies; besides slices of ham and smoked beef; and moreover delectable dishes of preserved plums, and peaches, and pears, and quinces; not to mention broiled shad and roasted chickens; together with bowls of milk and cream, all mingled higgledy-piggledy, pretty much as I have enumerated them, with the motherly tea-pot sending up its clouds of vapor from the midst—Heaven bless the mark! I want breath and time to discuss this banquet as it deserves, and am too eager to get on with my story. Happily, Ichabod Crane was not in so great a hurry as his historian, but did ample justice to every dainty.

He was a kind and thankful creature, whose heart dilated in proportion as his skin was filled with good cheer; and whose spirits rose with eating as some men's do with drink. He could not help, too, rolling his large eyes round him as he ate, and chuckling with the possibility that he might one day be lord of all this scene of almost unimaginable luxury and splendor. Then, he thought, how soon he'd turn his back upon the old school-house; snap his fingers in the face of Hans Van Ripper, and every other niggardly patron, and kick any itinerant pedagogue out-of-doors that should dare to call him comrade!

Old Baltus Van Tassel moved about among his guests with a face dilated with content and good-humor, round and jolly as the harvest-moon. His hospitable attentions were brief, but expressive, being confined to a shake of the hand, a slap on the shoulder, a loud laugh, and a pressing invitation to "fall to, and help themselves."

And now the sound of the music from the common room, or hall, summoned to the dance. The musician was an old gray-headed Negro, who had been the itinerant orchestra of the neighborhood for more than half a century. His instrument was as old and battered as himself. The greater part of the time he scraped on two or three strings, accompanying every movement of the bow with a motion of the head; bowing almost to the ground, and stamping with his foot whenever a fresh couple were to start.

Ichabod prided himself upon his dancing as much as upon his vocal powers. Not a limb, not a fibre about him was idle; and to have seen his loosely hung frame in full motion, and clattering about the room, you would have thought Saint Vitus himself, that blessed patron of the dance, was figuring before you in person. He was the admiration of all the Negroes; who, having gathered, of all ages and sizes, from the farm and the neighborhood, stood forming a pyramid of shining black faces at every door and window, gazing with delight at the scene, rolling their white eyeballs, and showing grinning rows of ivory from ear to ear. How could the flogger of urchins be otherwise than animated and joyous? The lady of his heart was his partner in the dance, and smiling graciously in reply to all his amorous oglings; while Brom Bones, sorely smitten with love and jealousy, sat brooding by himself in one corner.

When the dance was at an end, Ichabod was attracted to a knot of the sager folks, who, with old Van Tassel, sat smoking at one end of the piazza, gossiping over former times, and drawing out long stories about the war.

This neighborhood, at the time of which I am speaking, was one of those highly favored places which abound with chronicle and great men. The British and American line had run near it during the war; it had, therefore, been the scene of marauding, and infested with refugees, cowboys, and all kinds of border chivalry. Just sufficient time has elapsed to enable each story-teller to dress up his tale with a little becoming fiction, and, in the indistinctness of his recollection, to make himself the hero of every exploit.

There was the story of Doffue Martling, a large blue-bearded Dutchman, who had nearly taken a British frigate with an old iron nine-pounder from a mud breastwork, only that his gun burst at the sixth discharge. And there was an old gentleman who shall be nameless, being too rich a mynheer to be lightly mentioned, who, in the battle of White Plains, being an excellent master of defence, parried a musket-ball with a small sword, insomuch that he absolutely felt it whiz round the blade, and glance off at the hilt; in proof of which he was ready at any time to show the sword, with the hilt a little bent. There were several more that had been equally great in the field, not one of whom but was persuaded that he had a considerable hand in bringing the war to a happy termination.

But all these were nothing to the tales of ghosts and apparitions that succeeded. The neighborhood is rich in legendary treasures of the kind. Local tales and superstitions thrive best in these sheltered long-settled retreats; but are trampled underfoot by the shifting throng that forms the population of most of our country places. Besides, there is no encouragement for ghosts in most of our villages, for they have scarcely had time to finish their first nap, and turn themselves in their graves before their surviving friends have travelled away from the neighbor-

hood; so that when they turn out at night to walk their rounds, they have no acquaintance left to call upon. This is perhaps the reason why we so seldom hear of ghosts, except in our long-established Dutch communities.

The immediate cause, however, of the prevalence of supernatural stories in these parts was doubtless owing to the vicinity of Sleepy Hollow. There was a contagion in the very air that blew from the haunted region; it breathed forth an atmosphere of dreams and fancies infecting all the land. Several of the Sleepy Hollow people were present at Van Tassel's and, as usual, were doling out their wild and wonderful legends. Many dismal tales were told about funeral trains, and mourning cries and wailings heard and seen about the great tree where the unfortunate Major André was taken, and which stood in the neighborhood. Some mention was made also of the woman in white, that haunted the dark glen at Raven Rock, and was often heard to shriek on winter nights before a storm, having perished there in the snow. The chief part of the stories, however, turned upon the favorite spectre of Sleepy Hollow, the headless horseman, who had been heard several times of late, patrolling the country; and, it was said, tethered his horse nightly among the graves in the churchyard.

The sequestered situation of this church seems always to have made it a favorite haunt of troubled spirits. It stands on a knoll, surrounded by locust-trees and lofty elms, from among which its decent white-washed walls shine modestly forth, like Christian purity beaming through the shades of retirement. A gentle slope descends from it to a silver sheet of water, bordered by high trees, between which, peeps may be caught at the blue hills of the Hudson. To look upon its grass-grown yard, where the sunbeams seem to sleep so quietly, one would think that there at least the dead might rest in peace. On one side of the church extends a wide woody dell, along which raves a large brook among broken rocks and trunks of fallen trees. Over a deep black part of the stream, not far from the church, was formerly thrown a wooden bridge; the road that led to it, and the bridge itself, were thickly shaded by overhanging trees, which cast a gloom about it, even in the daytime, but occasioned a fearful darkness at night. This was one of the favorite haunts of the headless horseman; and the place where he was most frequently encountered. The tale was told of old Brouwer, a most heretical disbeliever in ghosts, how he met the horseman returning from his foray into Sleepy Hollow, and was obliged to get up behind him; how they galloped over bush and brake, over hill and swamp, until they reached the bridge; when the horseman suddenly turned into a skeleton, threw old Brouwer into the brook, and sprang away over the tree-tops with a clap of thunder.

This story was immediately matched by a thrice marvellous adventure of Brom Bones, who made light of the galloping Hessian as an arrant jockey. He affirmed that, on returning one night from the neighboring village of Sing Sing, he had been overtaken by this midnight trooper; that he had offered to race with him for a bowl of punch, and should have won it too, for Daredevil beat the goblin horse all hollow, but, just as they came to the church bridge, the Hessian bolted, and vanished in a flash of fire.

All these tales, told in that drowsy undertone with which men talk in the dark, the countenances of the listeners only now and then receiving a casual gleam from the glare of a pipe, sank deep in the mind of Ichabod. He repaid them in kind with large extracts from his invaluable author, Cotton Mather, and added many marvellous events that had taken place in his native State of Connecticut, and fearful sights which he had seen in his nightly walks about the Sleepy Hollow.

The revel now gradually broke up. The old farmers gathered together their families in their wagons, and were heard for some time rattling along the hollow roads, and over the distant hills. Some of the damsels mounted on pillions behind their favorite swains, and their light-hearted laughter, mingling with the clatter of hoofs, echoed along the silent woodlands, sounding fainter and fainter until they gradually died away—and the late scene of noise and frolic was all silent and deserted. Ichabod only lingered behind, according to the custom of country lovers, to have a *tête-à-tête* with the heiress, fully convinced that he was now on the high road to success. What passed at this interview I will not pretend to say, for in fact I do not know. Something, however, I fear me, must have gone wrong, for he certainly sallied forth, after no very great interval, with an air quite desolate and chop-fallen.—Oh, these women! these women! Could that girl have been playing off any of her coquettish tricks?—Was her encouragement of the poor pedagogue all a mere sham to secure her conquest of his rival?—Heaven only knows, not I!—Let it suffice to say, Ichabod stole forth with the air of one who had been sacking a hen-roost, rather than a fair lady's heart. Without looking to the right or left to notice the scene of rural wealth on which he had so often gloated, he went straight to the stable, and with several hearty cuffs and kicks, roused his steed most uncourteously from the comfortable quarters in which he was soundly sleeping, dreaming of mountains of corn and oats, and whole valleys of timothy and clover.

It was the very witching time of night that Ichabod, heavy-hearted and crestfallen, pursued his travel homewards, along the sides of the lofty hills which rise above Tarry Town, and which he had traversed so cheerily in the afternoon. The hour was as dismal as himself. Far below him, the Tappan Zee spread its dusky and indistinct waste of waters, with here and there the tall mast of a sloop riding quietly at anchor under the land. In the dead hush of midnight he could even hear the barking of the watch-dog from the opposite shore of the Hudson; but it was so vague and faint as only to give an idea of his distance from this faithful companion of man. Now and then, too, the long-drawn crowing of a cock, accidentally awakened, would sound far, far off, from some farm-house away among the hills—but it was like a dreaming sound in his ear. No signs of life occurred near him, but occasionally the melancholy chirp of a cricket, or perhaps the gutteral twang of a bull-frog, from a neighboring marsh, as if sleeping uncomfortably, and turning suddenly in his bed.

All the stories of ghosts and goblins that he had heard in the afternoon, now came crowding upon his recollection. The night grew darker and darker; the stars seemed to sink deeper in the sky, and driving clouds occasionally hid them from his sight. He had never felt so lonely and dismal. He was, moreover, approaching the very place where many of the scenes of the ghost-stories had been laid. In the centre of the road stood an enormous tulip-tree, which towered like a giant above all the other trees of the neighborhood, and formed a kind of landmark. Its limbs were gnarled, and fantastic, large enough to form trunks for ordinary trees, twisting down almost to the earth, and rising again into the air. It was connected with the tragical story of the unfortunate

André, who had been taken prisoner hard by; and was universally known by the name of Major André's tree. The common people regarded it with a mixture of respect and superstition, partly out of sympathy for the fate of its ill-starred namesake, and partly from the tales of strange sights and doleful lamentations told concerning it.

As Ichabod approached this fearful tree, he began to whistle: he thought his whistle was answered—it was but a blast sweeping sharply through the dry branches. As he approached a little nearer, he thought he saw something white, hanging in the midst of the tree—he paused and ceased whistling; but on looking more narrowly, perceived that it was a place where the tree had been scathed by lightning, and the white wood laid bare. Suddenly he heard a groan—his teeth chattered and his knees smote against the saddle: it was but the rubbing of one huge bough upon another, as they were swayed about by the breeze. He passed the tree in safety; but new perils lay before him.

About two hundred yards from the tree a small brook crossed the road, and ran into a marshy and thickly wooded glen, known by the name of Wiley's Swamp. A few rough logs, laid side by side, served for a bridge over this stream. On that side of the road where the brook entered the wood, a group of oaks and chestnuts, matted thick with wild grape-vines, threw a cavernous gloom over it. To pass this bridge was the severest trial. It was at this identical spot that the unfortunate André was captured, and under the covert of those chestnuts and vines were the sturdy yeomen concealed who surprised him. This has ever since been considered a haunted stream, and fearful are the feelings of the school boy who has to pass it alone after dark.

As he approached the stream, his heart began to thump; he summoned up, however, all his resolution, gave his horse half a score of kicks in the ribs, and attempted to dash briskly across the bridge; but instead of starting forward, the perverse old animal made a lateral movement, and ran broadside against the fence. Ichabod, whose fears increased with the delay, jerked the reins on the other side, and kicked lustily with the contrary foot: it was all in vain; his steed started, it is true, but it was only to plunge to the opposite side of the road into a thicket of brambles and alder bushes. The schoolmaster now bestowed both whip and heel upon the starveling ribs of old Gunpowder, who dashed forward, snuf-

fling and snorting, but came to a stand just by the bridge, with a suddenness that had nearly sent his rider sprawling over his head. Just at this moment a plashy tramp by the side of the bridge caught the sensitive ear of Ichabod. In the dark shadow of the grove, on the margin of the brook, he beheld something huge, misshapen, black, and towering. It stirred not, but seemed gathered up in the gloom, like some gigantic monster ready to spring upon the traveller.

The hair of the affrighted pedagogue rose upon his head with terror. What was to be done? To turn and fly was now too late; and besides, what chance was there of escaping ghost or goblin, if such it was, which could ride upon the wings of the wind? Summoning up, therefore, a show of courage, he demanded in stammering accents— "Who are you?" He received no reply. He repeated his demand in a still more agitated voice. Still there was no answer. Once more he cudgelled the sides of the inflexible Gunpowder, and, shutting his eyes, broke forth with involuntary fervor into a psalm-tune. Just then the shadowy object of alarm put itself in motion, and, with a scramble and a bound, stood at once in the middle of the road. Though the night was dark and dismal, yet the form of the unknown might now in some degree be ascertained. He appeared to be a horseman of large dimensions, and mounted on a black horse of powerful frame. He made no offer of molestation or sociability, but kept aloof on one side of the road, jogging along on the blind side of old Gunpowder, who had now got over his fright and waywardness.

Ichabod, who had no relish for this strange midnight companion, and bethought himself of the adventure of Brom Bones with the Galloping Hessian, now quickened his steed, in hopes of leaving him behind. The stranger, however, quickened his horse to an equal pace. Ichabod pulled up, and fell into a walk, thinking to lag behind—the other did the same. His heart began to sink within him; he endeavored to resume his psalm-tune, but his parched tongue clove to the roof of his mouth, and he could not utter a stave. There was something in the moody and dogged silence of this pertinacious companion, that was mysterious and appalling. It was soon fearfully accounted for. On mounting a rising ground, which brought the figure of his fellow-traveller in relief against the sky, gigantic in height, and muffled in a cloak, Ichabod was horror-struck, on perceiving that he was headless!—but his horror was still more increased, on observing that the head, which should have rested on his shoulders, was carried before him on the pommel of the saddle: his terror rose to desperation; he rained a shower of kicks and blows upon Gunpowder, hoping, by a sudden movement, to give his companion the slip—but the spectre started full jump with him. Away then they dashed, through thick and thin; stones flying, and sparks flashing at every bound. Ichabod's flimsy garments fluttered in the air, as he stretched his long lank body away over his horse's head, in the eagerness of his flight.

They had now reached the road which turns off to Sleepy Hollow; but Gunpowder, who seemed possessed with a demon, instead of keeping up it, made an opposite turn, and plunged headlong downhill to the left. This road leads through a sandy hollow, shaded by trees for about a quarter of a mile, where it crosses the bridge famous in goblin story, and just beyond swells the green knoll on which stands the white-washed church.

As yet the panic of the steed had given his unskilful rider an apparent advantage in the chase; but just as he had got half-way through the hollow, the girths of the saddle gave way, and he felt it slipping from under him. He seized it by the pommel, and endeavored to hold it firm, but in vain; and had just time to save himself by clasping old Gunpowder round the neck, when the saddle fell to the earth, and he heard it trampled underfoot by his pursuer. For a moment, the terror of Hans Van Ripper's wrath passed across his mind—for it was his Sunday saddle; but this was no time for petty fears; the goblin was hard on his haunches; and (unskilful rider that he was!) he had much ado to maintain his seat; sometimes slipping on one side, sometimes on another, and sometimes jolted on the high ridge of his horse's backbone, with a violence that he verily feared would cleave him asunder.

An opening in the trees now cheered him with the hopes that the church-bridge was at hand. The wavering reflection of a silver star in the bosom of the brook told him that he was not mistaken. He saw the walls of the church dimly glaring under the trees beyond. He recollected the place where Brom Bones' ghostly competitor had disappeared. "If I can but reach that bridge," thought Ichabod, "I am safe." Just then he heard the black steed panting and blowing close behind him; he even fancied that he felt his hot breath. Another convulsive kick in the ribs, and old Gunpowder sprang upon the bridge; he thundered over the resounding planks; he gained the opposite side; and now Ichabod cast a look behind to see if his pursuer should vanish, according to rule, in a flash of fire and brimstone. Just then he saw the goblin rising in his stirrups, and in the very act of hurling his head at him. Ichabod endeavored to dodge the horrible missile, but too late. It encountered his cranium with a tremendous crash—he was tumbled headlong into the dust, and Gunpowder, the black steed, and the goblin rider, passed by like a whirlwind.

The next morning the old horse was found without his saddle, and with the bridle under his feet, soberly cropping the grass at his master's gate. Ichabod did not make his appearance at breakfast;—dinner-hour came, but no Ichabod. The boys assembled at the school-house, and strolled idly about the banks of the brook; but no schoolmaster. Hans Van Ripper now began to feel some uneasiness about the fate of poor Ichabod, and his saddle. An inquiry was sent on foot, and after diligent investigation they came upon his traces. In one part of the road leading to the church was found the saddle trampled in the dirt; the tracks of horses' hoofs deeply dented in the road, and evidently at furious speed, were traced to the bridge, beyond which, on the bank of a broad part of the brook, where the water ran deep and black, was found the hat of the unfortunate Ichabod, and close beside it a shattered pumpkin.

The brook was searched, but the body of the schoolmaster was not to be discovered. Hans Van Ripper, as executor of his estate, examined the bundle which contained all his worldly effects. They consisted of two shirts and a half; two stocks for the neck; a pair or two of worsted stockings, an old pair of corduroy small-clothes; a rusty razor; a book of psalm-tunes, full of dogs' ears; and a broken pitch-pipe. As to the books and furniture of the school-house, they belonged to the community, excepting Cotton Mather's *History of Witchcraft,* a *New England Almanac,* and a book of dreams and fortune-telling; in which last was a sheet of foolscap much scribbled and blotted in several fruitless attempts to make a copy of verses in honor of the heiress of Van Tassel. These magic books and the poetic scrawl were forthwith consigned to the flames by Hans Van Ripper; who from that time forward determined to send his children no more to school; observing, that he never knew any good come of this same reading and writing. Whatever money the schoolmaster possessed, and he had received his quarter's pay but a day or two before, he must have had about his person at the time of his disappearance.

The mysterious event caused much speculation at the church on the following Sunday. Knots of gazers and gossips were collected in the churchyard, at the bridge, and at the spot where the hat and pumpkin had been found. The stories of Brouwer, of Bones, and a whole budget of others, were called to mind; and when they had diligently considered them all, and compared them with the symptoms of the present case, they shook their heads, and came to the conclusion that Ichabod had been carried off by the Galloping Hessian. As he was a bachelor, and in nobody's debt, nobody troubled his head any more about him. The school was removed to a different quarter of the Hollow, and another pedagogue reigned in his stead.

It is true, an old farmer, who had been down to New York on a visit several years after, and from whom this account of the ghastly adventure was received, brought home the intelligence that Ichabod Crane was still alive; that he had left the neighborhood, partly through fear of the goblin and Hans Van Ripper, and partly in mortification at having been suddenly dismissed by the heiress; that he had changed his quarters to a distant part of the country; had kept school and studied law at the same time, had been admitted to the bar, turned politician, electioneered, written for the newspapers, and finally had been made a justice of the Ten Pound Court. Brom Bones too, who shortly after his rival's disappearance conducted the blooming Katrina in triumph to the altar, was observed to look exceedingly knowing whenever the story of Ichabod was related, and always burst into a hearty laugh at the mention of the pumpkin; which led some to suspect that he knew more about the matter than he chose to tell.

The old country wives, however, who are the best judges of these matters, maintain to this day that Ichabod was spirited away by supernatural means; and it is a favorite story often told about the neighborhood round the winter evening fire. The bridge became more than ever an object of superstitious awe, and that may be the reason why the road has been altered of late years, so as to approach the church by the border of the mill-pond. The school-house, being deserted, soon fell to decay, and was reported to be haunted by the ghost of the unfortunate pedagogue; and the plough-boy, loitering homeward of a still summer evening, has often fancied his voice at a distance, chanting a melancholy psalm-tune, among the tranquil solitudes of Sleepy Hollow.

POSTSCRIPT,

Found in the Handwriting of Mr. Knickerbocker.

The preceding Tale is given, almost in the precise words in which I heard it related at a Corporation meeting of the ancient city of Manhattoes, at which were present many of its sagest and most illustrious burghers. The narrator was a pleasant, shabby, gentlemanly old fellow, in pepper-and-salt clothes, with a sadly humorous face; and one whom I strongly suspected of being poor—he made such efforts to be entertaining. When his story was concluded, there was much laughter and approbation, particularly from two or three deputy aldermen, who had been asleep the greater part of the time. There was, however, one tall, dry-looking old gentleman, with beetling eyebrows, who maintained a grave and rather severe face throughout; now and then folding his arms, inclining his head, and looking down upon the floor, as if turning a doubt over in his mind. He was one of your wary men, who never laugh, but on good grounds—when they have reason and the law on their side. When the mirth of the rest of the company had subsided and silence was restored, he leaned one arm on the elbow of his chair, and sticking the other akimbo, demanded, with a slight but exceedingly sage motion of the head, and contraction of the brow, what was the moral of the story, and what it went to prove?

The story-teller, who was just putting a glass of wine to his lips, as a refreshment after his toils, paused for a moment, looked at his inquirer with an air of infinite deference, and, lowering the glass slowly to the table, observed, that the story was intended most logically to prove:

"There is no situation in life but has its advantages and pleasures—provided we will but take a joke as we find it;

"That, therefore, he that runs races with goblin troopers is likely to have rough riding of it.

"*Ergo,* for a country schoolmaster to be refused the hand of a Dutch heiress, is a certain step to high preferment in the state."

The cautious old gentleman knit his brows tenfold closer after this explanation, being sorely puzzled by ratiocination of the syllogism; while, methought, the one in pepper-and-salt eyed him with something of a triumphant leer. At length he observed, that all this was very well, but still he thought the story a little on the extravagant—there were one or two points on which he had his doubts.

"Faith, sir," replied the story-teller, "as to that matter, I don't believe one half of it myself."

D.K.

The Stout Gentleman

A STAGE-COACH ROMANCE

I'll cross it though it blast me! — HAMLET

A favorite evening pastime at the Hall, and one which the worthy Squire is fond of promoting, is story-telling, a "good old-fashioned fireside amusement," as he terms it. Indeed, I believe he promotes it chiefly because it was one of the choice recreations in those days of yore when ladies and gentlemen were not much in the habit of reading. Be this as it may, he will often, at supper-table, when conversation flags, call on some one or other of the company for a story, as it was formerly the custom to call for a song; and it is edifying to see the exemplary patience, and even satisfaction, with which the good old gentleman will sit and listen to some hackneyed tale that he has heard for at least a hundred times.

In this way one evening the current of anecdotes and stories ran upon mysterious personages that have figured at different times, and filled the world with doubts and conjecture; such as the Wandering Jew; the Man with the Iron Mask, who tormented the curiosity of all Europe; the Invisible Girl; and last, though not least, the Pig-faced Lady.

At length one of the company was called upon who had the most unpromising physiognomy for a story-teller that ever I had seen. He was a thin, pale, weazen-faced man, extremely nervous, who had sat at one corner of the table, shrunk up, as it were, into himself, and almost swallowed up in the cape of his coat, as a turtle in its shell.

The very demand seemed to throw him into a nervous agitation, yet he did not refuse. He emerged his head out of his shell, made a few odd grimaces and gesticulations, before he could get his muscles into order, or his voice under command, and then offered to give some account of a mysterious personage whom he had recently encountered in the course of his travels, and one whom he thought fully entitled of being classed with the Man with the Iron Mask.

I was so much struck with his extraordinary narrative, that I have written it out to the best of my recollection, for the amusement of the reader. I think it has in it all the elements of that mysterious and romantic narrative so greedily sought after at the present day.

It was a rainy Sunday in the gloomy month of November. I had been detained, in the course of a journey, by a slight indisposition, from which I was recovering; but was still feverish, and obliged to keep within doors all day, in an inn of the small town of Derby. A wet Sunday in a country inn!—whoever has had the luck to experience one can alone judge of my situation. The rain pattered against the casements; the bells tolled for church with a melancholy sound. I went to the windows in quest of something to amuse the eye; but it seemed as if I had been placed completely out of the reach of all amusement. The windows of my bedroom looked out among tiled roofs and stacks of chimneys, while those of my sitting-room commanded a full view of the stable-yard. I know of nothing more calculated to make a man sick of this world than a stable-yard on a rainy day. The place was littered with wet straw that had been kicked about by travellers and stable-boys. In one corner was a stagnant pool of water, surrounding an island of muck; there were several half-drowned fowls crowded together under a cart, among which was a miserable, crestfallen cock, drenched out of all life and spirit; his drooping tail matted, as it were, into a single feather, along which the water trickled from his back; near the cart was a half-dozing cow, chewing the cud, and standing patiently to be rained on, with wreaths of vapor rising from her reeking hide; a wall-eyed horse, tired of the loneliness of the stable, was poking his spectral head out of a window, with the rain dripping on it from the eaves; an unhappy cur, chained to a dog-house hard by, uttered something, every now and then, between a bark and a yelp; a drab of a kitchen-wench tramped backwards and forwards through the yard in pattens, looking as sulky as the weather itself; everything, in short, was comfortless and forlorn, excepting a crew of hardened ducks, assembled like boon companions round a puddle, and making a riotous noise over their liquor.

I was lonely and listless, and wanted amusement. My room soon became insupportable. I abandoned it, and sought what is technically called the travellers' room. This is a public room set apart at most inns for the accommodation of a class of wayfarers called travellers, or riders; a kind of commercial knights-errant, who are incessantly scouring the kingdom in gigs, on horseback, or by coach. They are the only successors that I know of at the present day to the knights-errant of yore. They lead the same kind of roving, adventurous life, only changing the lance for a driving-whip, the buckler for a pattern-card, and the coat of mail for an upper Benjamin. Instead of vindicating the charms of peerless beauty, they rove about, spreading the fame and standing of some substantial tradesman, or manufacturer, and are ready at any time to bargain in his name; it being the fashion nowadays to trade, instead of fight, with one another. As the room of the hostel, in the good old fighting times, would be hung round at night with the armor of way-worn warriors, such as coats of mail, falchions, and yawning helmets, so the travellers' room is garnished with box-coats, whips of all kinds, spurs, gaiters, and oil-cloth covered hats.

I was in hopes of finding some of these worthies to talk with, but was disappointed. There were, indeed, two or three in the room; but I could make nothing of them. One was just finishing his breakfast, quarrelling with his bread and butter, and huffing the waiter; another buttoned on a pair of gaiters, with many execrations at Boots for not having cleaned his shoes well; a third sat drumming on the table with his fingers and looking at the rain as it streamed down the window-glass; they all appeared infected by the weather, and disappeared, one after the other, without exchanging a word.

I sauntered to the window, and stood gazing at the people, picking their way to church, with petticoats hoisted midleg high, and dripping umbrellas. The bell ceased to toll, and the streets became silent. I then amused myself with watching the daughters of a tradesman opposite; who, being confined to the house for fear of wetting their Sunday finery, played off their charms at the front windows, to fascinate the chance tenants of the inn. They at length were summoned away by a vigilant, vinegar-faced mother, and I had nothing further from without to amuse me.

What was I to do to pass away the long-lived day? I was sadly nervous and lonely; and everything about an inn seems calculated to make a dull day ten times duller. Old newspapers, smelling of beer and tobacco-smoke, and which I had already read half a dozen times. Good-for-nothing books, that were worse than rainy weather. I bored myself to death with an old volume of the *Lady's Magazine*. I read all the commonplace names of ambitious travellers scrawled on the panes of glass; the eternal families of the Smiths, and the Browns, and the Jacksons, and the Johnsons, and all the other sons; and I deciphered several scraps of fatiguing inn-window poetry which I have met with in all parts of the world.

The day continued lowering and gloomy; the slovenly, ragged, spongy cloud drifted heavily along; there was no variety even in the rain: it was one dull, continued, monotonous patter—patter—patter, except-ing that now and then I was enlivened by the idea of a brisk shower, from the rattling of the drops upon a passing umbrella.

It was quite *refreshing* (if I may be allowed a hackneyed phrase of the day) when, in the course of the morning, a horn blew, and a stage-coach whirled through the street, with outside passengers stuck all over it, cowering under cotton umbrellas, and seethed together, and reeking with the steams of wet box-coats and upper Benjamins.

The sound brought out from their lurking-places a crew of vagabond boys, and vagabond dogs, and the carroty-headed hostler, and that nondescript animal ycleped Boots, and all the other vagabond race that infest the purlieus of an inn. But the bustle was transient; the coach again whirled on its way; and boy and dog, and hostler and Boots, all slunk back again to their holes; the street again became silent, and the rain continued to rain on. In fact, there was no hope of its clearing up; the barometer pointed to rainy weather; mine hostess's tortoise-shell cat sat by the fire washing her face, and rubbing her paws over her ears; and, on referring to the Almanac, I found a direful prediction stretching from the top of the page to the bottom through the whole month, "expect—much—rain—about—this—time!"

I was dreadfully hipped. The hours seemed as if they would never creep by. The very ticking of the clock became irksome. At length the stillness of the house was interrupted by the ringing of a bell. Shortly after I heard the voice of a waiter at the bar: "The stout gentleman in No. 13 wants his breakfast. Tea and bread and butter, with ham and eggs; the eggs not to be too much done."

In such a situation as mine, every incident is of importance. Here was a subject of speculation presented to my mind, and ample exercise for my imagination. I am prone to paint pictures to myself, and on this occasion I had some materials to work upon. Had the guest upstairs been mentioned as Mr. Smith, or Mr. Brown, or Mr. Jackson, or Mr. Johnson, or merely as "the gentleman in No. 13," it would have been a perfect blank to me. I should have thought nothing of it; but "the stout gentleman"!—the very name had something in it of the picturesque. It at once gave the size; it embodied the personage to my mind's eye, and my fancy did the rest.

He was stout, or, as some term it, lusty; in all probability, therefore, he was advanced in life, some people expanding as they grow old. By his breakfasting rather late, and in his own room, he must be a man accustomed to live at his ease, and above the necessity of early rising; no doubt a round, rosy, lusty old gentleman.

There was another violent ringing. The stout gentleman was impatient for his breakfast. He was evidently a man of importance; "well to do in the world"; accustomed to be promptly waited upon; of a keen appetite, and a little cross when hungry; "perhaps," thought I, "he may be some London Alderman; or who knows but he may be a Member of Parliament?"

The breakfast was sent up, and there was a short interval of silence; he was, doubtless, making the tea. Presently there was a violent ringing; and before it could be answered, another ringing still more violent. "Bless me! what a choleric old gentleman!" The waiter came down in a huff. The butter was rancid, the eggs were overdone, the ham was too salt;—the stout gentleman was evidently nice in his eating; one of those who eat and growl, and keep the waiter on the trot, and live in a state militant with the household.

The hostess got into a fume. I should observe that she was a brisk,

coquettish woman; a little of a shrew, and something of a slammerkin, but very pretty withal; with a nincompoop for a husband, as shrews are apt to have. She rated the servants roundly for their negligence in sending up so bad a breakfast, but said not a word against the stout gentleman; by which I clearly perceived that he must be a man of consequence, entitled to make a noise and to give trouble at a country inn. Other eggs, and ham, and bread and butter were sent up. They appeared to be more graciously received; at least there was no further complaint.

I had not made many turns about the travellers' room, when there was another ringing. Shortly afterwards there was a stir and an inquest about the house. The stout gentleman wanted the *Times* or the *Chronicle* newspaper. I set him down, therefore, for a Whig; or rather, from his being so absolute and lordly where he had a chance, I suspected him of being a Radical. Hunt, I had heard, was a large man; "who knows," thought I, "but it is Hunt himself!"

My curiosity began to be awakened. I inquired of the waiter who was this stout gentleman that was making all this stir; but I could get no information. Nobody seemed to know his name. The landlords of bustling inns seldom trouble their heads about the names or occupations of their transient guests. The color of a coat, the shape or size of a person, is enough to suggest a travelling name. It is either the tall gentleman, or the short gentleman, or the gentleman in black, or the gentleman in snuff-color; or, as in the present instance, the stout gentleman. A designation of the kind once hit on, answers every purpose, and saves all further inquiry.

Rain—rain—rain! pitiless, ceaseless rain! No such thing as putting a foot out of doors, and no occupation or amusement within. By and by I heard some one walking overhead. It was in the stout gentleman's room. He evidently was a large man by the heaviness of his tread; and an old man from his wearing such creaking soles. "He is doubtless," thought I, "some rich old square-toes of regular habits, and is now taking exercise after breakfast."

I now read all the advertisements of coaches and hotels that were stuck about the mantelpiece. The *Lady's Magazine* had become an abomination to me; it was as tedious as the day itself. I wandered out, not knowing what to do, and ascended again to my room. I had not been there long, when there was a squall from a neighboring bedroom. A door opened and slammed violently; a chamber-maid, that I had re-marked for having a ruddy, good-humored face, went downstairs in a violent flurry. The stout gentleman had been rude to her!

This sent a whole host of my deductions to the deuce in a moment. The unknown personage could not be an old gentleman; for old gentle-men are not apt to be so obstreperous to chamber-maids. He could not be a young gentleman; for young gentlemen are not apt to inspire such indignation. He must be a middle-aged man, and confounded ugly into the bargain, or the girl would not have taken the matter in such terrible dudgeon. I confess I was sorely puzzled.

In a few minutes I heard the voice of my landlady. I caught a glance of her as she came tramping upstairs—her face glowing, her cap flaring, her tongue wagging the whole way. "She'd have no such doings in her house, she'd warrant. If gentlemen did spend money freely, it was no rule. She'd have no servant-maids of hers treated in that way, when they were about their work, that's what she wouldn't."

As I hate squabbles, particularly with women, and above all with pretty women, I slunk back into my room, and partly closed the door; but my curiosity was too much excited not to listen. The landlady marched intrepidly to the enemy's citadel, and entered it with a storm. The door closed after her. I heard her voice in high windy clamor for a moment or two. Then it gradually subsided, like a gust of wind in a garret; then there was a laugh; then I heard nothing more.

After a little while my landlady came out with an odd smile on her face, adjusting her cap, which was a little on one side. As she went downstairs, I heard the landlord ask her what was the matter. She said, "Nothing at all, only the girl's a fool." I was more than ever perplexed what to make of this unaccountable personage, who could put a good-natured chamber-maid in a passion, and send away a termagant landlady in smiles. He could not be so old, nor cross, nor ugly either.

I had to go to work at his picture again, and to paint him entirely different. I now set him down for one of those stout gentlemen that are frequently met with swaggering about the doors of country inns. Moist, merry fellows, in Belcher handkerchiefs, whose bulk is a little assisted by malt liquors. Men who have seen the world, and been sworn at High-gate; who are used to tavern-life, up to all the tricks of tapsters, and knowing in the ways of sinful publicans. Free-livers on a small scale; who are prodigal within the compass of a guinea, who call all the waiters by name, tousle the maids, gossip with the landlady at the bar, and prose over a pint of port, or a glass of negus, after dinner.

The morning wore away in forming these and similar surmises. As fast as I wove one system of belief, some movement of the unknown would completely overturn it, and throw all my thoughts again into confusion. Such are the solitary operations of a feverish mind. I was, as I have said, extremely nervous; and the continual meditation on the concerns of this invisible personage began to have its effect. I was getting a fit of the fidgets.

Dinner-time came. I hoped the stout gentleman might dine in the travellers' room, and that I might at length get a view of his person; but no—he had dinner served in his own room. What could be the meaning of this solitude and mystery? He could not be a Radical; there was something too aristocratical in thus keeping himself apart from the rest of the world, and condemning himself to his own dull company through-out a rainy day. And then, too, he lived too well for a discontented politician. He seemed to expatiate on a variety of dishes, and to sit over his wine like a jolly friend of good living. Indeed, my doubts on this head were soon at an end; for he could not have finished his first bottle before I could faintly hear him humming a tune; and on listening I found it to be "God save the King." 'Twas plain, then, he was no Radical, but a faithful subject; one who grew loyal over his bottle and was ready to stand by king and constitution, when he could stand by nothing else. But who could he be? My conjectures began to run wild. Was he not some personage of distinction travelling incog.? "God knows!" said I, at my wit's end; "it may be one of the royal family for aught I know, for they are all stout gentlemen!"

The weather continued rainy. The mysterious unknown kept his room, and, as far as I could judge, his chair, for I did not hear him move. In the meantime, as the day advanced, the travellers' room began to be frequented. Some, who had just arrived, came in buttoned up in box-coats; others came home who had been dispersed about the town; some took their dinners, and some their tea. Had I been in a different mood, I should have found entertainment in studying this peculiar class of men. There were two especially, who were regular wags of the road, and up to all the standing jokes of travellers. They had a thousand sly things to say to the waiting-maid, whom they called Louisa, and Ethelinda, and a dozen other fine names, changing the name every time, and chuckling amazingly at their own waggery. My mind, however, had been completely engrossed by the stout gentleman. He had kept my fancy in chase during a long day, and it was not now to be diverted from the scent.

The evening gradually wore away. The travellers read the papers two or three times over. Some drew round the fire and told long stories about their horses, about their adventures, their overturns, and breakings-down. They discussed the credit of different merchants and different inns; and the two wags told several choice anecdotes of pretty chamber-maids and kind landladies. All this passed as they were quietly taking what they called their night-caps, that is to say, strong glasses of brandy and water and sugar, or some other mixture of the kind; after which they one after another rang for Boots and the chamber-maid, and walked off to bed in old shoes cut down into marvellously uncomfortable slippers.

There was now only one man left: a short-legged, long-bodied, plethoric fellow, with a very large, sandy head. He sat by himself, with a glass of port-wine negus, and a spoon; sipping and stirring, and meditating and sipping, until nothing was left but the spoon. He gradually fell asleep bolt upright in his chair, with the empty glass standing before him; and the candle seemed to fall asleep too, for the wick grew long, and black, and cabbaged at the end, and dimmed the little light that remained in the chamber. The gloom that now prevailed was contagious. Around hung the shapeless, and almost spectral box-coats of departed travellers, long since buried in deep sleep. I only heard the ticking of the clock, with the deep-drawn breathings of the sleeping topers, and the drippings of the rain, drop—drop—drop, from the eaves of the house. The church-bells chimed midnight. All at once the stout gentleman began to walk overhead, pacing slowly backwards and forwards. There was something extremely awful in all this, especially to one in my state of nerves. These ghastly great-coats, these guttural breathings, and the creaking footsteps of this mysterious being. His steps grew fainter and fainter, and at length died away. I could bear it no longer. I was wound up to the desperation of a hero of romance. "Be he who or what he may," said I to myself, "I'll have a sight of him!" I seized a chamber-candle, and hurried up to No. 13. The door stood ajar. I hesitated—I entered; the room was deserted. There stood a large, broad-bottomed elbow-chair at a table, on which was an empty tumbler, and a *Times* newspaper, and the room smelt powerfully of Stilton cheese.

The mysterious stranger had evidently but just retired. I turned off, sorely disappointed, to my room, which had been changed to the front of the house. As I went along the corridor, I saw a large pair of boots, with dirty, waxed tops, standing at the door of a bed-chamber. They doubtless belonged to the unknown; but it would not do to disturb so redoubtable a personage in his den: he might discharge a pistol, or something worse, at my head. I went to bed, therefore, and lay awake half the night in a terribly nervous state; and even when I fell asleep, I was still haunted in my dreams by the idea of the stout gentleman and his wax-topped boots.

I slept rather late the next morning, and was awakened by some stir and bustle in the house, which I could not at first comprehend; until getting more awake, I found there was a mail-coach starting from the door. Suddenly there was a cry from below: "The gentleman has forgot his umbrella! Look for the gentleman's umbrella in No. 13!" I heard an immediate scampering of a chamber-maid along the passage, and a shrill reply as she ran. "Here it is! here's the gentleman's umbrella!"

The mysterious stranger then was on the point of setting off. This was the only chance I should ever have of knowing him. I sprang out of bed, scrambled to the window, snatched aside the curtains, and just caught a glimpse of the rear of a person getting in at the coach-door. The skirts of a brown coat parted behind, and gave me a full view of the broad disk of a pair of drab breeches. The door closed—"All right!" was the word—the coach whirled off;—and that was all I ever saw of the stout gentleman!

Annette Delarbre

The soldier frae the war returns,
And the merchant from the main,
But I hae parted wi' my love,
And ne'er to meet again,
                    My dear,
And ne'er to meet again.
When day is gone, and night is come,
And a' are boun to sleep,
I think on them that's far awa
The lee-lang night and weep,
                    My dear,
The lee-lang night and weep.
                    OLD SCOTCH BALLAD

Yesterday was a day of quiet and repose after the bustle of May-day. During the morning I joined the ladies in a small sitting-room, the windows of which came down to the floor, and opened upon a terrace of the garden, which was set out with delicate shrubs and flowers. The soft sunshine falling into the room through the branches of trees that overhung the windows, the sweet smell of flowers, and the singing of birds, produced a pleasing yet calming effect on the whole party. Some time elapsed without any one speaking. Lady Lillycraft and Miss Templeton were sitting by an elegant work-table, near one of the windows, occupied with some pretty lady-like work. The captain was on a stool at his mistress's feet, looking over some music; and poor Phoebe Wilkins, who has always been a kind of pet among the ladies, but who has risen vastly in favor with Lady Lillycraft in consequence of some tender confessions, sat in one corner of the room, with swollen eyes, working pensively at some of the fair Julia's wedding ornaments.

The silence was interrupted by her ladyship, who suddenly proposed a task to the captain. "I am in your debt," said she, "for that tale you read to us the other day; I will now furnish one in return, if you'll read it; and it is just suited to this sweet May morning, for it is all about love!"

The proposition seemed to delight every one present. The captain smiled assent. Her ladyship rang for her page, and despatched him to her room for the manuscript. "As the captain," said she, "gave us an account of the author of his story, it is but right I should give one of mine. It was written by the parson of the parish where I reside. He is a thin, elderly man, of a delicate constitution, but positively one of the most charming men that ever lived. He lost his wife a few years since; one of the sweetest women you ever saw. He has two sons, whom he educates himself; both of whom already write delightful poetry. His parsonage is a lovely place, close by the church, all overrun with ivy and honeysuckles, with the sweetest flower-garden about it; for, you know, our country clergymen are almost always fond of flowers, and make their parsonages perfect pictures.

"His living is a very good one, and he is very much beloved, and does a great deal of good in the neighborhood, and among the poor. And then such sermons as he preaches! Oh, if you could only hear one taken from a text in Solomon's Song, all about love and matrimony, one of the sweetest things you ever heard! He preaches it at least once a year, in springtime, for he knows I am fond of it. He always dines with me on Sundays, and often brings me some of the sweetest pieces of poetry, all about the pleasures of melancholy, and such subjects, that make me cry so, you can't think. I wish he would publish. I think he has some things as sweet as anything of Moore or Lord Byron.

"He fell into very ill health, some time ago, and was advised to go to the Continent; and I gave him no peace until he went, and promised to take care of his two boys until he returned.

"He was gone for above a year, and was quite restored. When he came back, he sent me the tale I'm going to show you—Oh, here it is!" said she, as the page put in her hands a beautiful box of satin-wood. She unlocked it, and among several parcels of notes on embossed paper, cards of charades, and copies of verses, she drew out a crimson velvet case, that smelt very much of perfumes. From this she took a manuscript, daintily written on gilt-edged vellum paper, and stitched with a light-blue ribbon. This she handed to the captain, who read the following tale, which I have procured for the entertainment of the reader.

In the course of a tour in Lower Normandy I remained for a day or two in the old town of Honfleur, which stands near the mouth of the Seine. It was the time of a fête, and all the world was thronging in the evening to dance at the fair, held before the chapel of Our Lady of Grace. As I like all kinds of innocent merry-making, I joined the throng.

The chapel is situated at the top of a high hill, or promontory, whence its bell may be heard at a distance by a mariner at night. It is said to have given the name to the port of Havre de Grace, which lies directly opposite, on the other side of the Seine. The road up to the chapel went in a zigzag course along the brow of the steep coast; it was shaded by trees, from between which I had beautiful peeps at the ancient towers of Honfleur below, the varied scenery of the opposite shore, the white buildings of Havre in the distance, and the wide sea beyond. The road was enlivened by groups of peasant girls, in bright crimson dresses, and tall caps, and I found all the flower of the neighborhood assembled on the green that crowds the summit of the hill.

The chapel of Notre Dame de Grace is a favorite resort of the inhabitants of Honfleur and its vicinity, both for pleasure and devotion. At this little chapel prayers are put up by the mariners of the port previous to their voyages, and by their friends during their absence; and votive offerings are hung about its walls, in fulfilment of vows made during times of shipwreck and disaster. The chapel is surrounded by trees. Over the portal is an image of the Virgin and Child, with an inscription which struck me as being quite poetical:

> "Etoile de la mer, priez pour nous!"
> (Star of the sea, pray for us.)

On a level spot near the chapel, under a grove of noble trees, the populace dance on fine summer evenings; and here are held frequent fairs and fêtes, which assemble all the rustic beauty of the loveliest parts of Lower Normandy. The present was an occasion of the kind. Booths and tents were erected among the trees; there were the usual displays of finery to tempt the rural coquette, and of wonderful shows to entice the curious; mountebanks were exerting their eloquence; jugglers and fortune-tellers astonishing the credulous; while whole rows of grotesque saints, in wood and wax-work, were offered for the purchase of the pious.

The fête had assembled in one view all the picturesque costumes of the Pays d'Auge and the Coté de Caux. I beheld tall, stately caps, and trim bodices, according to fashions which have been handed down from mother to daughter for centuries; the exact counterparts of those worn in the time of the Conqueror; and which surprised me by their faithful resemblance to those in the old pictures of Froissart's Chronicles, and in the paintings of illuminated manuscripts. Any one, also, who has been in Lower Normandy, must have remarked the beauty of the peasantry, and that air of native elegance which prevails among them. It is to this country, undoubtedly, that the English owe their good looks. It was hence that the bright carnation, the fine blue eye, the light auburn hair, passed over to England in the train of the Conqueror, and filled the land with beauty.

The scene before me was perfectly enchanting: the assemblage of so many fresh and blooming faces; the gay groups in fanciful dresses; some dancing on the green, others strolling about, or seated on the grass; the fine clumps of trees in the foreground, bordering the brow of this

airy height, and the broad green sea, sleeping in summer tranquillity, in the distance.

Whilst I was regarding this animated picture, I was struck with the appearance of a beautiful girl, who passed through the crowd without seeming to take any interest in their amusements. She was slender and delicate, without the bloom upon her cheek usual among the peasantry of Normandy, and her blue eyes had a singular and melancholy expression. She was accompanied by a venerable-looking man, whom I presumed to be her father. There was a whisper among the by-standers, and a wistful look after her as she passed; the young men touched their hats, and some of the children followed her at a little distance, watching her movements. She approached the edge of the hill, where there is a little platform, whence the people of Honfleur look out for the approach of vessels. Here she stood for some time waving her handkerchief, though there was nothing to be seen but two or three fishing-boats, like mere specks on the bosom of the distant ocean.

These circumstances excited my curiosity, and I made some inquiries about her, which were answered with readiness and intelligence by a priest of the neighboring chapel. Our conversation drew together several of the by-standers, each of whom had something to communicate, and from them all I gathered the following particulars.

Annette Delarbre was the only daughter of one of the higher order of farmers, or small proprietors, as they are called, of Pont l'Eveque, a pleasant village not far from Honfleur, in that rich pastoral part of Lower Normandy called the Pays d'Auge. Annette was the pride and delight of her parents, who brought her up with the fondest indulgence. She was gay, tender, petulant, and susceptible. All her feelings were quick and ardent; and having never experienced contradiction nor restraint she was little practised in self-control; nothing but the native

goodness of her heart kept her from running continually into error.

Even while a child, her susceptibility was evinced in an attachment formed to a playmate, Eugene la Forgue, the only son of a widow of the neighborhood. Their childish love was an epitome of maturer passion; it had its caprices, and jealousies, and quarrels, and reconciliations. It was assuming something of a graver character as Annette entered her fifteenth and Eugene his nineteenth year, when he was suddenly carried off to the army by the conscription.

It was a heavy blow to his widowed mother, for he was her only pride and comfort; but it was one of those sudden bereavements which mothers were perpetually doomed to feel in France, during the time that continual and bloody wars were incessantly draining her youth. It was a temporary affliction also to Annette, to lose her lover. With tender embraces, half childish, half womanish, she parted from him. The tears streamed from her blue eyes as she bound a braid of her fair hair round his wrist; but the smiles still broke through; for she was yet too young to feel how serious a thing is separation, and how many chances there are, when parting in this wide world, against our ever meeting again.

Weeks, months, years flew by. Annette increased in beauty as she increased in years, and was the reigning belle of the neighborhood. Her time passed innocently and happily. Her father was a man of some consequence in the rural community, and his house was the resort of the gayest of the village. Annette held a kind of rural court; she was always surrounded by companions of her own age, among whom she shone unrivalled. Much of their time was passed in making lace, the prevalent manufacture of the neighborhood. As they sat at this delicate and feminine labor, the merry tale and sprightly song went round. None laughed with a lighter heart than Annette; and if she sang, her voice was perfect melody. Their evenings were enlivened by the dance, or by those pleasant social games so prevalent among the French; and when she appeared at the village ball on Sunday evenings, she was the theme of universal admiration.

As she was a rural heiress, she did not want for suitors. Many advantageous offers were made her, but she refused them all. She laughed at the pretended pangs of her admirers, and triumphed over them with the caprice of buoyant youth and conscious beauty. With all her apparent levity, however, could any one have read the story of her heart, they might have traced in it some fond remembrance of her early playmate, not so deeply graven as to be painful, but too deep to be easily obliterated; and they might have noticed, amidst all her gayety, the tenderness that marked her manner towards the mother of Eugene. She would often steal away from her youthful companions and their amusements, to pass whole days with the good widow; listening to her fond talk about her boy, and blushing with secret pleasure, when his letters were read, at finding herself a constant theme of recollection and inquiry.

At length the sudden return of peace, which sent many a warrior to his native cottage, brought back Eugene, a young sunburnt soldier, to the village. I need not say how rapturously his return was greeted by his mother, who saw in him the pride and staff of her old age. He had risen in the service by his merit; but brought away but little from the wars excepting a soldier-like air, a gallant name, and, a scar across the forehead. He brought back however, a nature unspoiled by the camp. He was frank, open, generous, and ardent. His heart was quick and kind in its impulses, and was perhaps a little softer from having suffered. It was full of tenderness for Annette. He had received frequent accounts of her from his mother; and the mention of her kindness to his lonely parent had rendered her doubly dear to him. He had been wounded. He had been a prisoner; he had been in various troubles but had always preserved the braid of hair which she had bound round his arm. It had been a kind of talisman to him; he had many a time looked upon it as he lay on the hard ground, and the thought that he might one day see Annette again, and the fair fields about his native village, had cheered his heart, and enabled him to bear up against every hardship.

He had left Annette almost a child; he found her a blooming woman. If he had loved her before, he now adored her. Annette was equally struck with the improvement time had made in her lover. She noticed, with secret admiration, his superiority to the young men of the village; the frank, lofty, military air, that distinguished him from all the rest at their rural gatherings. The more she saw him, the more her light, playful fondness of former years deepened into ardent and powerful affection. But Annette was a rural belle. She had tasted the sweets of dominion, and had been rendered wilful and capricious by constant indulgence at home, and admiration abroad. She was conscious of her power over Eugene, and delighted in exercising it. She sometimes treated him with petulant caprice, enjoying the pain which she inflicted by her frowns, from the idea how soon she would chase it away again by her smiles. She took a pleasure in alarming his fears, by affecting a temporary preference for some one or other of his rivals; and then would delight in allaying them by an ample measure of returning kindness. Perhaps there was some degree of vanity gratified by all this; it might be a matter of triumph to show her absolute power over the young soldier, who was a universal object of female admiration. Eugene, however, was of too serious and ardent a nature to be trifled with. He loved too fervently not to be filled with doubt. He saw Annette surrounded by admirers, and full of animation, the gayest among the gay at all their rural festivities, and apparently most gay when he was most dejected. Every one saw through this caprice but himself; every one saw that in reality she doted on him; but Eugene alone suspected the sincerity of her affection. For some time he bore the coquetry with secret impatience and distrust; but his feelings grew sore and irritable, and overcame his self-command. A slight misunderstanding took place; a quarrel ensued. Annette, unaccustomed to being thwarted and contradicted, and full of the insolence of youthful beauty, assumed an air of disdain. She refused all explanations to her lover, and they parted in anger. That very evening Eugene saw her, full of gayety, dancing with one of his rivals; and as her eye caught his, fixed on her with unfeigned distress, it sparkled with more than usual vivacity. It was a finishing blow to his hopes, already so much impaired by secret distrust. Pride and resentment both struggled in his breast, and seemed to rouse his spirit to all his wonted energy. He retired from her presence with the hasty determination never to see her again.

A woman is more considerate in affairs of love than a man; because love is more the study and business of her life. Annette soon repented of her indiscretion; she felt that she had used her lover unkindly; she felt that she had trifled with his sincere and generous nature—and then he looked so handsome when he parted after their quarrel—his fine features lighted up by indignation. She had intended making up with him at the evening dance; but his sudden departure prevented her. She now promised herself that when next they met she would amply repay him by the sweets of a perfect reconciliation, and that, thenceforward, she would never—never tease him more! That promise was not to be fulfilled. Day after day passed; but Eugene did not make his appearance. Sunday evening came, the usual time when all the gayety of the village assembled; but Eugene was not there. She inquired after him; he had left the village. She now became alarmed, and, forgetting all coyness and affected indifference, called on Eugene's mother for an explanation. She found her full of affliction, and learnt with surprise and consternation that Eugene had gone to sea.

While his feelings were yet smarting with her affected disdain, and his heart a prey to alternate indignation and despair, he had suddenly embraced an invitation which had repeatedly been made him by a relative, who was fitting out a ship from the port of Honfleur, and who wished him to be the companion of his voyage. Absence appeared to him the only cure for his unlucky passion; and in the temporary transports of his feelings there was something gratifying in the idea of having half the world intervene between them. The hurry necessary for his departure left no time for cool reflection; it rendered him deaf to the remonstrances of his afflicted mother. He hastened to Honfleur just in time to make the needful preparations for the voyage; and the first news that Annette received of this sudden determination was a letter delivered by his mother, returning her pledges of affection, particularly the long-treasured braid of her hair, and bidding her a last farewell, in terms more full of sorrow and tenderness than upbraiding.

This was the first stroke of real anguish that Annette had ever received, and it overcame her. The vivacity of her spirits were apt to hurry her to extremes; she for a time gave way to ungovernable transports of affliction and remorse, and manifested, in the violence of her grief, the real ardor of her affection. The thought occurred to her that the ship might not yet have sailed; she seized on the hope with eagerness, and hastened with her father to Honfleur. The ship had sailed that very morning. From the heights above the town she saw it lessening to a speck on the broad bosom of the ocean, and before evening the white sail had faded from her sight. She turned, full of anguish, to the neighboring chapel of Our Lady of Grace, and throwing herself on the pavement, poured out prayers and tears for the safe return of her lover.

When she returned home, the cheerfulness of her spirits was at an end. She looked back with remorse and self-upbraiding on her past caprices; she turned with distaste from the adulation of her admirers, and had no longer any relish for the amusements of the village. With humiliation and diffidence she sought the widowed mother of Eugene; but was received by her with an overflowing heart, for she only beheld in Annette one who could sympathize in her doting fondness for her son. It seemed some alleviation of her remorse to sit by the mother all day, to study her wants, to beguile her heavy hours, to hang about her with the caressing endearments of a daughter, and to seek by every means, if possible, to supply the place of the son, whom she reproached herself with having driven away.

In the meantime the ship made a prosperous voyage to her destined port. Eugene's mother received a letter from him, in which he lamented the precipitancy of his departure. The voyage had given him time for sober reflection. If Annette had been unkind to him, he ought not to have forgotten what was due to his mother, who was now advanced in years. He accused himself of selfishness in only listening to the suggestions of his own inconsiderate passions. He promised to return with the ship, to make his mind up to his disappointment, and to think of nothing but making his mother happy——"And when he does return," said Annette, clasping her hands with transport, "it shall not be my fault if he ever leaves us again."

The time approached for the ship's return. She was daily expected, when the weather became dreadfully tempestuous. Day after day brought news of vessels foundered, or driven on shore, and the coast was strewed with wrecks. Intelligence was received of the looked-for ship having been seen dismasted in a violent storm, and the greatest fears were entertained for her safety.

Annette never left the side of Eugene's mother. She watched every change of her countenance with painful solicitude, and endeavored to cheer her with hopes, while her own mind was racked by anxiety. She tasked her efforts to be gay; but it was a forced and unnatural gayety. A sigh from the mother would completely check it; and when she could no longer restrain the rising tears, she would hurry away and pour out her agony in secret. Every anxious look, every anxious inquiry of the mother, whenever a door opened, or a strange face appeared, was an arrow to her soul. She considered every disappointment as a pang of her own infliction, and her heart sickened under the care-worn expression of the maternal eye. At length this suspense became insupportable. She left the village and hastened to Honfleur, hoping every hour, every moment, to receive some tidings of her lover. She paced the pier, and wearied the seamen of the port with her inquiries. She made a daily pilgrimage to the chapel of Our Lady of Grace, hung votive garlands on the wall, and passed hours either kneeling before the altar, or looking out from the brow of the hill upon the angry sea.

At length word was brought that the long-wished-for vessel was in sight. She was seen standing into the mouth of the Seine, shattered and crippled, bearing marks of having been sadly tempest-tossed. A general joy was diffused by her return; and there was not a brighter eye, nor a lighter heart, than Annette's in the little port of Honfleur. The ship came to anchor in the river; and a boat put off for the shore. The populace crowded down to the pier-head to welcome it. Annette stood blushing, and smiling, and trembling, and weeping; for a thousand painfully pleasing emotions agitated her breast at the thoughts of the meeting and reconciliation about to take place.

Her heart throbbed to pour itself out, and atone to her gallant lover for all its errors. At one moment she would place herself in a conspicuous situation, where she might catch his view at once, and surprise him by her welcome; but the next moment a doubt would come across her mind, and she would shrink among the throng, trembling and faint, and gasping with her emotions. Her agitation increased as the boat drew near, until it became distressing; and it was almost a relief to her when she perceived that her lover was not there. She presumed that some accident had detained him on board of the ship, and felt that the delay would enable her to gather more self-possession for the meeting. As the boat neared the shore, many inquiries were made, and laconic answers returned. At length Annette heard some inquiries after her lover. Her heart palpitated; there was a moment's pause; the reply was brief, but awful. He had been washed from the deck, with two of the crew, in the midst of a stormy night, when it was impossible to render any assistance. A piercing shriek broke from among the crowd, and Annette had nearly fallen into the waves.

The sudden revulsion of feelings after such a transient gleam of happiness was too much for her harassed frame. She was carried home senseless. Her life was for some time despaired of, and it was months before she recovered her health; but she never had perfectly recovered her mind. It still remained unsettled with respect to her lover's fate.

"The subject," continued my informer, "is never mentioned in her hearing; but she sometimes speaks of it herself, and it seems as though there were some vague train of impressions in her mind, in which hope and fear are strangely mingled; some imperfect idea of her lover's shipwreck, and yet some expectation of his return.

"Her parents have tried every means to cheer her, and to banish these gloomy images from her thoughts. They assemble round her the young companions in whose society she used to delight; and they will work and chat, and sing, and laugh, as formerly; but she will sit silently among them, and will sometimes weep in the midst of their gayety; and if spoken to, will make no reply, but look up with streaming eyes, and sing a dismal little song, which she has learned somewhere, about a shipwreck. It makes everyone's very heart ache to see her in this way, for she used to be the happiest creature in the village.

"She passes the greater part of the time with Eugene's mother; whose only consolation is her society, and who dotes on her with a mother's tenderness. She is the only one that has perfect influence over Annette in every mood. The poor girl seems, as formerly, to make an effort to be cheerful in her company; but will sometimes gaze upon her with the most piteous look, and then kiss her gray hairs, and fall on her neck and weep.

"She is not always melancholy, however; there are occasional intervals when she will be bright and animated for days together; but a degree of wildness attends these fits of gayety, that prevents their yielding any satisfaction to her friends. At such times she will arrange her room, which is all covered with pictures of ships and legends of saints; and will wreathe a white chaplet, as for a wedding, and prepare wedding ornaments. She will listen anxiously at the door, and look frequently out at the window, as if expecting some one's arrival. It is supposed that at such times she is looking for her lover's return; but, as no one touches upon the theme, or mentions his name in her presence, the current of her thoughts is a mere matter of conjecture. Now and then she will make a pilgrimage to the chapel of Notre Dame de Grace; where she will pray for hours at the altar, and decorate the images with wreathes that she has woven; or will wave her handkerchief from the terrace, as you have seen if there is any vessel in the distance."

Upwards of a year, he informed me, had now elapsed without effacing from her mind this singular taint of insanity; still her friends hoped it might gradually wear away. They had at one time removed her to a distant part of the country, in hopes that absence from the scenes connected with her story might have a salutary effect; but, when her periodical melancholy returned, she became more restless and wretched than usual, and, secretly escaping from her friends, set out on foot, without knowing the road, on one of her pilgrimages to the chapel.

This little story entirely drew my attention from the gay scene of the fête, and fixed it upon the beautiful Annette. While she was yet standing on the terrace, the vesper-bell rang from the neighboring chapel. She listened for a moment, and then drawing a small rosary from her bosom, walked in that direction. Several of the peasantry followed her in silence; and I felt too much interested not to do the same.

The chapel, as I said before, is in the midst of a grove, on the high promontory. The inside is hung round with little models of ships, and rude paintings of wrecks and perils at sea, and providential deliverances, the votive offerings of captains and crews that have been saved. On entering, Annette paused for a moment before a picture of the Virgin, which, I observed, had recently been decorated with a wreath of artificial flowers. When she reached the middle of the chapel she knelt down, and those who followed her involuntarily did the same at a little distance. The evening sun shone softly through the checkered grove into one window of the chapel. A perfect stillness reigned within; and this stillness was the more impressive, contrasted with the distant sound of music and merriment from the fair. I could not take my eyes off from the poor suppliant; her lips moved as she told her beads, but her prayers were breathed in silence. It might have been mere fancy excited by the scene, that, as she raised her eyes to heaven, I thought they had an expression truly seraphic. But I am easily affected by female beauty, and there was something in this mixture of love, devotion, and partial insanity, inexpressibly touching.

As the poor girl left the chapel, there was a sweet serenity in her looks; and I was told she would return home, and in all probability be calm and cheerful for days, and even weeks; in which time it was supposed that hope predominated in her mental malady; and when the dark side of her mind, as her friends call it, was about to turn up, it would be known by her neglecting her distaff or her lace, singing plaintive songs, and weeping in silence.

She passed on from the chapel without noticing the fête, but smiling and speaking to many as she passed. I followed her with my eyes as she descended the winding road towards Honfleur, leaning on her father's arm. "Heaven," thought I, "has ever its store of balms for the hurt mind and wounded spirit, and may in time rear up this broken flower to be once more the pride and joy of the valley. The very delusion in which the poor girl walks may be one of those mists kindly diffused by Providence over the regions of thought, when they become too fruitful of misery. The veil may gradually be raised which obscures the horizon of her mind, as she is enabled steadily and calmly to contemplate the sorrows at present hidden in mercy from her view."

On my return from Paris, about a year afterwards, I turned off from the beaten route at Rouen, to revisit some of the most striking scenes of Lower Normandy. Having passed through the lovely country of the Pays d'Auge, I reached Honfleur on a fine afternoon, intending to cross to Havre the next morning, and embark for England. As I had no better way of passing the evening, I strolled up the hill to enjoy the fine prospect from the chapel of Notre Dame de Grace; and while there, I thought of inquiring after the fate of poor Annette Delarbre. The priest who had told me her story was officiating at vespers, after which I accosted him, and learnt from him the remaining circumstances. He told me that from the time I had seen her at the chapel, her disorder took a sudden turn for the worse, and her health rapidly declined. Her cheerful intervals became shorter and less frequent, and attended with more incoherency. She grew languid, silent, and moody in her melancholy; her form was wasted, her looks were pale and disconsolate, and it was feared she would never recover. She became impatient of all sounds of gayety, and was never so contented as when Eugene's mother was near her. The good woman watched over her with patient, yearning solicitude; and in seeking to beguile her sorrows, would half forget her own. Sometimes, as she sat looking upon her pallid face, the tears would fill her eyes, which when Annette perceived, she would anxiously wipe them away, and tell her not to grieve, for that Eugene would soon return; and then she would effect a forced gayety, as in former times, and sing a lively air; but a sudden recollection would come over her, and she would burst into tears, hang on the poor mother's neck, and entreat her not to curse her for having destroyed her son.

Just at this time, to the astonishment of every one, news was received of Eugene; who, it appears, was still living. When almost drowned, he had fortunately seized upon a spar, washed from the ship's deck. Finding himself nearly exhausted, he fastened himself to it, and floated for a day and night, until all sense left him. On recovering, he found himself on board a vessel bound to India, but so ill as not to move without assistance. His health continued precarious throughout the voyage. On arriving in India, he experienced many vicissitudes, and was transferred from ship to ship, and hospital to hospital. His constitution enabled him to struggle through every hardship; and he was now in a distant port, waiting only for the sailing of a ship to return home.

Great caution was necessary in imparting these tidings to the mother, and even then she was nearly overcome by the transports of her joy. But how to impart them to Annette was a matter of still greater perplexity. Her state of mind had been so morbid, she had been subject to such violent changes, and the cause of her derangement had been of such an inconsolable and hopeless kind, that her friends had always forborne to tamper with her feelings. They had never even hinted at the subject of her griefs, nor encouraged the theme when she adverted to it, but had passed it over in silence, hoping that time would gradually wear the traces of it from her recollection, or, at least, would render them less painful. They now felt at a loss how to undeceive her even in her misery, lest the sudden recurrence of happiness might confirm the estrangement of her reason, or might overpower her feeble frame. They ventured, however, to probe those wounds which they formerly did not dare to touch, for they now had the balm to pour into them. They led the conversation to those topics which they had hitherto shunned, and endeavored to ascertain the current of her thoughts in those varying moods which had formerly perplexed them. They found her mind even more affected than they had imagined. All her ideas were confused and wandering. Her bright and cheerful moods, which now grew seldomer than ever, were all the effects of mental delusion. At such times she had no recollection of her lover's having been in danger, but was only anticipating his arrival. "When the winter has passed away," said she, "and the trees put on their blossoms, and the swallow comes back over the sea, he will return." When she was drooping and desponding, it was in vain to remind her of what she had said in her gayer moments, and to assure her that Eugene would indeed return shortly. She wept on in silence, and appeared insensible to their words. But at times her agitation became violent, when she would upbraid herself with having driven Eugene from his mother, and brought sorrow on her gray hairs. Her mind admitted but one leading idea at a time, which nothing could avert or efface; or if they ever succeeded in interrupting the current of her fancy, it only became the more incoherent, and increased the feverishness that preyed upon both mind and body. Her friends felt more alarm for her than ever, for they feared her senses were irrevocably gone, and her constitution completely undermined.

In the meantime Eugene returned to the village. He was violently affected when the story of Annette was told him. With bitterness of heart he upbraided his own rashness and infatuation that had hurried him away from her, and accused himself as the author of all her woes. His mother would describe to him all the anguish and remorse of poor Annette; the tenderness with which she clung to her, and endeavored, even in the midst of her insanity, to console her for the loss of her son; and the touching expressions of affection mingled with her most incoherent wanderings of thought, until his feelings would be wound up to agony, and he would entreat her to desist from the recital. They did not dare as yet to bring him into Annette's sight; but he was permitted to see her when she was sleeping. The tears streamed down his sunburnt cheeks as he contemplated the ravages which grief and malady had made; and his heart swelled almost to breaking as he beheld round her neck the very braid of hair which she once gave him in token of girlish affection, and which he had returned to her in anger.

At length the physician that attended her determined to adventure upon an experiment; to take advantage of one of those cheerful moods when her mind was visited by hope, and to engraft, as it were, the reality upon the delusions of her fancy. These moods had now become very rare, for nature was sinking under the continual pressure of her mental malady, and the principle of reaction was daily growing weaker. Every effort was tried to bring on a cheerful interval of the kind. Several of her most favorite companions were kept continually about her; they chatted gayly, they laughed, and sang, and danced; but Annette reclined with languid frame and hollow eye, and took no part in their gayety. At length the winter was gone; the trees put forth their leaves; the swallows began to build in the eaves of the house, and the robin and wren piped all day beneath the window. Annette's spirits gradually revived. She began to deck her person with unusual care; and bringing forth a basket of artificial flowers, went to work to wreathe a bridal chaplet of white roses. Her companions asked her why she prepared the chaplet. "What!" said she with a smile, "have you not noticed the trees putting on their wedding-dresses of blossoms? Has not the swallow flown back over the sea? Do you not know that the time is come for Eugene to return? That he will be home tomorrow, and that on Sunday we are to be married?"

Her words were repeated to the physician, and he seized on them at once. He directed that her idea should be encouraged and acted upon. Her words were echoed through the house. Every one talked of the return of Eugene as a matter of course; they congratulated her upon her approaching happiness, and assisted her in her preparations. The next morning the same theme was resumed. She was dressed out to receive her lover. Every bosom fluttered with anxiety. A cabriolet drove into the village. "Eugene is coming!" was the cry. She saw him alight at the door, and rushed with a shriek into his arms.

Her friends trembled for the result of this critical experiment; but she did not sink under it, for her fancy had prepared her for his return. She was as one in a dream, to whom a tide of unlooked-for prosperity, that would have overwhelmed his waking reason, seems but the natural current of circumstances. Her conversation, however, showed that her senses were wandering. There was an absolute forgetfulness of all past sorrow; a wild and feverish gayety that at times was incoherent.

The next morning she awoke languid and exhausted. All the occurrences of the preceding day had passed away from her mind as though they had been the mere illusions of her fancy. She rose melancholy and abstracted, and as she dressed herself, was heard to sing one of her plaintive ballads. When she entered the parlor, her eyes were swollen with weeping. She heard Eugene's voice without, and started; passed her hand across her forehead, and stood musing, like one endeavoring to recall a dream. Eugene entered the room, and advanced towards her. She looked at him with an eager, searching look, murmured some indistinct words, and, before he could reach her, sank upon the floor.

She relapsed into a wild and unsettled state of mind; but now that the first shock was over, the physician ordered that Eugene should keep continually in her sight. Sometimes she did not know him; at other times she would talk to him as if he were going to sea, and would implore him not to part from her in anger; and when he was not present, she would speak of him as if buried in the ocean, and would sit, with clasped hands, looking upon the ground, the picture of despair.

As the agitation of her feelings subsided, and her frame recovered from the shock it had received, she became more placid and coherent. Eugene kept almost continually near her. He formed the real object round which her scattered ideas once more gathered, and which linked them once more with the realities of life. But her changeful disorder now appeared to take a new turn. She became languid and inert, and would sit for hours silent, and almost in a state of lethargy. If roused from this stupor, it seemed as if her mind would make some attempt to follow up a train of thought, but would soon become confused. She would regard every one that approached her with an anxious and inquiring eye, that seemed continually to disappoint itself. Sometimes, as her lover sat holding her hand, she would look pensively in his face without saying a word, until his heart was overcome; and after these transient fits of intellectual exertion, she would sink again into lethargy.

By degrees this stupor increased; her mind appeared to have subsided into a stagnant and almost deathlike calm. For the greater part of the time her eyes were closed; her face was almost as fixed and passionless as that of a corpse. She no longer took any notice of surrounding objects. There was an awfulness in this tranquillity that filled her friends with apprehensions. The physician ordered that she should be kept perfectly quiet; or that, if she evinced any agitation, she should be gently lulled, like a child, by some favorite tune.

She remained in this state for hours, hardly seeming to breathe, and apparently sinking into the sleep of death. Her chamber was profoundly still. The attendants moved about it with noiseless tread; everything was communicated by signs and whispers. Her lover sat by her side watching her with painful anxiety, and fearing every breath which stole from her pale lips would be the last.

At length she heaved a deep sigh; and from some convulsive motions, appeared to be troubled in her sleep. Her agitation increased, accompanied by an indistinct moaning. One of her companions, remembering the physician's instructions, endeavored to lull her by singing, in a low voice, a tender little air, which was a particular favorite of Annette's. Probably it had some connection in her mind with her own story; for every fond girl has some ditty of the kind, linked in her thoughts with sweet and sad remembrances.

As she sang, the agitation of Annette subsided. A streak of faint color came into her cheeks; her eyelids became swollen with rising tears, which trembled there for a moment, and then, stealing forth, coursed down her pallid cheeks. When the song was ended, she opened her eyes, and looked about her, as one awaking in a strange place.

"Oh, Eugene! Eugene!" said she, "it seems as if I have had a long and dismal dream; what has happened, and what has been the matter with me?"

The questions were embarrassing; and before they could be answered, the physician, who was in the next room, entered. She took him by the hand, looked up in his face, and made the same inquiry. He endeavored to put her off with some evasive answer. "No, no!" cried she, "I know I have been ill, and I have been dreaming strangely. I thought Eugene had left us—and that he had gone to sea—and that—and that he was drowned!—but he *has* been to sea!" added she earnestly, as recollection kept flashing upon her, "and he has been wrecked—and we were all so wretched—and he came home again one bright morning—and—oh!" said she, pressing her hand against her forehead with a sickly smile, "I see how it is; all has not been right here. I begin to recollect—but it is all past now—Eugene is here! and his mother is happy—and we will never—never part again—shall we, Eugene?"

She sunk back in her chair exhausted; the tears streamed down her cheeks. Her companions hovered round her, not knowing what to make of this sudden dawn of reason. Her lover sobbed aloud. She opened her eyes again, and looked upon them with an air of the sweetest acknowledgment. "You are all so good to me!" said she, faintly.

The physician drew the father aside. "Your daughter's mind is restored," said he; "she is sensible that she has been deranged; she is growing conscious of the past, and conscious of the present. All that now remains is to keep her calm and quiet until her health is re-established, and then let her be married, in God's name!"

"The wedding took place," continued the good priest, "but a short time since; they were here at the last fête during their honeymoon, and a handsomer and happier couple was not to be seen as they danced under yonder trees. The young man, his wife, and mother, now live on a fine farm at Pont l'Eveque; and the model of a ship which you see yonder, with white flowers wreathed round it, is Annette's offering of thanks to our Lady of Grace, for having listened to her prayers, and protected her lover in the hour of peril."

The captain having finished, there was a momentary silence. The tender-hearted Lady Lillycraft, who knew the story by heart, had led the way in weeping, and indeed often began to shed tears before they came to the right place.

The fair Julia was a little flurried at the passage where wedding preparations were mentioned; but the auditor most affected was the simple Phoebe Wilkins. She had gradually dropped her work in her lap, and sat sobbing through the latter part of the story, until towards the end, when the happy reverse had nearly produced another scene of hysterics. "Go, take this case to my room again, child," said Lady Lillycraft kindly, "and don't cry so much."

"I won't, an't please your ladyship, if I can help it;—but I'm glad they made all up again, and were married!"

The Haunted House

FROM THE MSS. OF THE LATE DIEDRICH KNICKERBOCKER

Formerly almost every place had a house of this kind. If a house was seated on some melancholy place, or built in some old romantic manner, or if any particular accident had happened in it, such as murder, sudden death, or the like, to be sure that house had a mark set on it, and was afterwards esteemed the habitation of a ghost.

—BOURNE'S ANTIQUITIES

In the neighborhood of the ancient city of the Manhattoes there stood, not very many years since, an old mansion, which, when I was a boy, went by the name of the Haunted House. It was one of the very few remains of the architecture of the early Dutch settlers, and must have been a house of some consequence at the time when it was built. It consisted of a centre and two wings, the gable ends of which were shaped like stairs. It was built partly of wood and partly of small Dutch bricks, such as the worthy colonists brought with them from Holland, before they discovered that bricks could be manufactured elsewhere. The house stood remote from the road, in the centre of a large field, with an avenue of old locust-trees† leading up to it, several of which had been shivered by lightning, and two or three blown down. A few apple-trees grew straggling about the field; there were traces also of what had been a kitchen garden; but the fences were broken down, the vegetables had disappeared, or had grown wild, and turned to little better than weeds, with here and there a ragged rosebush, or a tall sunflower shooting up from among the brambles, and hanging its head sorrowfully, as if contemplating the surrounding desolation. Part of the roof of the old house had fallen in, the windows were shattered, the

†Acacias.

panels of the doors broken, and mended with rough boards, and two rusty weather-cocks at the ends of the house made a great jingling and whistling as they whirled about, but always pointed wrong. The appearance of the whole place was forlorn and desolate at the best of times; but, in unruly weather, the howling of the wind about the crazy old mansion, the screeching of the weather-cocks, and the slamming and banging of a few loose window-shutters, had altogether so wild and dreary an effect, that the neighborhood stood perfectly in awe of the place, and pronounced it the rendezvous of hobgoblins. I recollect the old building well; for many times, when an idle, unlucky urchin, I have prowled round its precinct, with some of my graceless companions, on holiday afternoons when out on a free-booting cruise among the orchards. There was a tree standing near the house that bore the most beautiful and tempting fruit; but then it was on enchanted ground, for the place was so charmed by frightful stories that we dreaded to approach it. Sometimes we would venture in a body, and get near the Hesperian tree, keeping an eye upon the old mansion, and darting fearful glances into its shattered windows, when, just as we were about to seize upon our prize, an exclamation from some one of the gang, or an accidental noise, would throw us all into a panic, and we would scamper headlong from the place, nor stop until we had got quite into the road. Then there was sure to be a host of fearful anecdotes told of strange cries and groans, or of some hideous face suddenly seen staring out of one of the windows. By degrees we ceased to venture into these lonely grounds, but would stand at a distance, and throw stones at the building; and there was something fearfully pleasing in the sound as they rattled along the roof, or sometimes struck some jingling fragments of glass out of the windows.

The origin of this house was lost in the obscurity that covers the early period of the province, while under the government of their high mightinesses the states-general. Some reported it to have been a country residence of Wilhelmus Kieft, commonly called the Testy, one of the Dutch governors of New Amsterdam; others said it had been built by a naval commander who served under Van Tromp, and who, on being disappointed of preferment, retired from the service in disgust, became a philosopher through sheer spite, and brought over all his wealth to the province, that he might live according to his humor, and despise the world. The reason of its having fallen to decay was likewise a matter of dispute. Some said it was in chancery, and had already cost more than its worth in legal expense; but the most current, and of course the most probable, account was that it was haunted, and that nobody could live quietly in it. There can, in fact, be very little doubt that this last was the case, there were so many corroborating stories to prove it—not an old woman in the neighborhood but could furnish at least a score. A gray-headed curmudgeon of a Negro who lived hard by had a whole budget of them to tell, many of which had happened to himself. I recollect many a time stopping with my schoolmates, and getting him to relate some. The old crone lived in a hovel, in the midst of a small patch of potatoes and Indian corn, which his master had given him on setting him free. He would come to us, with his hoe in his hand, and as we sat perched, like a row of swallows, on the rail of a fence, in the mellow twilight of a summer evening, would tell us such fearful stories, accompanied by such awful rollings of his white eyes, that we were almost afraid of our own footsteps as we returned home afterwards in the dark.

Poor old Pompey! Many years are past since he died, and went to keep company with the ghosts he was so fond of talking about. He was buried in a corner of his own little potato patch; the plough soon passed over his grave, and levelled it with the rest of the field, and nobody thought any more of the gray-headed Negro. By singular chance I was strolling in that neighborhood, several years afterwards, when I had grown up to be a young man, and I found a knot of gossips speculating on a skull which had just been turned up by a plough-share. They of course determined it to be the remains of some one who had been murdered, and they had raked up with it some of the traditionary tales of the Haunted House. I knew it at once to be the relic of poor Pompey, but I held my tongue; for I am too considerate of other people's enjoyment ever to mar a story of a ghost or a murder. I took care, however, to see the bones of my old friend once more buried in a place where they were not likely to be disturbed. As I sat on the turf and watched the interment, I fell into a long conversation with an old gentleman of the neighborhood, John Josse Vandermoere, a pleasant gossiping man, whose whole life was spent in hearing and telling the news of the province. He recollected old

Pompey, and his stories about the Haunted House; but he assured me he could give me one still more strange than any that Pompey had related, and on my expressing a great curiosity to hear it, he sat down beside me on the turf, and told the following tale. I have endeavored to give it as nearly as possible in his words; but it is now many years since, and I am grown old, and my memory is not over good. I cannot therefore vouch for the language, but I am always scrupulous as to facts.

D.K.

Dolph Heyliger

In the early time of the province of New York, while it groaned under the tyranny of the English governor, Lord Cornbury, who carried his cruelties towards the Dutch inhabitants so far as to allow no dominie or schoolmaster to officiate in their language without his special license; about this time there lived in the jolly little old city of the Manhattoes a kind motherly dame, known by the name of Dame Heyliger. She was the widow of a Dutch sea-captain, who died suddenly of a fever, in consequence of working too hard and eating too heartily, at a time when all the inhabitants turned out in a panic, to fortify the place against the invasion of a small French privateer.† He left her with very little money and one infant son, the only survivor of several children. The good woman had need of much management to make both ends meet, and keep up a decent appearance. However, as her husband had fallen a victim to his zeal for the public safety, it was universally agreed that "something ought to be done for the widow"; and on the hopes of this "something" she lived tolerably for some years; in the meantime everybody pitied and spoke well of her, and that helped along.

She lived in a small house, in a small street, called Garden Street, very probably from a garden which may have flourished there some time or

†1705.

other. As her necessities every year grew greater, and the talk of the public about doing "something for her" grew less, she had to cast about for some mode of doing something for herself, by way of helping out her slender means, and maintaining her independence, of which she was somewhat tenacious.

Living in a mercantile town, she had caught something of the spirit, and determined to venture a little in the great lottery of commerce. On a sudden, therefore, to the great surprise of the street, there appeared at her window a grand array of gingerbread kings and queens, with their arms stuck akimbo, after the invariable royal manner. There were also several broken tumblers, some filled with sugar-plums, some with marbles; there were, moreover, cakes of various kinds, and barley-sugar, and Holland dolls, and wooden horses, with here and there gilt-covered picture-books, and now and then a skein of thread, or a dangling pound of candles. At the door of the house sat the good old dame's cat, a decent demure-looking personage, who seemed to scan everybody that passed, to criticise their dress, and now and then to stretch her neck, and to look out with sudden curiosity, to see what was going on at the other end of the street; but if by chance any idle vagabond dog came by, and offered to be uncivil—hoity-toity!—how she would bristle up, and growl, and spit, and strike out her paws! She was as indignant as ever was an ancient and ugly spinster on the approach of some graceless profligate.

But though the good woman had to come down to those humble means of subsistence, yet she still kept up a feeling of family pride, being descended from the Vander Spiegels, of Amsterdam; and she had the family arms painted and framed, and hung over her mantel-piece. She was, in truth, much respected by all the poorer people of the place; her house was quite a resort of the old wives of the neighborhood; they would drop in there of a winter's afternoon, as she sat knitting on one side of her fireplace, her cat purring on the other, and the tea-kettle singing before it; and they would gossip with her until late in the evening. There was always an arm-chair for Peter de Groodt, sometimes called Long Peter, and sometimes Peter Longlegs, the clerk and sexton of the little Lutheran church, who was her great crony, and indeed the oracle of her fireside. Nay, the Dominie himself did not disdain, now and then, to step in, converse about the state of her mind, and take a glass of her special good cherry-brandy. Indeed, he never failed to call on New-Year's day, and wish her a happy New Year; and the good dame, who was a little vain on some points, always piqued herself on giving him as large a cake as any one in town.

I have said that she had one son. He was the child of her old age; but could hardly be called the comfort, for, of all unlucky urchins, Dolph Heyliger was the most mischievous. Not that the whipster was really vicious; he was only full of fun and frolic, and had that daring, game-some spirit which is extolled in a rich man's child, but execrated in a poor man's. He was continually getting into scrapes; his mother was incessantly harassed with complaints of some waggish pranks which he had played off; bills were sent in for windows that he had broken; in a word, he had not reached his fourteenth year before he was pronounced, by all the neighborhood, to be a "wicked dog, the wickedest dog in the street!" Nay, one old gentleman, in a claret-colored coat with a thin red face, and ferret eyes, went so far as to assure Dame Heyliger, that her son would, one day or other, come to the gallows!

Yet, notwithstanding all this, the poor old soul loved her boy. It seemed as though she loved him the better the worse he behaved, and that he grew more in her favor the more he grew out of favor with the world. Mothers are foolish, fond-hearted beings; there's no reasoning them out of their dotage; and, indeed, this poor woman's child was all that was left to love her in this world;—so we must not think it hard that she turned a deaf ear to her good friends, who sought to prove to her that Dolph would come to a halter.

To do the varlet justice, too, he was strongly attached to his parent. He would not willingly have given her pain on any account; and when he had been doing wrong, it was but for him to catch his poor mother's eye fixed wistfully and sorrowfully upon him, to fill his heart with bitterness and contrition. But he was a heedless youngster, and could not, for the life of him, resist any new temptation to fun and mischief. Though quick at his learning, whenever he could be brought to apply himself, he was always prone to be led away by idle company, and would play truant to hunt after birds' nests, to rob orchards, or to swim in the Hudson.

In this way he grew up, a tall, lubberly boy; and his mother began to be greatly perplexed what to do with him, or how to put him in a way to do for himself; for he had acquired such an unlucky reputation, that no one seemed willing to employ him.

Many were the consultations that she held with Peter de Groodt, the clerk and sexton, who was her prime counsellor. Peter was as much perplexed as herself, for he had no great opinion of the boy, and thought he would never come to good. He at once advised her to send him to sea; a piece of advice only given in the most desperate cases; but Dame Heyliger would not listen to such an idea; she could not think of letting Dolph go out of her sight. She was sitting one day knitting by her fireside, in great perplexity, when the sexton entered with an air of unusual vivacity and briskness. He had just come from a funeral. It had been that of a boy of Dolph's years, who had been apprentice to a famous German doctor, and had died of a consumption. It is true, there had been a whisper that the deceased had been brought to his end by being made the subject of the doctor's experiments, on which he was apt to try the effects of a new compound, or a quieting draught. This, however, it is likely, was a mere scandal; at any rate, Peter de Groodt did not think it worth mentioning; though, had we time to philosophize, it would be a curious matter for speculation, why a doctor's family is apt to be so lean and cadaverous, and a butcher's so jolly and rubicund.

Peter de Groodt, as I said before, entered the house of Dame Heyliger with unusual alacrity. A bright idea had popped into his head at the funeral, over which he had chuckled as he shovelled the earth into the grave of the doctor's disciple. It had occurred to him, that, as the situation of the deceased was vacant at the doctor's, it would be the very place for Dolph. The boy had parts, and could pound a pestle, and run an errand with any boy in the town; and what more was wanted in a student?

The suggestion of the sage Peter was a vision of glory to the mother. She already saw Dolph, in her mind's eye, with a cane at his nose, a knocker at his door, and an M.D. at the end of his name—one of the established dignitaries of the town.

The matter, once undertaken, was soon effected; the sexton had some influence with the doctor, they having had much dealing together in the way of their separate professions; and the very next morning he called and conducted the urchin, clad in his Sunday clothes, to undergo the inspection of Dr. Karl Lodovick Knipperhausen.

They found the doctor seated in an elbow-chair, in one corner of his study, or laboratory, with a large volume, in German print, before him. He was a short fat man, with a dark square face, rendered more dark by a black velvet cap. He had a little nobbed nose, not unlike the ace of spades, with a pair of spectacles gleaming on each side of his dusky countenance, like a couple of bow-windows.

Dolph felt struck with awe on entering into the presence of this learned man; and gazed about him with boyish wonder at the furniture of this chamber of knowledge; which appeared to him almost as the den of a magician. In the centre stood a claw-footed table, with pestle and mortar, phials and gallipots, and a pair of small burnished scales. At one end was a heavy clothes-press, turned into a receptacle for drugs and compounds; against which hung the doctor's hat and cloak, and gold-headed cane, and on the top grinned a human skull. Along the mantel-piece were glass vessels, in which were snakes and lizards, and a human foetus preserved in spirits. A closet, the doors of which were taken off, contained three whole shelves of books, and some, too, of mighty folio dimensions—a collection the like of which Dolph had never before beheld. As, however, the library did not take up the whole of the closet, the doctor's thrifty housekeeper had occupied the rest with pots of pickles and preserves; and had hung about the room, among awful implements of the healing art, strings of red pepper and corpulent cucumbers, carefully preserved for seed.

Peter de Groodt and his protégé were received with great gravity and stateliness by the doctor, who was a very wise, dignified little man, and never smiled. He surveyed Dolph from head to foot, above, and under, and through his spectacles, and the poor lad's heart quailed as these great glasses glared on him like two full moons. The doctor heard all that Peter de Groodt had to say in favor of the youthful candidate; and then wetting his thumb with the end of his tongue, he began deliberately to turn over page after page of the great black volume before him. At length, after many hums and haws, and strokings of the chin, and all that hesitation and deliberation with which a wise man proceeds to do what he intended to do from the very first, the doctor agreed to take the lad as a disciple; to give him bed, board, and clothing, and to instruct him in the healing art; in return for which he was to have his services until his twenty-first year.

Behold, then, our hero, all at once transformed from an unlucky urchin running wild about the streets, to a student of medicine, diligently pounding a pestle, under the auspices of the learned Doctor Karl Lodovick Knipperhausen. It was a happy transition for his fond old mother. She was delighted with the idea of her boy's being brought up worthy of his ancestors; and anticipated the day when he would be able to hold up his head with the lawyer, that lived in the large house opposite; or, peradventure, with the Dominie himself.

Doctor Knipperhausen was a native of the Palatinate in Germany; whence, in company with many of his countrymen, he had taken refuge in England, on account of religious persecution. He was one of nearly three thousand Palatines, who came over from England in 1710, under the protection of Governor Hunter. Where the doctor had studied, how he had acquired his medical knowledge, and where he had received his diploma, it is hard at present to say, for nobody knew at the time; yet it is certain that his profound skill and abstruse knowledge were the talk and wonder of the common people, far and near.

His practice was totally different from that of any other physician— consisting in mysterious compounds, known only to himself, in the preparing and administering of which, it was said, he always consulted the stars. So high an opinion was entertained of his skill, particularly by the German and Dutch inhabitants, that they always resorted to him in desperate cases. He was one of those infallible doctors that are always effecting sudden and surprising cures, when the patient has been given up by all the regular physicians; unless, as is shrewdly observed, the case has been left too long before it was put into their hands. The doctor's library was the talk and marvel of the neighborhood, I might almost say of the entire burgh. The good people looked with reverence at a man who had read three whole shelves full of books, and some of them, too, as large as a family Bible. There were many disputes among the members of the little Lutheran church, as to which was the wisest man, the doctor or the Dominie. Some of his admirers even went so far as to say, that he knew more than the governor himself. In a word, it was thought that there was no end to his knowledge!

No sooner was Dolph received into the doctor's family, than he was put in possession of the lodging of his predecessor. It was a garret room of a steep-roofed Dutch house, where the rain had pattered on the shingles, and the lightning gleamed, and the wind piped through the crannies in stormy weather; and where whole troops of hungry rats, like Don Cossacks, galloped about, in defiance of traps and ratsbane.

He was soon up to his ears in medical studies, being employed, morning, noon and night, in rolling pills, filtering tinctures, or pounding the pestle and mortar in one corner of the laboratory; while the doctor would take his seat in another corner, when he had nothing else to do, or expected visitors, and arrayed in his morning gown and velvet cap, would pore over the contents of some folio volume. It is true, that the regular thumping of Dolph's pestle, or perhaps the drowsy buzzing of the summer flies, would now and then lull the little man into a slumber; but then his spectacles were always wide awake, and studiously regarding the book.

There was another personage in the house, however, to whom Dolph was obliged to pay allegiance. Though a bachelor, and a man of such great dignity and importance, the doctor was, like many other wise men, subject to petticoat government. He was completely under the sway of his housekeeper—a spare, busy, fretting housewife, in a little, round, quilted German cap, with a huge bunch of keys jingling at the girdle of an exceedingly long waist. Frau Ilsé (or Frow Ilsy, as it was pronounced) had accompanied him in his various migrations from Germany to England, and from England to the province; managing his establishment and himself too; ruling him, it is true, with a gentle hand, but carrying a high hand with all the world beside. How she had acquired such ascendency I do not pretend to say. People, it is true, did talk—but have not people been prone to talk ever since the world began? Who can tell how women generally continue to get the upper-hand? A husband, it is true, may now and then be master in his own house; but who ever knew a bachelor that was not managed by his housekeeper?

Indeed, Frau Ilsy's power was not confined to the doctor's household. She was one of those prying gossips who know every one's business better than they do themselves; and whose all-seeing eyes, and all-telling tongues, are terrors throughout a neighborhood.

Nothing of any moment transpired in the world of scandal of this little burgh, but it was known to Frau Ilsy. She had her crew of cronies, that were perpetually hurrying to her little parlor with some precious bit of news; nay, she would sometimes discuss a whole volume of secret history, as she held the street-door ajar, and gossiped with one of these garrulous cronies in the very teeth of a December blast.

Between the doctor and the housekeeper it may easily be supposed that Dolph had a busy life of it. As Frau Ilsy kept the keys, and literally ruled the roost, it was starvation to offend her, though he found the study of her temper more perplexing even than that of medicine. When not busy in the laboratory, she kept him running hither and thither on her errands; and on Sundays he was obliged to accompany her to and from church, and carry her Bible. Many a time has the poor varlet stood shivering and blowing his fingers, or holding his frost-bitten nose, in the churchyard, while Ilsy and her cronies were huddled together, wagging their heads, and tearing some unlucky character to pieces.

With all his advantages, however, Dolph made very slow progress in his art. This was no fault of the doctor's, certainly, for he took unwearied pains with the lad, keeping him close to the pestle and mortar, or on the trot about town with phials and pill-boxes; and if he ever flagged in his industry, which he was rather apt to do, the doctor would fly into a passion, and ask him if he ever expected to learn his profession, unless he applied himself closer to the study. The fact is, he still retained the fondness for sport and mischief that had marked his childhood; the habit, indeed, had strengthened with his years, and gained force from being thwarted and constrained. He daily grew more and more untractable, and lost favor in the eyes, both of the doctor and the housekeeper.

In the meantime the doctor went on, waxing wealthy and renowned. He was famous for his skill in managing cases not laid down in the books. He had cured several old women and young girls of witchcraft— a terrible complaint, and nearly as prevalent in the province in those days as hydrophobia is at present. He had even restored one strapping country girl to perfect health, who had gone so far as to vomit crooked pins and needles; which is considered a desperate stage of the malady. It was whispered, also, that he was possessed of the art of preparing love-powders; and many applications had he in consequence from love-sick patients of both sexes. But all these cases formed the mysterious part of his practice, in which, according to the cant phrase, "secrecy and honor might be depended on." Dolph, therefore, was obliged to turn out of the study whenever such consultations occurred, though it is said he learnt more of the secrets of the art at the keyhole than by all the rest of his studies put together.

As the doctor increased in wealth, he began to extend his possessions, and to look forward, like other great men, to the time when he should

retire to the repose of a country-seat. For this purpose he had purchased a farm, or as the Dutch settlers called it, a *bowerie*, a few miles from town. It had been the residence of a wealthy family, that had returned some time since to Holland. A large mansion-house stood in the centre of it, very much out of repair, and which, in consequence of certain reports, had received the appellation of the Haunted House. Either from these reports, or from its actual dreariness, the doctor found it impossible to get a tenant; and that the place might not fall to ruin before he could reside in it himself, he placed a country boor, with his family, in one wing, with the privilege of cultivating the farm on shares.

The doctor now felt all the dignity of a landholder rising within him. He had a little of the German pride of territory in his composition, and almost looked upon himself as owner of a principality. He began to complain of the fatigue of business; and was fond of riding out "to look at his estate." His little expeditions to his lands were attended with a bustle and parade that created a sensation throughout the neighborhood. His wall-eyed horse stood, stamping and whisking off the flies, for a full hour before the house. Then the doctor's saddle-bags would be brought out and adjusted; then, after a little while, his cloak would be rolled up and strapped to the saddle; then his umbrella would be buttoned to the cloak; while, in the meantime, a group of ragged boys, that observant class of beings, would gather before the door. At length the doctor would issue forth, in a pair of jackboots that reached above his knees, and a cocked hat flapped down in front. As he was a short, fat man, he took some time to mount into the saddle; and when there, he took some time to have the saddle and stirrups properly adjusted, enjoying the wonder and admiration of the urchin crowd. Even after he had set off, he would pause in the middle of the street, or trot back two or three times to give some parting orders; which were answered by the house-keeper from the door, or Dolph from the study, or the black cook from the cellar, or the chambermaid from the garret window; and there were generally some last words bawled after him, just as he was turning the corner.

The whole neighborhood would be aroused by this pomp and circum-stance. The cobbler would leave his last; the barber would thrust out his frizzled head, with a comb sticking in it; a knot would collect at the grocer's door, and the word would be buzzed from one end of the street to the other, "The doctor's riding out to his country-seat!"

These were golden moments for Dolph. No sooner was the doctor out of sight, than pestle and mortar were abandoned; the laboratory was left to take care of itself, and the student was off on some mad-cap frolic.

Indeed, it must be confessed, the youngster, as he grew up, seemed in a fair way to fulfil the prediction of the old claret-colored gentleman. He was the ringleader of all holiday sports and midnight gambols; ready for all kinds of mischievous pranks and hare-brained adventures.

There is nothing so troublesome as a hero on a small scale, or, rather a hero in a small town. Dolph soon became the abhorrence of all drowsy, housekeeping old citizens, who hated noise, and had no relish for waggery. The good dames, too, considered him as little better than a reprobate, gathered their daughters under their wings whenever he approached, and pointed him out as a warning to their sons. No one seemed to hold him in much regard except the wild striplings of the place, who were captivated by his open-hearted, daring manners—and the Negroes, who always looked upon every idle, do-nothing youngster as a kind of gentleman. Even the good Peter de Groodt, who had considered himself a kind of patron of the lad, began to despair of him; and would shake his head dubiously, as he listened to a long complaint from the housekeeper, and sipped a glass of her raspberry-brandy.

Still his mother was not to be wearied out of her affection by all the waywardness of her boy; nor disheartened by the stories of his misdeeds, with which her good friends were continually regaling her. She had, it is true, very little of the pleasure which rich people enjoy, in always hearing their children praised; but she considered all this ill-will as a kind of persecution which he suffered, and she liked him the better on that account. She saw him growing up a fine, tall, good-looking youngster, and she looked at him with the secret pride of a mother's heart. It was her great desire that Dolph should appear like a gentleman, and all the money she could save went towards helping out his pocket and his wardrobe. She would look out of the window after him, as he sallied forth in his best array, and her heart would yearn with delight; and once, when Peter de Groodt, struck with the youngster's gallant appearance on a bright Sunday morning, observed, "Well, after all, Dolph does grow a comely fellow!" the tear of pride started into the mother's eye. "Ah, neighbor! neighbor!" exclaimed she, "they may say what they please; poor Dolph will yet hold up his head with the best of them!"

Dolph Heyliger had now nearly attained his one-and-twentieth year, and the term of his medical studies was just expiring; yet it must be confessed that he knew little more of the profession than when he first entered the doctor's doors. This, however, could not be from any want of quickness of parts, for he showed amazing aptness in mastering other branches of knowledge, which he could only have studied at intervals. He was, for instance, a sure marksman, and won all the geese and turkeys at Christmas holidays. He was a bold rider; he was famous for leaping and wrestling; he played tolerably on the fiddle; could swim like a fish; and was the best hand in the whole place at fives and ninepins.

All these accomplishments, however, procured him no favor in the eyes of the doctor, who grew more and more crabbed and intolerant the nearer the term of apprenticeship approached. Frau Ilsy, too, was forever finding some occasion to raise a windy tempest about his ears, and seldom encountered him about the house without a clatter of the tongue; so that at length the jingling of her keys, as she approached, was to Dolph like the ringing of the prompter's bell, that gives notice of a theatrical thunder-storm. Nothing but the infinite good-humor of the heedless youngster enabled him to bear all this domestic tyranny without open rebellion. It was evident that the doctor and his housekeeper were preparing to beat the poor youth out of the nest, the moment his term should have expired—a short-hand mode which the doctor had of providing for useless disciples.

Indeed, the little man had been rendered more than usually irritable lately in consequence of various cares and vexations which his country estate had brought upon him. The doctor had been repeatedly annoyed by the rumors and tales which prevailed concerning the old mansion, and found it difficult to prevail even upon the country-man and his family to remain there rent-free. Every time he rode out to the farm he was teased by some fresh complaint of strange noises and fearful sights, with which the tenants were disturbed at night; and the doctor would come home fretting and fuming, and vent his spleen upon the whole household. It was indeed a sore grievance that affected him both in pride and purse. He was threatened with an absolute loss of the profits of his property; and then, what a blow to his territorial consequence, to be the landlord of a haunted house!

It was observed, however, that with all his vexation, the doctor never proposed to sleep in the house himself; nay, he could never be prevailed upon to remain on the premises after dark, but made the best of his way for town as soon as the bats began to flit about in the twilight. The fact was, the doctor had a secret belief in ghosts, having passed the early part of his life in a country where they particularly abound; and indeed the story went, that, when a boy, he had once seen the devil upon the Hartz Mountains in Germany.

At length the doctor's vexations on this head were brought to a crisis. One morning as he sat dozing over a volume in his study, he was suddenly startled from his slumbers by the bustling in of the housekeeper.

"Here's a fine to-do!" cried she, as she entered the room. "Here's Claus

Hopper come in, bag and baggage, from the farm, and swears he'll have nothing more to do with it. The whole family have been frightened out of their wits; for there's such racketing and rummaging about the old house, that they can't sleep quiet in their beds!"

"Donner and blitzen!" cried the doctor, impatiently; "will they never have done chattering about that house? What a pack of fools, to let a few rats and mice frighten them out of good quarters!"

"Nay, nay," said the housekeeper, wagging her head knowingly, and piqued at having a good ghost-story doubted, "there's more in it than rats and mice. All the neighborhood talks about the house; and then such sights as have been seen in it! Peter de Groodt tells me, that the family that sold you the house, and went to Holland, dropped several strange hints about it, and said, 'they wished you joy of your bargain'; and you know yourself there's no getting any family to live in it."

"Peter de Groodt's a ninny—an old woman," said the doctor, peevishly; "I'll warrant he's been filling these people's heads full of stories. It's just like his nonsense about the ghost that haunted the church belfry, as an excuse for not ringing the bell that cold night when Harmanus Brinkerhoff's house was on fire. Send Claus to me."

Claus Hopper now made his appearance: a simple country lout, full of awe at finding himself in the very study of Dr. Knipperhausen, and too much embarrassed to enter in much detail of the matters that had caused his alarm. He stood twirling his hat in one hand, resting sometimes on one leg, sometimes on the other, looking occasionally at the doctor, and now and then stealing a fearful glance at the death's-head that seemed ogling him from the top of the clothes-press.

The doctor tried every means to persuade him to return to the farm, but all in vain; he maintained a dogged determination on the subject; and at the close of every argument or solicitation would make the same brief, inflexible reply: "Ich kan nicht, mynheer." The doctor was a "little pot, and soon hot"; his patience was exhausted by these continual vexations about his estate. The stubborn refusal of Claus Hopper seemed to him like flat rebellion; his temper suddenly boiled over, and Claus was glad to make a rapid retreat to escape scalding.

When the bumpkin got to the housekeeper's room, he found Peter de Groodt, and several other true believers, ready to receive him. Here he indemnified himself for the restraint he had suffered in the study, and opened a budget of stories about the haunted house that astonished all his hearers. The housekeeper believed them all, if it was only to spite the doctor for having received her intelligence so uncourteously. Peter de Groodt matched them with many a wonderful legend of the times of the Dutch dynasty, and of the Devil's Stepping-stones; and of the pirate hanged at Gibbet Island, that continued to swing there at night long after the gallows was taken down; and of the ghost of the unfortunate Governor Leisler, hanged for treason, which haunted the old fort and the government house. The gossiping knot dispersed, each charged with direful intelligence. The sexton disburdened himself at a vestry meeting that was held that very day, and the black cook forsook her kitchen, and spent half the day at the street pump, that gossiping-place of servants, dealing forth the news to all that came for water. In a little time the whole town was in a buzz with tales about the Haunted House. Some said that Claus Hopper had seen the devil, while others hinted that the house was haunted by the ghosts of some of the patients whom the doctor had physicked out of the world, and that was the reason why he did not venture to live in it himself.

All this put the little doctor in a terrible fume. He threatened vengeance on any one who should affect the value of his property by exciting popular prejudices. He complained loudly of thus being in a manner dispossessed of his territories by mere bugbears; but he secretly determined to have the house exorcised by the Dominie. Great was his relief, therefore, when in the midst of his perplexities, Dolph stepped forward and undertook to garrison the Haunted House. The youngster had been listening to all the stories of Claus Hopper and Peter de Groodt: he was fond of adventure, he loved the marvellous, and his imagination had become quite excited by these tales of wonder. Besides, he had led such an uncomfortable life at the doctor's, being subjected to the intolerable thraldom of early hours, that he was delighted at the prospect of having a house to himself, even though it should be a haunted one. His offer was eagerly accepted, and it was determined he should mount guard that very night. His only stipulation was, that the enterprise should be kept secret from his mother; for he knew the poor soul would not sleep a wink if she knew her son was waging war with the powers of darkness.

When night came on he set out on this perilous expedition. The old black cook, his only friend in the household, had provided him with a little mess for supper, and a rushlight; and she tied round his neck an amulet, given her by an African conjurer, as a charm against evil spirits. Dolph was escorted on his way by the doctor and Peter de Groodt, who had agreed to accompany him to the house, and to see him safe lodged. The night was overcast, and it was very dark when they arrived at the grounds which surrounded the mansion. The sexton led the way with the lantern. As they walked along the avenue of acacias, the fitful light, catching from bush to bush, and tree to tree, often startled the doughty Peter, and made him fall back upon his followers; and the doctor grappled still closer hold of Dolph's arm, observing that the ground was very slippery and uneven. At one time they were nearly put to total rout by a bat, which came flitting about the lantern; and the notes of the insects from the trees and the frogs from a neighboring pond, formed a most drowsy and doleful concert. The front door of the mansion opened with a grating sound, that made the doctor turn pale. They entered a tolerably large hall, such as is common in American country houses, and which serves for a sitting-room in warm weather. From this they went up a wide staircase, that groaned and creaked as they trod, every step making its particular note, like the key of a harpsichord. This led to another hall on the second story, whence they entered the room where Dolph was to sleep. It was large, and scantily furnished; the shutters were closed; but as they were much broken, there was no want of a circulation of air. It appeared to have been that sacred chamber, known among Dutch housewives by the name of "the best bedroom"; which is the best furnished room in the house, but in which scarce anybody is ever permitted to sleep. Its splendor, however, was all at an end. There were a few broken articles of furniture about the room, and in the centre stood a heavy deal table and a large arm-chair, both of which had the look of being coeval with the mansion. The fireplace was wide, and had been faced with Dutch tiles, representing Scripture stories; but some of them had fallen out of their places, and lay scattered about the hearth. The sexton lit the rushlight; and the doctor, looking fearfully about the room, was just exhorting Dolph to be of good cheer, and to pluck up a stout heart, when a noise in the chimney, like voices and struggling, struck a sudden panic into the sexton. He took to his heels with the lantern; the doctor followed hard after him; the stairs groaned and creaked as they hurried down, increasing their agitation and speed by its noise. The front door slammed after them; and Dolph heard them scrabbling down the avenue, till the sound of their feet was lost in the distance. That he did not join in this precipitate retreat might have been owing to his possessing a little more courage than his companions, or perhaps that he had caught a glimpse of the cause of their dismay, in a nest of chimney-swallows, that came tumbling down into the fireplace.

Being now left to himself, he secured the front door by a strong bolt and bar; and having seen that the other entrances were fastened, returned to his desolate chamber. Having made his supper from the basket which the good old cook had provided, he locked the chamber door, and retired to rest on a mattress in one corner. The night was calm and still; and nothing broke upon the profound quiet but the lonely chirping of a cricket from the chimney of a distant chamber. The rushlight, which stood in the centre of the deal table, shed a feeble yellow ray, dimly illumining the chamber, and making uncouth shapes and shadows on the walls, from the clothes which Dolph had thrown over a chair.

With all his boldness of heart, there was something subduing in this desolate scene; and he felt his spirits flag within him, as he lay on his hard bed and gazed about the room. He was turning over in his mind his idle habits, his doubtful prospects, and now and then heaving a heavy sigh as he thought on his poor old mother; for there is nothing like the silence and loneliness of night to bring dark shadows over the brightest mind. By and by he thought he heard a sound as of some one walking below stairs. He listened, and distinctly heard a step on the great staircase. It approached solemnly and slowly, tramp—tramp—tramp! It was evidently the tread of some heavy personage; and yet how could he have got into the house without making a noise? He had examined all the fastenings, and was certain that every entrance was secure. Still the steps advanced, tramp—tramp—tramp! It was evident that the person approaching could not be a robber, the step was too loud and deliberate; a robber would either be stealthy or precipitate. And now the footsteps had ascended the staircase; they were slowly advancing along the passage, resounding through the silent and empty apartments. The very cricket had ceased its melancholy note, and nothing interrupted their awful distinctness. The door, which had been locked on the inside, slowly swung open, as if self-moved. The footsteps entered the room; but no one was to be seen. They passed slowly and audibly across it, tramp—tramp—tramp! but whatever made the sound was invisible. Dolph rubbed his eyes, and stared about him; he could see to every part of the dimly lighted chamber; all was vacant; yet still he heard those mysterious footsteps, solemnly walking about the chamber. They ceased, and all was dead silence. There was something more appalling in this invisible visitation than there would have been in anything that addressed itself to the eyesight. It was awfully vague and indefinite. He felt his heart beat against his ribs; a cold sweat broke out upon his forehead; he lay for some time in a state of violent agitation: nothing, however, occurred to increase his alarm. His light gradually burnt down into the socket, and he fell asleep. When he awoke it was broad daylight; the sun was peering through the cracks of the window-shutters, and the birds were merrily singing about the house. The bright cheery day soon put to flight all the terrors of the preceding night. Dolph laughed, or rather tried to laugh, at all that had passed, and endeavored to persuade himself that it was a mere freak of the imagination, conjured up by the stories he had heard; but he was a little puzzled to find the door of his room locked on the inside, notwithstanding that he had positively seen it swing open as the footsteps had entered. He returned to town in a state of considerable perplexity; but he determined to say nothing on the subject, until his doubts were either confirmed or removed by another night's watching. His silence was a grievous disappointment to the gossips who had gathered at the doctor's mansion. They had prepared their minds to hear direful tales, and were almost in a rage of being assured he had nothing to relate.

The next night, then, Dolph repeated his vigil. He now entered the house with some trepidation. He was particular in examining the fastenings of all the doors, and securing them well. He locked the door of his chamber, and placed a chair against it; then having despatched his supper, he threw himself on his mattress and endeavored to sleep. It was all in vain; a thousand crowding fancies kept him waking. The time slowly dragged on, as if minutes were spinning themselves out into hours. As the night advanced, he grew more and more nervous; and he almost started from his couch when he heard the mysterious footstep again on the staircase. Up it came, as before, solemnly and slowly, tramp—tramp—tramp! It approached along the passage; the door again swung open, as if there had been neither lock nor impediment, and a strange looking figure stalked into the room. It was an elderly man,

large and robust, clothed in the old Flemish fashion. He had on a kind of short cloak, with a garment under it, belted round the waist; trunk-hose, with great bunches or bows at the knees; and a pair of russet boots, very large at top, and standing widely from his legs. His hat was broad and slouched, with a feather trailing over one side. His iron-gray hair hung in thick masses on his neck; and he had a short grizzled beard. He walked slowly round the room, as if examining that all was safe; then, hanging his hat on a peg beside the door, he sat down in the elbow-chair, and, leaning his elbow on the table, fixed his eyes on Dolph with an unmoving and deadening stare.

Dolph was not naturally a coward; but he had been brought up in an implicit belief in ghosts and goblins. A thousand stories came swarming to his mind that he had heard about this building; and as he looked at this strange personage, with his uncouth garb, his pale visage, his grizzly beard, and his fixed, staring, fishlike eyes, his teeth began to chatter, his hair to rise on his head, and a cold sweat to break out all over his body. How long he remained in this situation he could not tell, for he was like one fascinated. He could not take his gaze off from the spectre; but lay staring at him, with his whole intellect absorbed in the contemplation.

The old man remained seated behind the table, without stirring, or turning an eye, always keeping a dead steady glare upon Dolph. At length the household cock, from a neighboring farm, clapped his wings, and gave a loud cheerful crow that rung over the fields. At the sound the old man slowly rose, and took down his hat from the peg; the door opened, and closed after him; he was heard to go slowly down the staircase, tramp—tramp—tramp!—and when he had got to the bottom, all was again silent. Dolph lay and listened earnestly; counted every footfall; listened, and listened, if the steps should return, until, exhausted by watching and agitation, he fell into a troubled sleep.

Daylight again brought fresh courage and assurance. He would fain have considered all that had passed as a mere dream; yet there stood the chair in which the unknown had seated himself; there was the table on which he had leaned; there was the peg on which he had hung his hat; and there was the door, locked precisely as he himself had locked it, with the chair placed against it. He hastened downstairs, and examined the doors and windows; all were exactly in the same state in which he had left them, and there was no apparent way by which any being could have entered and left the house, without leaving some trace behind. "Pooh!" said Dolph to himself, "it was all a dream" —but it would not do. The more he endeavored to shake the scene off from his mind, the more it haunted him.

Though he persisted in a strict silence as to all that he had seen or heard, yet his looks betrayed the uncomfortable night that he had passed. It was evident that there was something wonderful hidden under this mysterious reserve. The doctor took him into the study, locked the door, and sought to have a full and confidential communication; but he could get nothing out of him. Frau Ilsy took him aside into the pantry, but to as little purpose; and Peter de Groodt held him by the button for a full hour, in the churchyard, the very place to get at the bottom of a ghost-story, but came off not a whit wiser than the rest. It is always the case, however, that one truth concealed makes a dozen current lies. It is like a guinea locked up in a bank, that has a dozen paper representatives. Before the day was over, the neighborhood was full of reports. Some said that Dolph Heyliger watched in the haunted house, with pistols loaded with silver bullets; others, that he had a long talk with a spectre without a head; others, that Doctor Knipperhausen and the sexton had been hunted down the Bowery lane, and quite into town, by a legion of ghosts of their customers. Some shook their heads, and thought it a shame the doctor should put Dolph to pass the night alone in that dismal house, where he might be spirited away no one knew whither; while others observed, with a shrug, that if the devil did carry off the youngster, it would be but taking his own.

These rumors at length reached the ears of the good Dame Heyliger, and, as may be supposed, threw her into a terrible alarm. For her son to have opposed himself to danger from living foes would have been nothing so dreadful in her eyes, as to dare alone the terrors of the Haunted House. She hastened to the doctor's, and passed a great part of the day in attempting to dissuade Dolph from repeating his vigil; she told him a score of tales, which her gossiping friends had just related to her, of persons who had been carried off when watching alone in old ruinous houses. It was all to no effect. Dolph's pride, as well as curiosity, was piqued. He endeavored to calm the apprehensions of his mother, and to assure her that there was no truth in all the rumors she had heard; she looked at him dubiously and shook her head; but finding his determination was not to be shaken, she brought him a little thick Dutch Bible, with brass clasps, to take with him, as a sword wherewith to fight the powers of darkness; and, lest that might not be sufficient, the housekeeper gave him the Heidelberg catechism by way of dagger.

The next night, therefore, Dolph took up his quarters for the third time in the old mansion. Whether dream or not, the same thing was repeated. Towards midnight, when everything was still, the same sound echoed through the empty halls, tramp—tramp—tramp! The stairs were again ascended; the door again swung open; the old man entered; walked round the room; hung up his hat, and seated himself by the table. The same fear and trembling came over poor Dolph, though not in so violent a degree. He lay in the same way, motionless and fascinated, staring at the figure, which regarded him as before, with a dead, fixed, chilling gaze. In this way they remained for a long time, till, by degrees, Dolph's courage began gradually to revive. Whether alive or dead, this being had certainly some object in his visitation; and he recollected to have heard it said, spirits have no power to speak until spoken to. Summoning up resolution, therefore, and making two or three attempts, before he could get his parched tongue in motion, he addressed the unknown in the most solemn form of adjuration, and demanded to know what was the motive of his visit.

No sooner had he finished, than the old man rose, took down his hat, the door opened, and he went out, looking back upon Dolph just as he crossed the threshold, as if expecting him to follow. The youngster did not hesitate an instant. He took the candle in his hand and the Bible under his arm, and obeyed the tacit invitation. The candle emitted a feeble, uncertain ray, but still he could see the figure before him slowly descend the stairs. He followed trembling. When it had reached the bottom of the stairs, it turned through the hall towards the back door of the mansion. Dolph held the light over the balustrades; but, in his eagerness to catch a sight of the unknown, he flared his feeble taper so suddenly, that it went out. Still there was sufficient light from the pale moonbeams, that fell through a narrow window, to give him an indistinct view of the figure near the door. He followed, therefore, downstairs, and turned towards the place; but when he arrived there the unknown had disappeared. The door remained fast barred and bolted; there was no other mode of exit, yet the being, whatever he might be, was gone. He unfastened the door, and looked out into the fields. It was a hazy, moonlit night, so that the eye could distinguish objects at some distance. He thought he saw the unknown in a footpath which led from the door. He was not mistaken; but how had he got out of the house? He did not pause to think, but followed on. The old man proceeded at a measured pace, without looking about him, his footsteps sounding on the hard ground. He passed through the orchard of apple-trees, always keeping the footpath. It led to a well, situated in a little hollow, which had supplied the farm with water. Just at this well Dolph lost sight of him. He rubbed his eyes and looked again; but nothing was to be seen of the unknown. He reached the well, but nobody was there. All the surrounding ground was open and clear; there was no bush nor hiding-place. He looked down the well, and saw, at a great depth, the reflection of the sky in the still water. After remaining here for some time, without seeing or hearing anything more of his mysterious conductor, he returned to the house, full of awe and wonder. He bolted the door, groped his way back to bed, and it was long before he could compose himself to sleep.

His dreams were strange and troubled. He thought he was following the old man along the side of a great river, until they came to a vessel on the point of sailing, and that his conductor led him on board and vanished. He remembered the commander of the vessel, a short, swarthy man, with crisped black hair, blind of one eye, and lame of one leg; but the rest of his dream was very confused. Sometimes he was sailing, sometimes on shore; now amidst storms and tempests, and now wandering quietly in unknown streets. The figure of the old man was strangely mingled up with the incidents of the dream, and the whole distinctly wound up by his finding himself on board of the vessel again, returning home, with a great bag of money!

When he woke, the gray, cool light of dawn was streaking the horizon, and the cocks passing the reveille from farm to farm throughout the country. He rose more harassed and perplexed than ever. He was singularly confounded by all that he had seen and dreamt, and began to doubt whether his mind was not affected, and whether all that passing in his thoughts might not be mere feverish fantasy. In his present state of mind, he did not feel disposed to return immediately to the doctor's, and undergo the cross-questioning of the household. He made a scanty breakfast, therefore, on the remains of the last night's provisions, and then wandered out into the fields to meditate on all that had befallen him. Lost in thought, he rambled about, gradually approaching the town, until the morning was far advanced, when he was aroused by a hurry and bustle around him. He found himself near the water's edge, in a throng of people, hurrying to a pier, where was a vessel ready to make sail. He was unconsciously carried along by the impulse of the crowd, and found that it was a sloop, on the point of sailing up the Hudson to Albany. There was much leave-taking, and kissing of old women and children, and great activity in carrying on board baskets of bread and cakes, and provisions of all kinds, notwithstanding the mighty joints of meat that dangled over the stern; for a voyage to Albany was an expedition of great moment in those days. The commander of the sloop was hurrying about, and giving a world of orders, which were not very strictly attended to; one man being busy in lighting his pipe, and another in sharpening his snicker-snee.

The appearance of the commander suddenly caught Dolph's attention. He was short and swarthy, with crisped black hair; blind of one eye, and lame of one leg—the very commander that he had seen in his dream! Surprised and aroused, he considered the scene more attentively, and recalled still further traces of his dream: the appearance of the vessel, of the river, and of images, a variety of other objects accorded with the imperfect images vaguely rising to recollection.

As he stood musing on these circumstances, the captain suddenly called out to him in Dutch: "Step on board, young man, or you'll be left behind!" He was startled by the summons; he saw that the sloop was cast loose, and was actually moving from the pier. It seemed as if he was actuated by some irresistible impulse; he sprang upon the deck, and the next moment the sloop was hurried off by the wind and tide. Dolph's thoughts and feelings were all in tumult and confusion. He had been strongly worked upon by the events which had recently befallen him, and could not but think there was some connection between his present situation and his last night's dream. He felt as if under supernatural influence, and tried to assure himself with an old and favorite maxim of his, that "one way or other all would turn out for the best." For a moment, the indignation of the doctor at his departure, without leave, passed across his mind; but that was matter of little moment. Then he thought of the distress of his mother at his strange disappearance, and the idea gave him a sudden pang. He would have entreated to be put on shore; but he knew with such wind and tide the entreaty would have been in vain. Then the inspiring love of novelty and adventure came rushing in full tide through his bosom. He felt himself launched strangely and suddenly on the world, and under full way to explore the regions of wonder that lay up this mighty river, and beyond those blue mountains which had bounded his horizon since childhood. While he was lost in this whirl of thought, the sails strained to the breeze; the shores seemed to hurry away behind him; and before he perfectly recovered his self-possession, the sloop was ploughing her way past Spiking-Devil and Yonkers, and the tallest chimney of the Manhattoes had faded from his sight.

I have said that a voyage up the Hudson in those days was an undertaking of some moment; indeed, it was as much thought of as a voyage to Europe is at present. The sloops were often many days on the way, the cautious navigators taking in sail when it blew fresh, and coming to anchor at night; and stopping to send the boat ashore for milk for tea, without which it was impossible for the worthy old lady passengers to subsist. And there were the much-talked-of perils of the Tappan Zee and the highlands. In short, a prudent Dutch burgher would talk of such a voyage for months, and even years, beforehand; and never undertook it without putting his affairs in order, making his will, and having prayers said for him in the Low Dutch churches.

In the course of such a voyage, therefore, Dolph was satisfied he would have time enough to reflect, and to make up his mind as to what he should do when he arrived at Albany. The captain, with his blind eye, and lame leg, would, it is true, bring his strange dream to mind, and perplex him sadly for a few moments; but of late his life had been made up so much of dreams and realities, his nights and days had been so jumbled together, that he seemed to be moving continually in a delusion. There is always, however, a kind of vagabond consolation in a man's having nothing in this world to lose; with this Dolph comforted his heart, and determined to make the most of the present enjoyment.

In the second day of the voyage they came to the highlands. It was the latter part of a calm, sultry day, that they floated gently with the tide between these stern mountains. There was that perfect quiet which prevails over nature in the languor of summer heat; the turning of a plank, or the accidental falling of an oar on deck, was echoed from the mountain-side, and reverberated along the shores; and if by chance the captain gave a shout of command, there were airy tongues which mocked it from every cliff.

Dolph gazed about him in mute delight and wonder at these scenes of nature's magnificence. To the left the Dunderberg reared its woody precipices, height over height, forest over forest, away into the deep summer sky. To the right strutted forth the bold promontory of Antony's Nose, with a solitary eagle wheeling about it; while beyond, mountain succeeded to mountain, until they seemed to lock their arms together, and confine this mighty river in their embraces. There was a feeling of quiet luxury in gazing at the broad, green bosoms here and there scooped out among the precipices; or at woodlands high in air, nodding over the edge of some beetling bluff, and their foliage all transparent in the yellow sunshine.

In the midst of his admiration, Dolph remarked a pile of bright, snowy clouds, peering above the western heights. It was succeeded by another, and another, each seemingly pushing onwards its predecessor, and towering, with dazzling brilliancy, in the deep blue atmosphere. And now muttering peals of thunder were faintly heard rolling behind the mountains. The river, hitherto still and glassy, reflecting pictures of the sky and land, now showed a dark ripple at a distance, as the breeze came creeping up it. The fish-hawks wheeled and screamed, and sought their nests on the high dry trees. The crows flew clamorously to the crevices of the rocks, and all nature seemed conscious of the approaching thunder-gust.

The clouds now rolled in volumes over the mountain-tops; their summits still bright and snowy, but the lower parts of an inky blackness. The rain began to patter down in broad and scattered drops; the wind freshened, and curled up the waves. At length it seemed as if the bellying clouds were torn open by the mountain-tops, and complete torrents of rain came rattling down. The lightning leaped from cloud to cloud, and streamed quivering against the rocks, splitting and rending the stoutest forest trees. The thunder burst in tremendous explosions; the peals were echoed from mountain to mountain; they crashed upon Dunderberg, and rolled up the long defile of the highlands, each headland making a new echo, until old Bull Hill seemed to bellow back the storm.

For a time the scudding rack and mist, and the sheeted rain, almost hid the landscape from the sight. There was a fearful gloom, illumined still more fearfully by the streams of lighting which glittered among the raindrops. Never had Dolph beheld such an absolute warring of the elements; it seemed as if the storm was tearing and rending its way through this mountain defile, and had brought all the artillery of heaven into action.

The vessel was hurried on by the increasing wind, until she came to where the river makes a sudden bend, the only one in the whole course of its majestic career.† Just as they turned the point, a violent flaw of wind came sweeping down a mountain gully, bending the forest before it, and, in a moment, lashing up the river into white froth and foam. The captain saw the danger, and cried out to lower the sail. Before the order could be obeyed, the flaw struck the sloop, and threw her on her beam ends. Everything now was fright and confusion; the flapping of the sails,

†This must have been the bend at West Point.

the whistling and rushing of the wind, the bawling of the captain and crew, the shrieking of the passengers, all mingled with the rolling and bellowing of the thunder. In the midst of the uproar the sloop righted; at the same time the mainsail shifted, the boom came sweeping the quarter-deck, and Dolph, who was gazing unguardedly at the clouds, found himself, in a moment, floundering in the river.

For once in his life one of his idle accomplishments was of use to him. The many truant hours he had devoted to sporting in the Hudson had made him an expert swimmer. Yet with all his strength and skill he found great difficulty in reaching the shore. His disappearance from the deck had not been noticed by the crew, who were all occupied by their own danger. The sloop was driven along with inconceivable rapidity. She had hard work to weather a long promontory on the eastern shore, round which the river turned, and which completely shut her from Dolph's view.

It was on a point of the western shore that he landed, and, scrambling up the rocks, threw himself, faint and exhausted, at the foot of a tree. By degrees the thunder-gust passed over. The clouds rolled away to the east, where they lay piled in feathery masses, tinted with the last rosy rays of the sun. The distant play of the lightning might be seen about the dark bases, and now and then might be heard the faint muttering of the thunder. Dolph rose, and sought about to see if any path led from the shore, but all was savage and trackless. The rocks were piled upon each other; great trunks of trees lay shattered about, as they had been blown down by the strong winds which draw through these mountains, or had fallen through age. The rocks, too, were overhung with wild vines and briers, which completely matted themselves together, and opposed a barrier to all ingress; every movement that he made shook down a shower from the dripping foliage. He attempted to scale one of these almost perpendicular heights; but, though strong and agile, he found it a Herculean undertaking. Often he was supported merely by crumbling projections of the rock, and sometimes he clung to roots and branches of trees, and hung almost suspended in the air. The wood-pigeon came cleaving his whistling flight by him, and the eagle screamed from the brow of the impending cliff. As he was thus clambering, he was on the point of seizing hold of a shrub to aid his ascent, when something rustled among the leaves, and he saw a snake quivering along like lightning, almost from under his hand. It coiled itself up immediately, in an attitude of defiance, with flattened head, distended jaws, and quickly vibrating tongue, that played like a little flame about its mouth. Dolph's heart turned faint within him, and he had well-nigh let go his hold and tumbled down the precipice. The serpent stood on the defensive but for an instant; and finding there was no attack, glided away into a cleft of the rock. Dolph's eye followed it with fearful intensity, and saw a nest of adders, knotted, and writhing, and hissing in the chasm. He hastened with all speed from so frightful a neighborhood. His imagination, full of this new horror, saw an adder in every curling vine, and heard the tail of a rattlesnake in every dry leaf that rustled.

At length he succeeded in scrambling to the summit of a precipice; but it was covered by a dense forest. Wherever he could gain a lookout between trees, he beheld heights and cliffs, one rising beyond another, until huge mountains overtopped the whole. There were no signs of cultivation; no smoke curling among the trees to indicate a human residence. Everything was wild and solitary. As he was standing on the edge of a precipice overlooking a deep ravine fringed with trees, his feet detached a great fragment of rock; it fell, crashing its way through the tree-tops, down into the chasm. A loud whoop, or rather yell, issued from the bottom of the glen; the moment after there was a report of a gun; and a ball came whistling over his head, cutting the twigs and leaves, and burying itself deep in the bark of a chestnut-tree.

Dolph did not wait for a second shot, but made a precipitate retreat; fearing every moment to hear the enemy in pursuit. He succeeded, however, in returning unmolested to the shore, and determined to penetrate no farther into a country so beset with savage perils.

He sat himself down, dripping, disconsolately, on a stone. What was to be done? Where was he to shelter himself? The hour of repose was approaching; the birds were seeking their nests, the bat began to flit about in the twilight, and the night-hawk, soaring high in the heaven, seemed to be calling out the stars. Night gradually closed in, and wrapped everything in gloom; and though it was the latter part of summer, the breeze stealing along the river, and among these dripping forests, was chilly and penetrating, especially to a half-drowned man.

As he sat drooping and despondent in this comfortless condition, he perceived a light gleaming through the trees near the shore, where the winding of the river made a deep bay. It cheered him with the hope of a human habitation, where he might get something to appease the clamorous cravings of his stomach, and what was equally necessary in his shipwrecked condition, a comfortable shelter for the night. With extreme difficulty he made his way toward the light, along ledges of rocks, down which he was in danger of sliding into the river, and over great trunks of fallen trees; some of which had been blown down in the late storm, and lay so thickly together that he had to struggle through their branches. At length he came to the brow of a rock overhanging a small dell, whence the light proceeded. It was from a fire at the foot of a great tree in the midst of a grassy interval or plat among the rocks. The fire cast up a red glare among the gray crags, and impending trees; leaving chasms of deep gloom, that resembled entrances to caverns. A small brook rippled close by, betrayed by the quivering reflection of the flame. There were two figures moving about the fire, and others squatted before it. As they were between him and the light, they were in complete shadow; but one of them happening to move round to the opposite side, Dolph was startled at perceiving, by the glare falling on painted features, and glittering on silver ornaments, that he was an Indian. He now looked more narrowly, and saw guns leaning against a tree, and a dead body lying on the ground. Here was the very foe that had fired at him from the glen. He endeavored to retreat quietly, not caring to intrust himself to these half-human beings in so savage and lonely a place. It was too late; the Indian, with that eagle quickness of eye so remarkable in his race, perceived something stirring among the bushes on the rock; he seized one of the guns that leaned against the tree; one moment more, and Dolph might have had his passion for adventure cured by a bullet. He halloed loudly, with the Indian salutation of friendship; the whole party sprang upon their feet; the salutation was returned, and the straggler was invited to join them at the fire.

On approaching, he found, to his consolation, the party was composed of white men as well as Indians. One, evidently the principal personage, or commander, was seated on a trunk of a tree before the fire. He was a large, stout man, somewhat advanced in life, but hale and hearty. His face was bronzed almost to the color of an Indian's; he had strong but rather jovial features, an aquiline nose, and a mouth shaped like a mastiff's. His face was half thrown in shade by a broad hat, with a buck's tail in it. His gray hair hung short on his neck. He wore a hunting-frock, with Indian leggins, and moccasins, and a tomahawk in the broad wampum-belt round his waist. As Dolph caught a distinct view of his person and features, something reminded him of the old man of the haunted house. The man before him, however, was different in dress and age; he was more cheery too in aspect, and it was hard to find where the vague resemblance lay; but a resemblance there certainly was. Dolph felt some degree of awe in approaching him; but was assured by a frank, hearty welcome. He was still further encouraged by perceiving that the dead body, which had caused him some alarm, was that of a deer; and his satisfaction was complete in discerning by savory steams from a kettle, suspended by a hooked stick over the fire, that there was a part cooking for the evening's repast.

He had, in fact, fallen in with a rambling hunting-party, such as often took place in those days among the settlers along the river. The hunter is always hospitable; and nothing makes men more social and unceremonious than meeting in the wilderness. The commander of the party poured out a dram of cheering liquor, which he gave him with a merry leer, to warm his heart; and ordered one of his followers to fetch some garments from a pinnace, moored in a cove close by, while those in which our hero was dripping might be dried before the fire.

Dolph found, as he had suspected, that the shot from the glen, which had come so near giving him his quietus when on the precipice, was from the party before him. He had nearly crushed one of them by the fragments of rock which he had detached; and the jovial old hunter, in the broad hat and buck-tail, had fired at the place where he saw the bushes move, supposing it to be the sound of some wild animal. He laughed heartily at the blunder, it being what is considered an exceeding good joke among hunters: "But faith, my lad," said he, "if I had but caught a glimpse of you to take sight at, you would have followed the rock. Antony Vander Heyden is seldom known to miss his aim." These last words were at once a clue to Dolph's curiosity; and a few questions let him completely into the character of the man before him, and of his band of woodland rangers. The commander in the broad hat and hunting-frock was no less a personage than the Heer Antony Vander Heyden, of Albany, of whom Dolph had many a time heard. He was, in fact, the hero of many a story, his singular humors and whimsical habits

115

being matters of wonder to his quiet Dutch neighbors. As he was a man of property, having had a father before him from whom he inherited large tracts of wild land, and whole barrels full of wampum, he could indulge his humors without control. Instead of staying quietly at home, eating and drinking at regular meal-times, amusing himself by smoking his pipe on the bench before the door, and then turning into a comfortable bed at night, he delighted in all kinds of rough, wild expeditions; never so happy as when on a hunting-party in the wilderness, sleeping under trees or bark sheds, or cruising down the river, or on some woodland lake, fishing and fowling, and living the Lord knows how.

He was a great friend to Indians, and to an Indian mode of life; which he considered true natural liberty and manly enjoyment. When at home he had always several Indian hangers-on who loitered about his house, sleeping like hounds in the sunshine; or preparing hunting and fishing tackle for some new expedition; or shooting at marks with bows and arrows.

Over these vagrant beings Heer Antony had as perfect command as a huntsman over his pack; though they were great nuisances to the regular people of his neighborhood. As he was a rich man, no one ventured to thwart his humors; indeed, his hearty, joyous manner made him universally popular. He would troll a Dutch song as he tramped along the street; hail everyone a mile off, and when he entered a house, would slap the good man familiarly on the back, shake him by the hand till he roared, and kiss his wife and daughter before his face—in short, there was no pride nor ill humor about Heer Antony.

Besides his Indian hangers-on, he had three or four humble friends among the white men, who looked up to him as a patron, and had the run of his kitchen, and the favor of being taken with him occasionally on his expeditions. With a medley of such retainers he was at present on a cruise along the shores of the Hudson, in a pinnace kept for his own recreation. There were two white men with him, dressed partly in the Indian style, with moccasins and hunting-shirts; the rest of his crew consisted of four favorite Indians. They had been prowling about the river, without any definite object, until they found themselves in the highlands; where they had passed two or three days, hunting the deer which still lingered among these mountains.

"It is lucky for you, young man," said Antony Vander Heyden, "that you happened to be knocked overboard today, as tomorrow morning we start early on our return homewards; and you might then have looked in vain for a meal among the mountains—but come, lads, stir about! stir about! Let's see what prog we have for supper; the kettle has boiled long enough; my stomach cries cupboard; and I'll warrant our guest is in no mood to dally with his trencher."

There was a bustle now in the little encampment; one took off the kettle and turned a part of the contents into a huge wooden bowl. Another prepared a flat rock for a table; while a third brought various utensils from the pinnace; Heer Antony himself brought a flask or two of precious liquor from his own private locker; knowing his boon companions too well to trust any of them with the key.

A rude but hearty repast was soon spread; consisting of venison smoking from the kettle, with cold bacon, boiled Indian corn, and mighty loaves of good brown household bread. Never had Dolph made a more delicious repast; and when he had washed it down with two or three draughts from the Heer Antony's flask, and felt the jolly liquor sending its warmth through his veins, and glowing round his very heart, he would not have changed his situation, no, not with the governor of the province.

The Heer Antony, too, grew chirping and joyous; told half a dozen fat stories, at which his white followers laughed immoderately, though the Indians, as usual, maintained an invincible gravity.

"This is your true life, my boy!" said he, slapping Dolph on the shoulder; "a man is never a man till he can defy wind and weather, range woods and wilds, sleep under a tree, and live on basswood leaves!"

And then would he sing a stave or two of a Dutch drinking-song, swaying a short swab Dutch bottle in his hand, while his myrmidons would join in the chorus, until the woods echoed again;—as the good old song has it,

> "They all with a shout made the elements ring
> So soon as the office was o'er,
> To feasting they went, with true merriment,
> And tippled strong liquor gillore."

In the midst of his joviality, however, Heer Antony did not lose sight of discretion. Though he pushed the bottle without reserve to Dolph, he always took care to help his followers himself, knowing the beings he had to deal with; and was particular in granting but a moderate allowance to the Indians. The repast being ended, the Indians having drunk their liquor, and smoked their pipes, now wrapped themselves in their blankets, stretched themselves on the ground, with their feet to the fire, and soon fell asleep, like so many tired hounds. The rest of the party remained chatting before the fire, which the gloom of the forest, and the dampness of the air from the late storm, rendered extremely grateful and comforting. The conversation gradually moderated from the hilarity of supper-time, and turned upon hunting-adventures, and exploits and perils in the wilderness, many of which were so strange and improbable, that I will not venture to repeat them, lest the veracity of Antony Vander Heyden and his comrades should be brought into question. There were many legendary tales told, also, about the river, and the settlements on its borders; in which valuable kind of lore the Heer Antony seemed deeply versed. As the sturdy bush-beater sat in a twisted root of a tree, that served him for an arm-chair, dealing forth these wild stories, with the fire gleaming on his strongly marked visage, Dolph was again repeatedly perplexed by something that reminded him of the phantom of the haunted house; some vague resemblance not to be fixed upon any precise feature or lineament, but pervading the general air of his countenance and figure.

The circumstances of Dolph's falling overboard led to the relation of divers disasters and singular mishaps that had befallen voyagers on this great river, particularly in the earlier periods of colonial history; most of which the Heer deliberately attributed to supernatural causes. Dolph stared at this suggestion; but the old gentleman assured him it was very currently believed by the settlers along the river, that these highlands were under the dominion of supernatural and mischievous beings, which seemed to have taken some pique against the Dutch colonists in the early time of the settlement. In consequence of this, they have ever taken particular delight in venting their spleen, and indulging their humors upon the Dutch skippers; bothering them with flaws, head-winds, counter-currents, and all kinds of impediments, insomuch, that a Dutch navigator was always obliged to be exceedingly wary and deliberate in his proceedings; to come to anchor at dusk; to drop his peak, or take in sail, whenever he saw a swag-bellied cloud rolling over the mountains; in short, to take so many precautions, that he was often apt to be an incredible time in toiling up the river.

Some, he said, believed these mischievous powers of the air to be the evil spirits conjured up by the Indian wizards, in the early times of the province, to revenge themselves on the strangers who had dispossessed them of their country. They even attributed to their incantations the misadventure which befell the renowned Hendrick Hudson, when he sailed so gallantly up this river in quest of a northwest passage, and, as he thought, ran his ship aground; which they affirm was nothing more nor less than a spell of these same wizards, to prevent his getting to China in this direction.

The greater part, however, Heer Antony observed, accounted for all the extraordinary circumstances attending this river, and the perplexities of the skippers who navigated it, by the old legend of the *Storm-Ship* which haunted Point-no-point. On finding Dolph to be utterly ignorant of this tradition, the Heer stared at him for a moment with surprise, and wondered where he had passed his life, to be uninformed on so important a point of history. To pass away the remainder of the evening, therefore, he undertook the tale, as far as his memory would serve, in the very words in which it had been written out by Mynheer Selyne, an early poet of the New Netherlands. Giving, then, a stir to the fire, that sent up its sparks among the trees like a little volcano, he adjusted himself comfortably in his root of a tree, and throwing back his head, and closing his eyes for a few moments, to summon up his recollection, he related the following legend.

The Storm-Ship

In the golden age of the province of the New Netherlands, when under the sway of Wouter Van Twiller, otherwise called the Doubter, the people of the Manhattoes were alarmed one sultry afternoon, just about the time of the summer solstice, by a tremendous storm of thunder and lightning. The rain fell in such torrents as absolutely to spatter up and smoke along the ground. It seemed as if the thunder rattled and rolled over the very roofs of the houses; the lightning was seen to play about the church of St. Nicholas, and to strive three times, in vain, to strike its weather-cock. Garret Van Horne's new chimney was split almost from top to bottom; Doffue Mildeberger was struck speechless from his baldfaced mare, just as he was riding into town. In a word, it was one of those unparalleled storms which only happen once within the memory of that venerable personage known in all towns by the appellation of "the oldest inhabitant."

Great was the terror of the good old women of the Manhattoes. They gathered their children together, and took refuge in the cellars; after having hung a shoe on the iron point of every bedpost, lest it should attract the lightning. At length the storm abated; the thunder sank into a growl, and the setting sun, breaking from under the fringed borders of the clouds, made the broad bosom of the bay to gleam like a sea of molten gold.

The word was given from the fort that a ship was standing up the bay. It passed from mouth to mouth, and street to street, and soon put the little capital in a bustle. The arrival of a ship, in those early times of the settlement, was an event of vast importance to the inhabitants. It brought them news from the old world, from the land of their birth, from which they were so completely severed; to the yearly ship, too, they looked for their supply of luxuries, of finery, of comforts, and almost of necessaries. The good *vrouw* could not have her new cap nor new gown until the arrival of the ship; the artist waited for it for his tools, the burgomaster for his pipe and his supply of Hollands, the schoolboy for his top and marbles, and the lordly landholder for the bricks with which he was to build his new mansion. Thus every one, rich and poor, great and small, looked out for the arrival of the ship. It was the great yearly event of the town of New Amsterdam; and from one end of the year to the other, the ship—the ship—the ship—was the continual topic of conversation.

The news from the fort, therefore, brought all the populace down to the Battery, to behold the wished-for sight. It was not exactly the time when she had been expected to arrive, and the circumstance was a matter of some speculation. Many were the groups collected about the Battery. Here and there might be seen a burgomaster, of slow and pompous gravity, giving his opinion with great confidence to a crowd of old women and idle boys. At another place was a knot of old weather-beaten fellows, who had been seamen or fishermen in their times, and were great authorities on such occasions. These gave different opinions, and caused great disputes among their several adherents; but the man most looked up to, and followed and watched by the crowd, was Hans Van Pelt, an old Dutch sea-captain retired from service, the nautical oracle of the place. He reconnoitred the ship through an ancient tele-scope, covered with tarry canvas, hummed a Dutch tune to himself, and said nothing. A hum, however, from Hans Van Pelt, had always more weight with the public than a speech from another man.

In the meantime the ship became more distinct to the naked eye: she was a stout, round, Dutch-built vessel, with high bow and poop, and bearing Dutch colors. The evening sun gilded her bellying canvas, as she came riding over the long waving billows. The sentinel who had given notice of her approach, declared, that he first got sight of her when she was in the centre of the bay; and that she broke suddenly on his sight, just as if she had come out of the bosom of the black thunder-cloud. The

bystanders looked at Hans Van Pelt, to see what he would say to this report; Hans Van Pelt screwed his mouth closer together, and said nothing; upon which some shook their heads, and others shrugged their shoulders.

The ship was now repeatedly hailed, but made no reply, and passing by the fort, stood on up the Hudson. A gun was brought to bear on her, and, with some difficulty, loaded and fired by Hans Van Pelt, the garrison not being expert in artillery. The shot seemed absolutely to pass through the ship, and to skip along the water on the other side, but no notice was taken of it! What was strange, she had all her sails set, and sailed right against wind and tide, which were both down the river. Upon this Hans Van Pelt, who was likewise harbor-master, ordered his boat, and set off to board her; but after rowing two or three hours, he returned without success. Sometimes he would get within one or two hundred yards of her, and then, in a twinkling, she would be half a mile off. Some said it was because his oarsmen, who were rather pursy and short-winded, stopped every now and then to take breath, and spit on their hands; but this it is probable was a mere scandal. He got near enough, however, to see the crew; who were all dressed in the Dutch style, the officers in doublets and high hats and feathers. Not a word was spoken by any one on board; they stood as motionless as so many statues, and the ship seemed as if left to her own government. Thus she kept on, away up the river, lessening and lessening in the evening sunshine, until she faded from sight, like a little white cloud melting away in the summer sky.

The appearance of this ship threw the governor into one of the deepest doubts that ever beset him in the whole course of his administration. Fears were entertained for the security of the infant settlements on the river, lest this might be an enemy's ship in disguise, sent to take possession. The governor called together his council repeatedly to assist him with their conjectures. He sat in his chair of state, built of timber from the sacred forest of the Hague, smoking his long jasmin pipe, and listening to all that his counsellors had to say on a subject about which they knew nothing; but in spite of all the conjecturing of the sagest and oldest heads, the governor still continued to doubt.

Messengers were despatched to different places on the river; but they returned without any tidings—the ship had made no port. Day after day, and week after week, elapsed, but she never returned down the Hudson. As, however, the council seemed solicitous for intelligence, they had it in abundance. The captains of the sloops seldom arrived without bringing some report of having seen the strange ship at different parts of the river; sometimes near the Palisadoes, sometimes off Croton

Point, and sometimes in the highlands; but she never was reported as having been seen above the highlands. The crews of the sloops, it is sure, generally differed among themselves in their accounts of these apparitions; but that may have arisen from the uncertain situations in which they saw her. Sometimes it was by the flashes of the thunder-storm lighting up a pitchy night, and giving glimpses of her careering across Tappan Zee, or the wide waste of Haverstraw Bay. At one moment she would appear close upon them, as if likely to run them down, and would throw them into great bustle and alarm; but the next flash would show her far off, always sailing against the wind. Sometimes, in quiet moon-lit nights, she would be seen under some high bluff of the highlands, all in deep shadow, excepting her topsails glittering in the moonbeams; by the time, however, that the voyagers reached the place, no ship was to be seen; and when they had passed on for some distance, and looked back, behold! there she was again, with her topsails in the moonshine! Her appearance was always just after, or just before, or just in the midst of unruly weather; and she was known among the skippers and voyagers of the Hudson by the name of the *Storm-Ship*.

These reports perplexed the governor and his council more than ever; and it would be endless to repeat the conjectures and opinions uttered on the subject. Some quoted cases in point, of ships seen off the coast of New England, navigated by witches and goblins. Old Hans Van Pelt, who had been more than once to the Dutch colony at the Cape of Good Hope, insisted that this must be the *Flying Dutchman,* which had so long haunted Table Bay; but being unable to make port, had now sought another harbor. Others suggested, that, if it really was a supernatural apparition, as there was every natural reason to believe, it might be Hendrick Hudson, and his crew of the *Half-Moon;* who, it was well known, had once run aground in the upper part of the river in seeking a northwest passage to China. This opinion had very little weight with the governor, but it passed current out of doors; for indeed it had already been reported, that Hendrick Hudson and his crew haunted the Kaatskill Mountains; and it appeared very reasonable to suppose, that his ship might infest the river where the enterprise was baffled, or that it might bear the shadowy crew to their periodical revels in the mountain.

Other events occurred to occupy the thoughts and doubts of the sage

Wouter and his council, and the *Storm-Ship* ceased to be a subject of deliberation at the board. It continued, however, a matter of popular belief and marvellous anecdote through the whole time of the Dutch government, and particularly just before the capture of New Amsterdam, and the subjugation of the province by the English squadron. About that time the *Storm-Ship* was repeatedly seen in the Tappan Zee; and about Weehawk, and even down as far as Hoboken; and her approaching squall in public affairs, and the downfall of Dutch domination.

Since that time we have no authentic accounts of her; though it is said she still haunts the highlands, and cruises about Point-no-point. People who live along the river insist that they sometimes see her in summer moonlight; and that in a deep still midnight they have heard the chant of her crew, as if heaving the lead; but sights and sounds are so deceptive along the mountainous shores, and about the wide bays and long reaches of this great river, that I confess I have very strong doubts upon the subject.

It is certain, nevertheless, that strange things have been seen in these highlands in storms, which are considered as connected with the old story of the ship. The captains of the river craft talk of a little bulbous-bottomed Dutch goblin, in trunk-hose and sugar-loafed hat, with a speaking-trumpet in his hand, which they say keeps about the Dunderberg.† They declare that they have heard him, in stormy weather, in the midst of the turmoil, giving orders in Low Dutch for the piping up of a fresh gust of wind, or the rattling off of another thunder-clap. That sometimes he has been seen surrounded by a crew of little imps in broad breeches and short doublets; tumbling head-over-heels in the rack and mist, and playing a thousand gambols in the air; or buzzing like a swarm of flies about Antony's Nose; and that, at such times, the hurry-scurry of the storm was always greatest. One time a sloop, in passing by the Dunderberg, was overtaken by a thunder-gust, that came scouring round the mountain, and seemed to burst just over the vessel. Though tight and well ballasted, she labored dreadfully, and the water came over the gunwale. All the crew were amazed when it was discovered that there was a little white sugar-loaf hat on the mast-head, known at once to be the hat of the Heer of the Dunderberg. Nobody, however, dared to climb to the mast-head, and get rid of this terrible hat. The sloop

---

†*i.e.*, The "Thunder-Mountain," so called from its echoes.

continued laboring and rocking, as if she would have rolled her mast overboard, and seemed in continual danger either of upsetting or of running on shore. In this way she drove quite through the highlands, until she had passed Pollopol's Island, where, it is said, the jurisdiction of the Dunderberg potentate ceases. No sooner had she passed this bourn, than the little hat spun up into the air like a top, whirled up all the clouds into a vortex, and hurried them back to the summit of the Dunderberg; while the sloop righted herself, and sailed on as quietly as if in a mill-pond. Nothing saved her from utter wreck but the fortunate circumstances of having a horse-shoe nailed against the mast—a wise precaution against evil spirits, since adopted by all the Dutch captains that navigate this haunted river.

There is another story told of this foul-weather urchin, by Skipper Daniel Ouselsticker, of Fishkill, who was never known to tell a lie. He declared, that, in a severe squall, he saw him seated astride of his bowsprit, riding the sloop ashore, full butt against Antony's Nose, and that he was exorcised by Dominie Van Gieson, of Esopus, who happened to be on board, and who sang the hymn of St. Nicholas; whereupon the goblin threw himself up in the air like a ball, and went off in a whirlwind, carrying away with him the nightcap of the Dominie's wife; which was discovered the next Sunday morning hanging on the weather-cock of Esopus church-steeple, at least forty miles off! Several events of this kind having taken place, the regular skippers of the river, for a long time, did not venture to pass the Dunderberg without lowering their peaks, out of homage to the Heer of the mountain; and it was observed that all such as paid this tribute of respect were suffered to pass unmolested.†

†Among the superstitions which prevailed in the colonies, during the early times of the settlements, there seems to have been a singular one about phantom ships. The superstitious fancies of men are always apt to turn upon those objects which concern their daily occupations. The solitary ship, which, from year to year, came like a raven in the wilderness, bringing to the inhabitants of a settlement the comforts of life from the world from which they were cut off, was apt to be present to their dreams, whether sleeping or waking. The accidental sight from shore of a sail gliding along the horizon in those as yet lonely seas, was apt to be a matter of much talk and speculation. There is mention made in one of the early New England writers of a ship navigated by witches, with a great horse that stood by the mainmast. I have met with another story, somewhere, of a ship that drove on shore, in fair, sunny, tranquil weather, with sails all set, and a table spread in the cabin, as if to regale a number of guests, yet not a living being on board. These phantom ships always sailed in the eye of the wind; or ploughed their way with great velocity, making the smooth sea foam before their bows, when not a breath of air was stirring.

"Such," said Antony Vander Heyden, "are a few of the stories written down by Selyne, the poet, concerning the *Storm-Ship*—which he affirms to have brought a crew of mischievous imps into the province, from some old ghost-ridden country of Europe. I could give a host more, if necessary; for all the accidents that so often befall the river craft in the highlands are said to be tricks played off by these imps of the Dunderberg; but I see that you are nodding, so let us turn in for the night."

The moon had just raised her silver horns above the round back of Old Bull Hill, and lit up the gray rocks and shagged forests, and glittered on the waving bosom of the river. The night dew was falling, and the late gloomy mountains began to soften and put on a gray aërial tint in the dewy light. The hunters stirred the fire, and threw on fresh fuel to qualify the damp of the night air. They then prepared a bed of branches and dry leaves under a ledge of rocks for Dolph; while Antony Vander Heyden, wrapping himself in a huge coat of skins, stretched himself before the fire. It was some time, however, before Dolph could close his eyes. He lay contemplating the strange scene before him: the wild woods and rocks around; the fire throwing fitful gleams on the faces of the sleeping savages; and the Heer Antony, too, who so singularly, yet vaguely, reminded him of the nightly visitant to the haunted house. Now and then he heard the cry of some wild animal from the forest; or the hooting of the owl; or the notes of the whippoorwill, which seemed to abound among these solitudes; or the splash of a sturgeon, leaping out of the river and falling back full-length on its placid surface. He contrasted all this with his accustomed nest in the garret room of the doctor's mansion;—where the only sounds at night were the church clock telling the hour; the drowsy voice of the watchman, drawling out all was well; the deep snoring of the doctor's clubbed nose from below stairs; or the cautious labors of some carpenter rat gnawing in the wainscot. His thoughts then wandered to his poor old mother: what would she think of his mysterious disappearance—what anxiety and distress would she not suffer? This thought would continually intrude itself to mar his present enjoyment. It brought with it a feeling of pain and compunction, and he fell asleep with the tears yet standing in his eyes.

Were this a mere tale of fancy, here would be a fine opportunity for weaving in strange adventures among these wild mountains, and roving hunters; and, after involving my hero in a variety of perils and difficulties, rescuing him from them all by some miraculous contrivance. But as this is absolutely a true story, I must content myself with simple facts, and keep to probabilities.

At an early hour of the next day, therefore, after a hearty morning's meal, the encampment broke up, and our adventurers embarked in the pinnace of Antony Vander Heyden. There being no wind for the sails, the Indians rowed her gently along, keeping time to a kind of chant of one of the white men. The day was serene and beautiful; the river without a wave; and as the vessel cleft the glassy water, it left a long, undulating track behind. The crows, who had scented the hunters' banquet, were already gathering and hovering in the air, just where a column of thin, blue smoke, rising from among the trees, showed the place of their last night's quarters. As they coasted along the bases of the mountains, the Heer Antony pointed out to Dolph a bald eagle, the sovereign of these regions, who sat perched on a dry tree that projected over the river, and, with eye turned upwards, seemed to be drinking in the splendor of the morning sun. Their approach disturbed the monarch's meditations. He first spread one wing, and then the other; balanced himself for a moment, and then, quitting his perch with dignified composure, wheeled slowly over their heads. Dolph snatched up a gun, and sent a whistling ball after him, that cut some of the feathers from his wing. The report of the gun leaped sharply from rock to rock, and awakened a thousand echoes. But the monarch of the air sailed calmly on, ascending higher and higher, and wheeling widely as he ascended, soaring up the green bosom of the woody mountain, until he disappeared over the brow of a beetling precipice. Dolph felt in a manner rebuked by this proud tranquillity, and almost reproached himself for having so wantonly insulted this majestic bird. Heer Antony told him, laughing, to remember that he was not yet out of the territories of the lord of the Dunderberg; and an old Indian shook his head, and observed, that there was bad luck in killing an eagle. The hunter, on the contrary, should always leave him a portion of his spoils.

Nothing, however, occurred to molest them on their voyage. They passed pleasantly through magnificent and lonely scenes, until they came to where Pollopol's Island lay, like a floating bower at the extremity of the highlands. Here they landed, until the heat of the day should abate, or a breeze spring up that might supersede the labor of the oar. Some prepared the mid-day meal, while others reposed under the shade of the trees, in luxurious summer indolence, looking drowsily forth upon the beauty of the scene. On the one side were the highlands, vast and cragged, feathered to the top with forests, and throwing their shadows on the glassy water that dimpled at their feet. On the other side was a wide expanse of the river, like a broad lake, with long sunny reaches, and green headlands; and the distant line of the Shawangunk Mountains waving along a clear horizon, or checkered by a fleecy cloud.

But I forbear to dwell on the particulars of their cruise along the river. This vagrant, amphibious life, careering across silver sheets of water, coasting wild woodland shores, banqueting on shady promontories, with the spreading tree overhead, the river curling its light foam to one's feet, and distant mountain, and rock, and tree, and snowy cloud, and deep-blue sky, all mingling in summer beauty before one—all this, though never cloying in the enjoyment, would be but tedious in narration.

When encamped by the water-side, some of the party would go into the woods and hunt; others would fish. Sometimes they would amuse themselves by shooting at a mark, by leaping, by running, by wrestling; and Dolph gained great favor in the eyes of Antony Vander Heyden, by his skill and adroitness in all these exercises, which the Heer considered as the highest of manly accomplishments.

Thus did they coast jollily on, choosing only the pleasant hours for voyaging; sometimes in the cool morning dawn, sometimes in the sober evening twilight, and sometimes when the moonshine spangled the crisp curling waves that whispered along the sides of their little bark. Never had Dolph felt so completely in his element; never had he met with anything so completely to his taste as this wild haphazard life. He was the very man to second Antony Vander Heyden in his rambling humors, and gained continually on his affections. The heart of the old bush-whacker yearned toward the young man, who seemed thus growing up in his own likeness; and as they approached to the end of their voyage, he could not help inquiring a little into his history. Dolph frankly told him his course of life, his severe medical studies, his little proficiency, and his very dubious prospects. The Heer was shocked to find that such amazing talents and accomplishments were to be cramped and buried under a doctor's wig. He had a sovereign contempt for the healing art, having never had any other physician than the butcher. He bore a mortal grudge to all kinds of study also, ever since he had been flogged about an unintelligible book when he was a boy. But to think that a young fellow like Dolph, of such wonderful abilities, who could shoot, fish, run, jump, ride, and wrestle, should be obliged to roll pills, and administer juleps for a living—'twas monstrous! He told Dolph never to despair, but to "throw physic to the dogs"; for a young fellow of his prodigious talents could never fail to make his way. "As you seem to have no acquaintance in Albany," said Heer Antony, "you shall go home with me, and remain under my roof until you can look about you; and in the meantime we can take an occasional bout at shooting and fishing, for it is a pity that such talents should lie idle."

Dolph, who was at the mercy of chance, was not hard to be persuaded. Indeed, on turning over matters in his mind, which he did very sagely and deliberately, he could not but think that Antony Vander Heyden was, "somehow or other," connected with the story of the Haunted House; that the misadventure in the highlands, which had thrown them so strangely together, was, "somehow or other," to work out something good: in short, there is nothing so convenient as this "somehow-or-other" way of accommodating one's self to circumstances; it is the mainstay of a heedless actor, and tardy reasoner, like Dolph Heyliger; and he who can, in this loose, easy way, link foregone evil to anticipated good, possesses a secret of happiness almost equal to the philosopher's stone.

On their arrival at Albany, the sight of Dolph's companion seemed to cause universal satisfaction. Many were the greetings at the river-side, and the salutations in the streets; the dogs bounded before him; the boys whooped as he passed; everybody seemed to know Antony Vander Heyden. Dolph followed on in silence, admiring the neatness of this worthy burgh; for in those days Albany was in all its glory, and inhabited almost exclusively by the descendants of the original Dutch settlers, not having as yet been discovered and colonized by the restless people of New England. Everything was quiet and orderly; everything was conducted calmly and leisurely; no hurry, no bustle, no struggling and scrambling for existence. The grass grew about the unpaved streets, and relieved the eye by its refreshing verdure. Tall sycamores or pendent willows shaded the houses, with caterpillars swinging in long silken strings from their branches; or moths, fluttering about like coxcombs, in joy at their gay transformation. The houses were built in the old Dutch style, with the gable-ends toward the street. The thrifty housewife was seated on a bench before her door, in close-crimped cap, bright-flowered gown, and white apron, busily employed in knitting. The husband smoked his pipe on the opposite bench; and the little pet Negro girl, seated on the step at her mistress's feet, was industriously plying her needle. The swallows sported about the eaves, or skimmed along the streets, and brought back some rich booty for their clamorous young; and the little housekeeping wren flew in and out of a Liliputian house, or an old hat nailed against the wall. The cows were coming home, lowing through the streets, to be milked at their owner's door; and if, perchance, there were any loiterers, some Negro urchin, with a long goad, was gently urging them homewards.

As Dolph's companion passed on, he received a tranquil nod from the burghers, and a friendly word from their wives; all calling him familiarly by the name of Antony; for it was the custom in this stronghold of the patriarchs, where they had all grown up together from childhood, to call each other by the Christian name. The Heer did not pause to have his usual jokes with them, for he was impatient to reach his home. At length they arrived at his mansion. It was of some magnitude, in the Dutch style, with large iron figures on the gables, that gave the date of its erection, and showed that it had been built in the earliest times of the settlement.

The news of Heer Antony's arrival had preceded him, and the whole household was on the look-out. A crew of Negroes, large and small, had collected in front of the house to receive him. The old, white-headed ones, who had grown gray in his service, grinned for joy, and made many awkward bows and grimaces, and the little ones capered about his knees. But the most happy being in the household was a little, plump, blooming lass, his only child, and the darling of his heart. She came bounding out of the house; but the sight of a strange young man with her father called up, for a moment, all the bashfulness of a home-bred damsel. Dolph gazed at her with wonder and delight; never had he seen, as he thought, anything so comely in the shape of a woman. She was dressed in the good old Dutch taste, with long stays, and full, short petticoats, so admirably adapted to show and set off the female form. Her hair, turned up under a small round cap, displayed the fairness of her forehead; she had fine blue, laughing eyes, a trim, slender waist, and soft swell—but, in a word, she was a little Dutch divinity; and Dolph, who never stopped half-way in a new impulse, fell desperately in love with her.

Dolph was now ushered into the house with a hearty welcome. In the interior was a mingled display of Heer Antony's taste and habits, and of the opulence of his predecessors. The chambers were furnished with good old mahogany; the buffets and cupboards glittered with embossed silver and painted china. Over the parlor fireplace was, as usual, the family coat-of-arms, painted and framed; above which was a long duck fowling-piece, flanked by an Indian pouch and a powder-horn. The room was decorated with many Indian articles, such as pipes of peace, tomahawks, scalping-knives, hunting-pouches, and belts of wampum; and there were various kinds of fishing-tackle, and two or three fowling-pieces in the corners. The household affairs seemed to be conducted, in some measure, after the master's humors; corrected, perhaps, by a little quiet management of the daughter's. There was a great degree of patriarchal simplicity, and good-humored indulgence. The Negroes came into the room without being called, merely to look at their master, and hear of his adventures; they would stand listening at the door until he had finished a story, and then go off on a broad grin, to repeat it in the kitchen. A couple of pet Negro children were playing about the floor with the dogs, and sharing with them their bread and butter. All the domestics looked hearty and happy; and when the table was set for the evening repast, the variety and abundance of good household luxuries bore testimony to the open-handed liberality of the Heer, and the notable housewifery of his daughter.

In the evening there dropped in several of the worthies of the place, the Van Renssellaers, and the Gansevoorts, and the Rosebooms, and others of Antony Vander Heyden's intimates, to hear an account of his expedition; for he was the Sinbad of Albany, and his exploits and adventures were favorite topics of conversation among the inhabitants. While these sat gossiping together about the door of the hall, and telling long twilight stories, Dolph was cosily seated, entertaining the daughter, on a window-bench. He had already got on intimate terms; for those were not times of false reserve and idle ceremony; and, besides, there is something wonderfully propitious to a lover's suit in the delightful dusk of a long summer evening; it gives courage to the most timid tongue, and hides the blushes of the bashful. The stars alone twinkled brightly, and now and then a fire-fly streamed his transient light before the window, or, wandering into the room, flew gleaming about the ceiling.

What Dolph whispered in her ear that long summer evening, it is impossible to say; his words were so low and indistinct, that they never reached the ear of the historian. It is probable, however, that they were to the purpose; for he had a natural talent at pleasing the sex, and was never long in company with a petticoat without paying proper court to it. In the meantime the visitors, one by one, departed; Antony Vander Heyden, who had fairly talked himself silent, sat nodding alone in his chair by the door, when he was suddenly aroused by a hearty salute with which Dolph Heyliger had unguardedly rounded off one of his periods, and which echoed through the still chamber like the report of a pistol. The Heer started up, rubbed his eyes, called for lights, and observed that it was high time to go to bed; though, on parting for the night, he squeezed Dolph heartily by the hand, looked kindly in his face, and shook his head knowingly; for the Heer well remembered what he himself had been at the youngster's age.

The chamber in which our hero was lodged was spacious, and panelled with oak. It was furnished with clothes-presses, and mighty chests of drawers, well waxed, and glittering with brass ornaments. These contained ample stock of family linen; for the Dutch housewives had always a laudable pride in showing off their household treasures to strangers.

Dolph's mind, however, was too full to take particular note of the objects around him; yet he could not help continually comparing the free, open-hearted cheeriness of this establishment with the starveling, sordid, joyless housekeeping at Doctor Knipperhausen's. Still, something marred the enjoyment: the idea that he must take leave of his hearty host and pretty hostess, and cast himself once more adrift upon the world. To linger here would be folly. He should only get deeper in love; and for a poor varlet, like himself, to aspire to the daughter of the great Heer Vander Heyden—it was madness to think of such a thing! The very kindness that the girl had shown towards him prompted him, on reflection, to hasten his departure; it would be a poor return for the frank hospitality of his host to entangle his daughter's heart in an injudicious attachment. In a word, Dolph was like many other young reasoners of exceeding good hearts and giddy heads—who think after they act, and act differently from what they think—who make excellent determinations overnight, and forget to keep them the next morning.

"This is a fine conclusion, truly, of my voyage," said he, as he almost buried himself in a sumptuous feather bed, and drew the fresh white sheets up to his chin. "Here am I, instead of finding a bag of money to carry home, launched in a strange place, with scarcely a stiver in my pocket; and, what is worse, have jumped ashore up to my very ears in love into the bargain. However," added he, after some pause, stretching himself, and turning himself in bed, "I'm in good quarters for the present, at least; so I'll e'en enjoy the present moment, and let the next take care of itself; I dare say all will work out, 'somehow or other,' for the best."

As he said these words, he reached out his hand to extinguish the candle, when he was suddenly struck with astonishment and dismay, for he thought he beheld the phantom of the Haunted House, staring on him from a dusky part of the chamber. A second look reassured him, as he perceived that what he had taken for the spectre was, in fact, nothing but a Flemish portrait, hanging in a shadowy corner, just behind a clothes-press. It was, however, the precise representation of his nightly visitor. The same cloak and belted jerkin, the same grizzled beard and fixed eye, the same broad slouched hat, with a feather hanging over one side. Dolph now called to mind the resemblance he had frequently remarked between his host and the old man of the Haunted House; and was fully convinced they were in some way connected, and that some especial destiny had governed his voyage. He lay gazing on the portrait with almost as much awe as he had gazed on the ghostly original, until the shrill house-clock warned him of the lateness of the hour. He put out the light, but remained for a long time turning over these curious circumstances and coincidences in his mind, until he fell asleep. His dreams partook of the nature of his waking thoughts. He fancied that he still lay gazing on the picture, until, by degrees, it became animated; that the figure descended from the wall, and walked out of the room; that he followed it, and found himself by the well to which the old man pointed, smiled on him, and disappeared.

In the morning, when he waked, he found his host standing by his bedside, who gave him a hearty morning's salutation, and asked him how he had slept. Dolph answered cheerily; but took occasion to inquire about the portrait that hung against the wall. "Ah," said Heer Antony, "that's a portrait of old Killian Vander Spiegel, once a burgomaster of Amsterdam, who, on some popular troubles, abandoned Holland, and came over to the province during the government of Peter Stuyvesant. He was my ancestor by the mother's side, and an old miserly curmudgeon he was. When the English took possession of New Amsterdam, in 1664, he retired into the country. He fell into a melancholy, apprehending that his wealth would be taken from him and he come to beggary. He turned all his property into cash, and used to hide it away. He was for a year or two concealed in various places, fancying himself sought after by the English, to strip him of his wealth; and finally he was found dead in his bed one morning, without any one being able to discover where he had concealed the greater part of his money."

When his host had left the room, Dolph remained for some time lost in thought. His whole mind was occupied by what he had heard. Vander Spiegel was his mother's family name; and he recollected to have heard her speak of this very Killian Vander Spiegel as one of her ancestors. He had heard her say, too, that her father was Killian's rightful heir, only that the old man died without leaving anything to be inherited. It now appeared that Heer Antony was likewise a descendant, and perhaps an heir also, of this poor rich man; and that thus the Heyligers and the Vander Heydens were remotely connected. "What," thought he, "if, after all, this is the interpretation of my dream, that this is the way I am to make my fortune by this voyage to Albany, and that I am to find the old man's hidden wealth in the bottom of that well? But what an odd roundabout mode of communicating the matter! Why the plague could not the old goblin have told me about the well at once, without sending me all the way to Albany, to hear a story that was to send me all the way back again?"

These thoughts passed through his mind while he was dressing. He descended the stairs, full of perplexity, when the bright face of Marie Vander Heyden suddenly beamed in smiles upon him, and seemed to give him a clue to the whole mystery. "After all," thought he, "the old goblin is in the right. If I am to get his wealth, he means that I shall marry his pretty descendant; thus both branches of the family will again be united, and the property go on in the proper channel."

No sooner did this idea enter his head, than it carried conviction with it. He was now all impatience to hurry back and secure the treasure, which, he did not doubt, lay at the bottom of the well, and which he feared every moment might be discovered by some other person. "Who knows," thought he, "but this night-walking old fellow of the haunted house may be in the habit of haunting every visitor, and may give a hint to some shrewder fellow than myself, who will take a shorter cut to the well than by the way of Albany?" He wished a thousand times that the babbling old ghost was laid in the Red Sea, and his rambling portrait with him. He was in a perfect fever to depart. Two or three days elapsed before any opportunity presented for returning down the river. They were ages to Dolph, notwithstanding that he was basking in the smiles of the pretty Marie, and daily getting more and more enamoured.

At length the very sloop from which he had been knocked overboard prepared to make sail. Dolph made an awkward apology to his host for his sudden departure. Antony Vander Heyden was sorely astonished. He had concerted half a dozen excursions into the wilderness; and his Indians were actually preparing for a grand expedition to one of the lakes. He took Dolph aside, and exerted his eloquence to get him to abandon all thoughts of business and to remain with him, but in vain; and he at length gave up the attempt, observing, "that it was a thousand pities so fine a young man should throw himself away." Heer Antony, however, gave him a hearty shake by the hand at parting, with a favorite fowling-piece, and an invitation to come to his house whenever he revisited Albany. The pretty little Marie said nothing; but as he gave her a farewell kiss, her dimpled cheek turned pale, and a tear stood in her eye.

Dolph sprang lightly on board of the vessel. They hoisted sail; the wind was fair; they soon lost sight of Albany, its green hills and embowered islands. They were wafted gayly past the Kaatskill Mountains, whose fairy heights were bright and cloudless. They passed prosperously through the highlands, without any molestation from the Dunderberg goblin and his crew; they swept on across Haverstraw Bay, and by Croton Point, and through the Tappan Zee, and under the Palisadoes, until, in the afternoon of the third day, they saw the promontory of Hoboken hanging like a cloud in the air; and, shortly after, the roofs of the Manhattoes rising out of the water.

Dolph's first care was to repair to his mother's house; for he was continually goaded by the idea of the uneasiness she must experience on his account. He was puzzling his brains, as he went along, to think how he should account for his absence without betraying the secrets of the Haunted House. In the midst of these cogitations he entered the street in which his mother's house was situated, when he was thunderstruck at beholding it a heap of ruins.

There had evidently been a great fire, which had destroyed several large houses, and the humble dwelling of poor Dame Heyliger had been involved in the conflagration. The walls were not so completely destroyed, but that Dolph could distinguish some traces of the scene of his childhood. The fireplace, about which he had often played, still remained, ornamented with Dutch tiles, illustrating passages in Bible history, on which he had many a time gazed with admiration. Among the rubbish lay the wreck of the good dame's elbow-chair, from which she had given him so many a wholesome precept; and hard by it was the family Bible, with brass clasps—now, alas! reduced almost to a cinder.

For a moment Dolph was overcome by this dismal sight, for he was seized with the fear that his mother had perished in the flames. He was relieved, however, from his horrible apprehension by one of the neighbors, who happened to come by and informed him that his mother was yet alive.

The good woman had, indeed, lost everything by this unlooked-for calamity; for the populace had been so intent upon saving the fine furniture of her rich neighbors, that the little tenement, and the little all of poor Dame Heyliger, had been suffered to consume without interruption; nay, had it not been for the gallant assistance of her old crony,

Peter de Groodt, the worthy dame and her cat might have shared the fate of their habitation.

As it was, she had been overcome with fright and affliction, and lay ill in body and sick at heart. The public, however, had showed her its wonted kindness. The furniture of her rich neighbors being, as far as possible, rescued from the flames; themselves duly and ceremoniously visited and condoled with on the injury of their property, and their ladies commiserated on the agitation of their nerves; the public, at length, began to recollect something about poor Dame Heyliger. She forthwith became again a subject of universal sympathy; everybody pitied her more than ever; and if pity could but have been coined into cash—good Lord! how rich she would have been!

It was now determined, in good earnest, that something ought to be done for her without delay. The Dominie, therefore, put up prayers for her on Sunday, in which all the congregation joined most heartily. Even Cobus Groesbeek, the alderman, and Mynheer Milledollar, the great Dutch merchant, stood up in their pews, and did not spare their voices on the occasion; and it was thought the prayers of such great men could not but have their due weight. Doctor Knipperhausen, too, visited her professionally, and gave her abundance of advice gratis, and was universally lauded for his charity. As to her old friend, Peter de Groodt, he was a poor man, whose pity and prayers and advice could be of but little avail, so he gave her all that was in his power—he gave her shelter.

To the humble dwelling of Peter de Groodt, then, did Dolph turn his steps. On his way thither he recalled all the tenderness and kindness of his simple-hearted parent, her indulgence of his errors, her blindness to his faults; and then he bethought himself of his own idle, harum-scarum life. "I've been a sad scapegrace," said Dolph, shaking his head sorrowfully. "I've been a complete sink-pocket, that's the truth of it. But," added he briskly, and clasping his hands, "only let her live—only let her live—and I will show myself indeed a son!"

As Dolph approached the house he met Peter de Groodt coming out of it. The old man started back aghast, doubting whether it was not a ghost that stood before him. It being bright daylight, however, Peter soon plucked up heart, satisfied that no ghost dare show his face in such clear sunshine. Dolph now learned from the worthy sexton the consternation and rumor to which his mysterious disappearance had given rise. It had been universally believed that he had been spirited away by those hobgoblin gentry that infested the Haunted House; and old Abraham Vandozer, who lived by the great buttonwood-trees, near the three-mile stone, affirmed that he had heard a terrible noise in the air, as he was going home late at night, which seemed just as if a flock of wild geese were overhead, passing off towards the northward. The Haunted House was, in consequence, looked upon with ten times more awe than ever; nobody would venture to pass a night in it for the world, and even the doctor had ceased to make his expeditions to it in the day-time.

It required some preparation before Dolph's return could be made known to his mother, the poor soul having bewailed him as lost; and her spirits having been sorely broken down by a number of comforters, who daily cheered her with stories of ghosts, and of people carried away by the devil. He found her confined to her bed, with the other member of the Heyliger family, the good dame's cat, purring beside her, but sadly singed, and utterly despoiled of those whiskers which were the glory of her physiognomy. The poor woman threw her arms about Dolph's neck. "My boy! my boy! art thou still alive?" For a time she seemed to have forgotten all her losses and troubles in her joy at his return. Even the sage grimalkin showed indubitable signs of joy at the return of the youngster. She saw, perhaps, that they were a forlorn and undone family, and felt a touch of that kindliness which fellow-sufferers only know. But, in truth, cats are a slandered people; they have more affection in them than the world commonly gives them credit for.

The good dame's eyes glistened as she saw one being at least, besides herself, rejoiced at her son's return. "Tib knows thee! poor dumb beast!" said she, smoothing down the mottled coat of her favorite; then recollecting herself, with a melancholy shake of the head, "Ah, my poor Dolph!" exclaimed she, "thy mother can help thee no longer! She can no longer help herself! What will become of thee, my poor boy!"

"Mother," said Dolph, "don't talk in that strain; I've been too long a charge upon you; it's now my part to take care of you in your old days. Come, be of good cheer! you and I and Tib will all see better days. I'm here, you see, young and sound and hearty; then don't let us despair; I dare say things will all, somehow or other, turn out for the best."

While this scene was going on with the Heyliger family, the news was carried to Doctor Knipperhausen of the safe return of his disciple. The little doctor scarce knew whether to rejoice or be sorry at the tidings. He was happy at having the foul reports which had prevailed concerning his country mansion thus disproved; but he grieved at having his disciple, of whom he had supposed himself fairly disencumbered, thus drifting back a heavy charge upon his hands. While balancing between these two feelings, he was determined by the councils of Frau Ilsy, who advised him to take advantage of the truant absence of the youngster, and shut the door upon him forever.

At the hour of bedtime, therefore, when it was supposed the recreant disciple would seek his old quarters, everything was prepared for his reception. Dolph, having talked his mother into a state of tranquillity, sought the mansion of his quondam master, and raised the knocker with a faltering hand. Scarcely, however, had it given a dubious rap, when the doctor's head, in a red nightcap, popped out of one window, and the housekeeper's, in a white nightcap, out of another. He was now greeted with a tremendous volley of hard names and hard language, mingled with invaluable pieces of advice, such as are seldom ventured to be given excepting to a friend in distress, or a culprit at the bar. In a few moments, not a window in the street but had its particular nightcap, listening to the shrill treble of Frau Ilsy, and the guttural croaking of Dr. Knipperhausen; and the word went from window to window, "Ah! here's Dolph Heyliger come back, and at his old pranks again." In short, poor Dolph found he was likely to get nothing from the doctor but good advice; a commodity so abundant as even to be thrown out of the window; so he was fain to beat a retreat, and take up his quarters for the night under the lowly roof of honest Peter de Groodt.

The next morning, bright and early, Dolph was out at the haunted house. Everything looked just as he had left it. The fields were grass-grown and matted, and appeared as if nobody had traversed them since his departure. With palpitating heart he hastened to the well. He looked down into it, and saw that it was of great depth, with water at the bottom. He had provided himself with a strong line, such as the fishermen use on the banks of Newfoundland. At the end was a heavy plummet and a large fish-hook. With this he began to sound the bottom of the well, and to angle about in the water. The water was of some depth; there was also much rubbish, stones from the top having fallen in. Several times his hook got entangled, and he came near breaking his line. Now and then, too, he hauled up mere trash, such as the skull of a horse, an iron hoop, and a shattered iron-bound bucket. He had now been several hours employed without finding anything to repay his trouble, or to encourage him to proceed. He began to think himself a great fool, to be thus decoyed into a wild-goose chase by mere dreams, and was on the point of throwing line and all into the well, and giving up all further angling.

"One more cast of the line," said he, "and that shall be the last." As he sounded, he felt the plummet slip, as it were, through the interstices of loose stones; and as he drew back the line, he felt that the hook had taken hold of something heavy. He had to manage his line with great caution, lest it should be broken by the strain upon it. By degrees the rubbish which lay upon the article he had hooked gave way; he drew it to the surface of the water, and what was his rapture at seeing something like silver glittering at the end of his line! Almost breathless with anxiety, he drew it up to the mouth of the well, surprised at its great weight, and fearing every instant that his hook would slip from its hold, and his prize tumble again to the bottom. At length he landed it safe beside the well. It was a great silver porringer, of an ancient form, richly embossed, and with armorial bearings engraved on its side, similar to those over his mother's mantel-piece. The lid was fastened on by several twists of wire; Dolph loosened them with a trembling hand, and, on lifting the lid, behold! the vessel was filled with broad golden pieces, of a coinage which he had never seen before! It was evident he had lit on the place where Killian Vander Spiegel had concealed his treasure.

Fearful of being seen by some straggler, he cautiously retired, and buried his pot of money in a secret place. He now spread terrible stories about the haunted house, and deterred every one from approaching it, while he made frequent visits to it in stormy days, when no one was stirring in the neighboring fields; though, to tell the truth, he did not care to venture there in the dark. For once in his life he was diligent and industrious, and followed up his new trade of angling with such perseverance and success, that in a little while he had hooked up wealth enough to make him, in those modern days, a rich burgher for life.

It would be tedious to detail minutely the rest of this story. To tell how he gradually managed to bring his property into use without exciting surprise and inquiry—how he satisfied all scruples with regard to retaining the property, and at the same time gratified his own feelings by marrying the pretty Marie Vander Heyden—and how he and Heer Antony had many a merry and roving expedition together.

I must not omit to say, however, that Dolph took his mother home to live with him, and cherished her in her old days. The good dame, too, had the satisfaction of no longer hearing her son made the theme of censure; on the contrary, he grew daily in public esteem; everybody spoke well of him and his wines; and the lordliest burgomaster was never known to decline his invitation to dinner. Dolph often related, at his own table, the wicked pranks which had once been the abhorrence of the town; but they were now considered excellent jokes, and the gravest dignitary was fain to hold his sides when listening to them. No one was more struck with Dolph's increasing merit than his old master the doctor; and so forgiving was Dolph, that he absolutely employed the doctor as his family physician, only taking care that his prescriptions should be always thrown out of the window. His mother had often her junto of old cronies to take a snug cup of tea with her in her comfortable little parlor; and Peter de Groodt, as he sat by the fireside, with one of her grandchildren on his knee, would many a time congratulate her upon her son turning out so great a man; upon which the good old soul would wag her head with exultation, and exclaim: "Ah, neighbor, neighbor! did I not say that Dolph would one day or other hold up his head with the best of them?"

Thus did Dolph Heyliger go on, cheerily and prosperously, growing merrier as he grew older and wiser, and completely falsifying the old proverb about money got over the devil's back; for he made good use of his wealth, and became a distinguished citizen, and a valuable member of the community. He was a great promoter of public institutions, such as beefsteak societies and catch-clubs. He presided at all public dinners, and was the first that introduced turtle from the West Indies. He improved the breed of race-horses and game cocks, and was so great a patron of modest merit, that any one who could sing a good song, or tell a good story, was sure to find a place at his table.

He was a member, too, of the corporation, made several laws for the protection of game and oysters, and bequeathed to the board a large silver punch-bowl, made out of the identical porringer before mentioned, and which is in the possession of the corporation to this very day.

Finally, he died, in a florid old age, of an apoplexy at a corporation feast, and was buried with great honors in the yard of the little Dutch church in Garden Street, where his tombstone may still be seen with a modest epitaph in Dutch, by his friend Mynheer Justus Benson, an ancient and excellent poet of the province.

The foregoing tale rests on better authority than most tales of the kind, as I have it at second-hand from the lips of Dolph Heyliger himself. He never related it till towards the latter part of his life, and then in great confidence (for he was very discreet), to a few of his particular cronies at his own table, over a supernumerary bowl of punch; and, strange as the hobgoblin parts of the story may seem, there never was a single doubt expressed on the subject by any of his guests. It may not be amiss, before concluding, to observe that, in addition to his other accomplishments, Dolph Heyliger was noted for being the ablest drawer of the long-bow in the whole province.

Rip Van Winkle

A POSTHUMOUS WRITING OF DIEDRICH KNICKERBOCKER

> By Woden, God of Saxons,
> From whence comes Wensday, that is Wodensday,
> Truth is a thing that ever I will keep
> Unto thylke day in which I creep into
> My sepulchre.
> —CARTWRIGHT

The following tale was found among the papers of the late Diedrich Knickerbocker, an old gentleman of New York, who was very curious in the Dutch history of the province, and the manners of the descendants from its primitive settlers. His historical researches, however, did not lie so much among books as among men; for the former are lamentably scanty on his favorite topics; whereas he found the old burghers, and still more their wives, rich in that legendary lore so invaluable to true history. Whenever, therefore, he happened upon a genuine Dutch family, snugly shut up in its low-roofed farm-house, under a spreading sycamore, he looked upon it as a little clasped volume of black-letter, and studied it with the zeal of a book-worm.

The result of all these researches was a history of the province during the reign of the Dutch governors, which he published some years since. There have been various opinions as to the literary character of his work, and, to tell the truth, it is not a whit better than it should be. Its chief merit is its scrupulous accuracy, which indeed was a little questioned on its first appearance, but has since been completely established; and it is now admitted into all historical collections as a book of unquestionable authority.

The old gentleman died shortly after the publication of his work; and now that he is dead and gone, it cannot do much harm to his memory to say that his time might have been much better employed in weightier labors. He, however, was apt to ride his hobby his own way; and though it did now and then kick up the dust a little in the eyes of his neighbors, and grieve the spirit of some friends, for whom he felt the truest deference and affection, yet his errors and follies are remembered "more in sorrow than in anger," and it begins to be suspected that he never intended to offend. But however his memory may be appreciated by critics, it is still held dear by many folk whose good opinion is well worth having; particularly by certain biscuit-makers, who have gone so far as to imprint his likeness on their New-Year cakes; and have thus given him a chance for immortality, almost equal to being stamped on a Waterloo Medal, or a Queen Anne's Farthing.

Whoever has made a voyage up the Hudson must remember the Kaatskill Mountains. They are a dismembered branch of the great Appalachian family, and are seen away to the west of the river, swelling up to a noble height, and lording it over the surrounding country. Every change of season, every change of weather, indeed, every hour of the day, produces some change in the magical hues and shapes of these mountains, and they are regarded by all the good wives, far and near, as perfect barometers. When the weather is fair and settled, they are clothed in blue and purple, and print their bold outlines on the clear evening sky; but sometimes, when the rest of the landscape is cloudless, they will gather a hood of gray vapors about their summits, which, in the last rays of the setting sun, will glow and light up like a crown of glory.

At the foot of these fairy mountains, the voyager may have descried the light smoke curling up from a village, whose shingle-roofs gleam among the trees, just where the blue tints of the upland melt away into the fresh green of the nearer landscape. It is a little village, of great antiquity, having been founded by some of the Dutch colonists in the early times of the province, just about the beginning of the government of the good Peter Stuyvesant (may he rest in peace!), and there were some of the houses of the original settlers standing within a few years, built of small yellow bricks brought from Holland, having latticed windows and gable fronts, surmounted with weather-cocks.

In that same village, and in one of these very houses (which, to tell the precise truth, was sadly time-worn and weather-beaten), there lived, many years since, while the country was yet a province of Great Britain, a simple, good-natured fellow, of the name of Rip Van Winkle. He was a descendant of the Van Winkles who figured so gallantly in the chivalrous days of Peter Stuyvesant, and accompanied him to the siege of Fort Christina. He inherited, however, but little of the martial character of his ancestors. I have observed that he was a simple, good-natured man; he was, moreover, a kind neighbor, and an obedient, hen-pecked husband. Indeed, to the latter circumstance might be owing that meekness of spirit which gained him such universal popularity; for those men are most apt to be obsequious and conciliating abroad, who are under the discipline of shrews at home. Their tempers, doubtless, are rendered pliant and malleable in the fiery furnace of domestic tribulation; and a curtain-lecture is worth all the sermons in the world for teaching the virtues of patience and long-suffering. A termagant wife may, therefore, in some respects, be considered a tolerable blessing; and if so, Rip Van Winkle was thrice blessed.

Certain it is, that he was a great favorite among all the good wives of the village, who, as usual with the amiable sex, took his part in all family squabbles; and never failed, whenever they talked those matters over in their evening gossipings, to lay all the blame on Dame Van Winkle. The children of the village, too, would shout with joy whenever he approached. He assisted at their sports, made their playthings, taught them to fly kites and shoot marbles, and told them long stories of ghosts, witches, and Indians. Whenever he went dodging about the village, he was surrounded by a troop of them, hanging on his skirts, clambering on his back, and playing a thousand tricks on him with impunity; and not a dog would bark at him throughout the neighborhood.

The great error in Rip's composition was an insuperable aversion to all kinds of profitable labor. It could not be from the want of assiduity or perseverance; for he would sit on a wet rock, with a rod as long and heavy as a Tartar's lance, and fish all day without a murmur, even though he should not be encouraged by a single nibble. He would carry a fowling-piece on his shoulder for hours together, trudging through woods and swamps, and up hill and down dale, to shoot a few squirrels or wild pigeons. He would never refuse to assist a neighbor even in the roughest toil, and was a foremost man at all country frolics for husking Indian corn, or building stone fences; the women of the village, too, used to employ him to run their errands, and to do such little odd jobs as their less obliging husbands would not do for them. In a word, Rip was ready to attend to anybody's business but his own; but as to doing family duty, and keeping his farm in order, he found it impossible.

In fact, he declared it was of no use to work on his farm; it was the most pestilent little piece of ground in the whole country; everything about it went wrong, and would go wrong, in spite of him. His fences were continually falling to pieces; his cow would either go astray, or get among the cabbages; weeds were sure to grow quicker in his fields than anywhere else; the rain always made a point of setting in just as he had some out-door work to do; so that though his patrimonial estate had dwindled away under his management, acre by acre, until there was little more left than a mere patch of Indian corn and potatoes, yet it was the worst-conditioned farm in the neighborhood.

His children, too, were as ragged and wild as if they belonged to nobody. His son Rip, an urchin begotten in his own likeness, promised to inherit the habits, with the old clothes, of his father. He was generally seen trooping like a colt at his mother's heels, equipped in a pair of his father's cast-off galligaskins, which he had much ado to hold up with one hand, as a fine lady does her train in bad weather.

Rip Van Winkle, however, was one of those happy mortals, of foolish, well-oiled dispositions, who take the world easy, eat white bread or brown, whichever can be got with least thought or trouble, and would rather starve on a penny than work for a pound. If left to himself, he would have whistled life away in perfect contentment; but his wife kept continually dinning in his ears about his idleness, his carelessness, and the ruin he was bringing on his family. Morning, noon, and night, her tongue was incessantly going, and everything he said or did was sure to produce a torrent of household eloquence. Rip had but one way of replying to all lectures of the kind, and that, by frequent use, had grown into a habit. He shrugged his shoulders, shook his head, cast up his eyes, but said nothing. This, however, always provoked a fresh volley from his wife; so that he was fain to draw off his forces, and take to the outside of the house—the only side which, in truth, belongs to a hen-pecked husband.

Rip's sole domestic adherent was his dog Wolf, who was as much hen-pecked as his master; for Dame Van Winkle regarded them as companions in idleness, and even looked upon Wolf with an evil eye, as the cause of his master's going so often astray. True it is, in all points of spirit befitting an honorable dog, he was as courageous an animal as ever

scoured the woods; but what courage can withstand the ever-enduring and all-besetting terrors of a woman's tongue? The moment Wolf entered the house his crest fell, his tail drooped to the ground, or curled between his legs, he sneaked about with a gallows air, casting many a sidelong glance at Dame Van Winkle, and at the least flourish of a broomstick or ladle he would fly to the door with yelping precipitation.

Times grew worse and worse with Rip Van Winkle as years of matrimony rolled on; a tart temper never mellows with age, and a sharp tongue is the only edged tool that grows keener with constant use. For a long while he used to console himself, when driven from home, by frequenting a kind of perpetual club of the sages, philosophers, and other idle personages of the village, which held its sessions on a bench before a small inn, designated by a rubicund portrait of His Majesty George the Third. Here they used to sit in the shade through a long, lazy summer's day, talking listlessly over village gossip, or telling endless sleepy stories about nothing. But it would have been worth any statesman's money to have heard the profound discussions that sometimes took place, when by chance an old newspaper fell into their hands from some passing traveller. How solemnly they would listen to the contents, as drawled out by Derrick Van Bummel, the schoolmaster, a dapper learned little man, who was not to be daunted by the most gigantic word in the dictionary; and how sagely they would deliberate upon public events some months after they had taken place.

The opinions of this junto were completely controlled by Nicholas Vedder, patriarch of the village, and landlord of the inn, at the door of which he took his seat from morning till night, just moving sufficiently to avoid the sun and keep in the shade of a large tree; so that the neighbors could tell the hour by his movements as accurately as by a sun-dial. It is true he was rarely heard to speak, but smoked his pipe incessantly. His adherents, however (for every great man has his adherents), perfectly understood him, and knew how to gather his opinions. When anything that was read or related displeased him, he was observed to smoke his pipe vehemently, and to send forth short, frequent, and angry puffs; but when pleased, he would inhale the smoke slowly and tranquilly, and emit it in light and placid clouds; and sometimes, taking the pipe from his mouth, and letting the fragrant vapor curl about his nose, would gravely nod his head in token of perfect approbation.

From even this stronghold the unlucky Rip was at length routed by his termagant wife, who would suddenly break in upon the tranquillity of the assemblage and call the members all to naught; nor was that august personage, Nicholas Vedder himself, sacred from the daring tongue of this terrible virago, who charged him outright with encouraging her husband in habits of idleness.

Poor Rip was at last reduced almost to despair; and his only alternative, to escape from the labor of the farm and clamor of his wife, was to take gun in hand and stroll away into the woods. Here he would sometimes seat himself at the foot of a tree, and share the contents of his wallet with Wolf, with whom he sympathized as a fellow-sufferer in persecution. "Poor Wolf," he would say, "thy mistress leads thee a dog's life of it, but never mind, my lad, whilst I live thou shalt never want a friend to stand by thee!" Wolf would wag his tail, look wistfully in his master's face, and if dogs can feel pity, I verily believe he reciprocated the sentiment with all his heart.

In a long ramble of the kind on a fine autumnal day, Rip had unconsciously scrambled to one of the highest parts of the Kaatskill Mountains. He was after his favorite sport of squirrel-shooting, and the still solitudes had echoed and re-echoed with the reports of his gun. Panting and fatigued, he threw himself, late in the afternoon, on a green knoll, covered with mountain herbage, that crowned the brow of a precipice. From an opening between the trees he could overlook all the lower country for many a mile of rich woodland. He saw at a distance the lordly Hudson, far, far below him, moving on its silent but majestic course, with the reflection of a purple cloud, or the sail of a lagging bark, here and there sleeping on its glassy bosom, and at last losing itself in the blue highlands.

On the other side he looked down into a deep mountain glen, wild, lonely, and shagged, the bottom filled with fragments from the impending cliffs, and scarcely lighted by the reflected rays of the setting sun. For some time Rip lay musing on this scene; evening was gradually advancing; the mountains began to throw their long blue shadows over the valleys; he saw that it would be dark long before he could reach the village, and he heaved a heavy sigh when he thought of encountering the terrors of Dame Van Winkle.

As he was about to descend, he heard a voice from a distance, hallooing, "Rip Van Winkle, Rip Van Winkle!" He looked around, but could see nothing but a crow winging its solitary flight across the mountain. He thought his fancy must have deceived him, and turned again to descend, when he heard the same cry ring through the still evening air: "Rip Van Winkle! Rip Van Winkle!"—at the same time Wolf bristled up his back, and giving a low growl, skulked to his master's side, looking fearfully down into the glen. Rip now felt a vague apprehension stealing over him; he looked anxiously in the same direction, and perceived a strange figure slowly toiling up the rocks, and bending under the weight of something he carried on his back. He was surprised to see any human being in this lonely and unfrequented place; but supposing it to be some one of the neighborhood in need of his assistance, he hastened down to yield it.

On nearer approach he was still more surprised at the singularity of the stranger's appearance. He was a short, square-built old fellow, with thick bushy hair, and a grizzled beard. His dress was of the antique Dutch fashion—a cloth jerkin strapped around the waist—several pair of breeches, the outer one of ample volume, decorated with rows of buttons down the sides, and bunches at the knees. He bore on his shoulders a stout keg, that seemed full of liquor, and made signs for Rip to approach and assist him with the load. Though rather shy and distrustful of this new acquaintance, Rip complied with his usual alacrity; and mutually relieving one another, they clambered up a narrow gully, apparently the dry bed of a mountain torrent. As they ascended, Rip every now and then heard long, rolling peals, like distant thunder, that seemed to issue out of a deep ravine, or rather cleft, between lofty rocks, toward which their rugged path conducted. He paused for an instant, but supposing it to be the muttering of one of those transient thunder-showers which often take place in mountain heights, he proceeded. Passing through the ravine, they came to a hollow, like a small amphi-theatre, surrounded by perpendicular precipices, over the brinks of which impending trees shot their branches, so that you only caught glimpses of the azure sky and the bright evening cloud. During the whole time Rip and his companion had labored on in silence; for though the former marvelled greatly what could be the object of carrying a keg of liquor up this wild mountain, yet there was something strange and incomprehensible about the unknown, that inspired awe and checked familiarity.

On entering the amphitheatre, new objects of wonder presented themselves. On a level spot in the centre was a company of odd-looking personages playing at ninepins. They were dressed in a quaint, outlandish fashion; some wore short doublets, others jerkins, with long knives in their belts, and most of them had enormous breeches, of similar style with that of the guide's. Their visages, too, were peculiar: one had a large beard, broad face, and small piggish eyes; the face of another seemed to consist entirely of nose, and was surmounted by a white sugar-loaf hat, set off with a little red cock's tail. They all had beards, of various shapes and colors. There was one who seemed to be the commander. He was a stout old gentleman, with a weather-beaten countenance; he wore a laced doublet, broad belt and hanger, high crowned hat and feather, red stockings, and high-heeled shoes, with roses in them. The whole group reminded Rip of the figures in an old Flemish painting, in the parlor of Dominie Van Shaick, the village parson, and which had been brought over from Holland at the time of the settlement.

What seemed particularly odd to Rip was, that, though these folks were evidently amusing themselves, yet they maintained the gravest faces, the most mysterious silence, and were, withal, the most melancholy party of pleasure he had ever witnessed. Nothing interrupted the stillness of the scene but the noise of the balls, which, whenever they rolled, echoed along the mountains like rumbling peals of thunder.

As Rip and his companion approached them, they suddenly desisted from their play, and stared at him with such fixed, statue-like gaze, and such strange, uncouth, lack-lustre countenances, that his heart turned within him, and his knees smote together. His companion now emptied the contents of the keg into large flagons, and made signs to him to wait upon the company. He obeyed with fear and trembling; they quaffed the liquor in profound silence, and then returned to their game.

By degrees Rip's awe and apprehension subsided. He even ventured, when no eye was fixed upon him, to taste the beverage, which he found had much of the flavor of excellent Hollands. He was naturally a thirsty soul, and was soon tempted to repeat the draught. One taste provoked another; and he reiterated his visits to the flagon so often that at length his senses were overpowered, his eyes swam in his head, his head gradually declined, and he fell into a deep sleep.

On waking, he found himself on the green knoll whence he had first seen the old man of the glen. He rubbed his eyes—it was a bright sunny morning. The birds were hopping and twittering among the bushes, and the eagle was wheeling aloft, and breasting the pure mountain breeze. "Surely," thought Rip, "I have not slept here all night." He recalled the occurrences before he fell asleep. The strange man with a keg of liquor—the mountain ravine—the wild retreat among the rocks—the woe-begone party at ninepins—the flagon—"Oh! that flagon! that wicked flagon!" thought Rip, "what excuse shall I make to Dame Van Winkle?"

He looked round for his gun, but in place of the clean, well-oiled fowling-piece, he found an old firelock lying by him, the barrel encrusted with rust, the lock falling off, and the stock worm-eaten. He now suspected that the grave roisters of the mountains had put a trick upon him, and, having dosed him with liquor, had robbed him of his gun. Wolf, too, had disappeared, but he might have strayed away after a squirrel or partridge. He whistled after him, and shouted his name, but all in vain; the echoes repeated his whistle and shout, but no dog was to be seen.

He determined to revisit the scene of the last evening's gambol, and if he met with any of the party, to demand his dog and gun. As he rose to walk, he found himself stiff in the joints, and wanting in his usual activity. "These mountain beds do not agree with me," thought Rip, "and if this frolic should lay me up with a fit of the rheumatism, I shall have a blessed time with Dame Van Winkle." With some difficulty he got down into the glen: he found the gully up which he and his companion had ascended the preceding evening; but to his astonishment a mountain stream was now foaming down it, leaping from rock to rock, and filling the glen with babbling murmurs. He, however, made shift to scramble up its sides, working his toilsome way through thickets of birch, sassafras, and witch-hazel, and sometimes tripped up or entangled by the wild grape-vines that twisted their coils or tendrils from tree to tree, and spread a kind of network in his path.

At length he reached to where the ravine had opened through the cliffs to the amphitheatre; but no traces of such opening remained. The rocks presented a high, impenetrable wall, over which the torrent came tumbling in a sheet of feathery foam, and fell into a broad deep basin, black from the shadows of the surrounding forest. Here, then, poor Rip was brought to a stand. He again called and whistled after his dog; he was only answered by the cawing of a flock of idle crows, sporting high in the air about a dry tree that overhung a sunny precipice; and who, secure in their elevation, seemed to look down and scoff at the poor man's perplexities. What was to be done? The morning was passing away, and Rip felt famished for want of his breakfast. He grieved to give up his dog and gun; he dreaded to meet his wife; but it would not do to starve among the mountains. He shook his head, shouldered the rusty firelock, and, with a heart full of trouble and anxiety, turned his footsteps homeward.

As he approached the village he met a number of people, but none whom he knew, which somewhat surprised him, for he had thought himself acquainted with every one in the country round. Their dress, too, was of a different fashion from that to which he was accustomed. They all stared at him with equal marks of surprise, and whenever they cast their eyes upon him, invariably stroked their chins. The constant recurrence of this gesture induced Rip, involuntarily, to do the same, when, to his astonishment, he found his beard had grown a foot long!

He had now entered the skirts of the village. A troop of strange children ran at his heels, hooting after him, and pointing at his gray beard. The dogs, too, not one of which he recognized for an old acquaintance, barked at him as he passed. The very village was altered; it was larger and more populous. There were rows of houses which he had never seen before, and those which had been his familiar haunts had disappeared. Strange names were over the doors—strange faces at the windows—everything was strange. His mind now misgave him; he began to doubt whether both he and the world around him were not bewitched. Surely this was his native village, which he had left but the day before. There stood the Kaatskill Mountains—there ran the silver Hudson at a distance—there was every hill and dale precisely as it had always been. Rip was sorely perplexed. "That flagon last night," thought he, "has addled my poor head sadly!"

It was with some difficulty that he found the way to his own house, which he approached with silent awe, expecting every moment to hear the shrill voice of Dame Van Winkle. He found the house gone to decay—the roof fallen in, the windows shattered, and the doors off the hinges. A half-starved dog that looked like Wolf was skulking about it. Rip called him by name, but the cur snarled, showed his teeth, and passed on. This was an unkind cut indeed. "My very dog," sighed poor Rip, "has forgotten me!"

He entered the house, which to tell the truth, Dame Van Winkle had always kept in neat order. It was empty, forlorn, and apparently abandoned. This desolateness overcame all his connubial fears—he called loudly for his wife and children—the lonely chambers rang for a moment with his voice, and then all again was silence.

He now hurried forth, and hastened to his old resort, the village inn, but it too was gone. A large rickety wooden building stood in its place, with great gaping windows, some of them broken and mended with old hats and petticoats, and over the door was painted, "The Union Hotel, by Jonathan Doolittle." Instead of the great tree that used to shelter the quiet little Dutch inn of yore, there now was reared a tall naked pole, with something on top that looked like a red night-cap, and from it was fluttering a flag, on which was a singular assemblage of stars and stripes;—all this was strange and incomprehensible. He recognized on the sign, however, the ruby face of King George, under which he had smoked so many a peaceful pipe; but even this was singularly metamorphosed. The red coat was changed for one of blue and buff, a sword was held in the hand instead of a sceptre, the head was decorated with a cocked hat, and underneath was painted in large characters, GENERAL WASHINGTON.

There was, as usual, a crowd of folk about the door, but none that Rip recollected. The very character of the people seemed changed. There was a busy, bustling, disputatious tone about it, instead of the accustomed phlegm and drowsy tranquillity. He looked in vain for the sage Nicholas Vedder, with his broad face, double chin, and fair long pipe, uttering clouds of tobacco-smoke instead of idle speeches; or Van Bummel, the schoolmaster, doling forth the contents of an ancient newspaper. In place of these, a lean, bilious-looking fellow, with his pockets full of handbills, was haranguing vehemently about rights of citizens—elections—members of congress—liberty—Bunker's Hill—

heroes of seventy-six—and other words, which were a perfect Babylonish jargon to the bewildered Van Winkle.

The appearance of Rip, with his long, grizzled beard, his rusty fowling-piece, his uncouth dress, and an army of women and children at his heels, soon attracted the attention of the tavern-politicians. They crowded round him, eying him from head to foot with great curiosity. The orator bustled up to him, and, drawing him partly aside, inquired "On which side he voted?" Rip stared in vacant stupidity. Another short but busy little fellow pulled him by the arm, and, rising on tiptoe, inquired in his ear, "Whether he was Federal or Democrat?" Rip was equally at a loss to comprehend the question; when a knowing, self-important old gentleman, in a sharp cocked hat, made his way through the crowd, putting them to the right and left with his elbow as he passed, and planting himself before Van Winkle, with one arm akimbo, the other resting on his cane, his keen eyes and sharp hat penetrating, as it were, into his very soul, demanded in an austere tone, "What brought him to the election with a gun on his shoulder, and a mob at his heels; and whether he meant to breed a riot in the village?"—"Alas! gentlemen," cried Rip, somewhat dismayed, "I am a poor quiet man, a native of the place, and a loyal subject of the King, God bless him!"

Here a general shout burst from the by-standers—"A tory! a tory! a spy! a refugee! hustle him! away with him!" It was with great difficulty that the self-important man in the cocked hat restored order; and, having assumed a tenfold austerity of brow, demanded again of the unknown culprit, what he came there for, and whom he was seeking? The poor man humbly assured him that he meant no harm, but merely came there in search of some of his neighbors, who used to keep about the tavern.

"Well—who are they?—name them."

Rip bethought himself a moment, and inquired, "Where's Nicholas Vedder?"

There was a silence for a little while, when an old man replied, in a thin piping voice, "Nicholas Vedder! why, he is dead and gone these eighteen years! There was a wooden tombstone in that churchyard that used to tell all about him, but that's rotten and gone too."

"Where's Brom Dutcher?"

"Oh, he went off to the army in the beginning of the war; some say he was killed at the storming of Stony Point—others say he was drowned in a squall at the foot of Antony's Nose. I don't know—he never came back again."

"Where's Van Bummel, the schoolmaster?"

"He went off to the wars too, was a great militia general, and is now in Congress."

Rip's heart died away at hearing of these sad changes in his home and friends, and finding himself thus alone in the world. Every answer puzzled him too, by treating of such enormous lapses of time, and of matters which he could not understand: war—Congress—Stony Point—he had no courage to ask after any more friends, but cried out in despair, "Does nobody here know Rip Van Winkle?"

"Oh, Rip Van Winkle!" exclaimed two or three, "oh, to be sure! that's Rip Van Winkle yonder, leaning against the tree."

Rip looked, and he beheld a precise counterpart of himself, as he went up the mountain; apparently as lazy, and certainly as ragged. The poor fellow was now completely confounded. He doubted his own identity, and whether he was himself or another man. In the midst of his bewilderment, the man in the cocked hat demanded who he was, and what was his name.

"God knows," exclaimed he, at his wit's end; "I'm not myself—I'm somebody else—that's me yonder—no—that's somebody else got into my shoes—I was myself last night, but I fell asleep on the mountain, and they've changed my gun, and everything's changed, and I'm changed, and I can't tell what's my name, or who I am!"

The by-standers began now to look at each other, nod, wink significantly, and tap their fingers against their foreheads. There was a whisper, also, about securing the gun, and keeping the old fellow from doing mischief, at the very suggestion of which the self-important man in the cocked hat retired with some precipitation. At this critical moment a fresh, comely woman pressed through the throng to get a peep at the gray-bearded man. She had a chubby child in her arms, which, frightened at his looks, began to cry. "Hush, Rip," cried she, "hush, you little fool; the old man won't hurt you." The name of the child, the air of the mother, the tone of her voice, all awakened a train of recollections in his mind. "What is your name, my good woman?" asked he.

"Judith Gardenier."

"And your father's name?"

"Ah, poor man, Rip Van Winkle was his name, but it's twenty years since he went away from home with his gun, and never has been heard of since—his dog came home without him; but whether he shot himself, or was carried away by the Indians, nobody can tell. I was then but a little girl."

Rip had but one question more to ask; but he put it with a faltering voice:

"Where's your mother?"

"Oh, she too has died but a short time since; she broke a blood vessel in a fit of passion at a New England peddler."

There was a drop of comfort, at least, in this intelligence. The honest man could contain himself no longer. He caught his daughter and her child in his arms. "I am your father!" cried he—"Young Rip Van Winkle once—old Rip Van Winkle now!—Does nobody know poor Rip Van Winkle?"

All stood amazed, until an old woman, tottering out from among the crowd, put her hand to her brow, and peering under it in his face for a moment, exclaimed, "Sure enough! it is Rip Van Winkle—it is himself! Welcome home again, old neighbor. Why, where have you been these twenty long years?"

Rip's story was soon told, for the whole twenty years had been to him but as one night. The neighbors stared when they heard it; some were seen to wink at each other, and put their tongues in their cheeks: and the self-important man in the cocked hat, who, when the alarm was over, had returned to the field, screwed down the corners of his mouth, and shook his head—upon which there was a general shaking of the head throughout the assemblage.

It was determined, however, to take the opinion of old Peter Vander-donk, who was seen slowly advancing up the road. He was a descendant of the historian of that name, who wrote one of the earliest accounts of the province. Peter was the most ancient inhabitant of the village, and well versed in all the wonderful events and traditions of the neighborhood. He recollected Rip at once, and corroborated his story in the most

satisfactory manner. He assured the company that it was a fact, handed down from his ancestor the historian, that the Kaatskill Mountains had always been haunted by strange beings. That it was affirmed that the great Hendrick Hudson, the first discoverer of the river and country, kept a kind of vigil there every twenty years, with his crew of the *Half-Moon*; being permitted in this way to revisit the scenes of his enterprise, and keep a guardian eye upon the river and the great city called by his name. That his father had once seen them in their old Dutch dresses playing at ninepins in a hollow of the mountain; and that he himself had heard, one summer afternoon, the sound of their balls, like distant peals of thunder.

To make a long story short, the company broke up and returned to the more important concerns of the election. Rip's daughter took him home to live with her; she had a snug, well-furnished house, and a stout, cheery farmer for a husband, whom Rip recollected for one of the urchins that used to climb upon his back. As to Rip's son and heir, who was the ditto of himself, seen leaning against the tree, he was employed to work on the farm; but evinced an hereditary disposition to attend to anything else but his business.

Rip now resumed his old walks and habits; he soon found many of his former cronies, though all rather the worse for the wear and tear of time; and preferred making friends among the rising generation, with whom he soon grew into great favor.

Having nothing to do at home, and being arrived at that happy age when a man can be idle with impunity, he took his place once more on the bench at the inn-door, and was reverenced as one of the patriarchs of the village, and a chronicler of the old times "before the war." It was some time before he could get into the regular track of gossip, or could be made to comprehend the strange events that had taken place during his torpor. How that there had been a revolutionary war—that the country had thrown off the yoke of old England—and that, instead of being a subject of His Majesty George the Third, he was now a free citizen of the United States. Rip, in fact, was no politician; the changes of states and empires made but little impression on him; but there was one species of despotism under which he long groaned, and that was—petticoat government. Happily that was at an end; he had got his neck

out of the yoke of matrimony, and could go in and out whenever he pleased, without dreading the tyranny of Dame Van Winkle. Whenever her name was mentioned, however, he shook his head, shrugged his shoulders, and cast up his eyes; which might pass either for an expression of resignation to his fate, or joy at his deliverance.

He used to tell his story to every stranger that arrived at Mr. Doolittle's hotel. He was observed, at first, to vary on some points every time he told it, which was, doubtless, owing to his having so recently awaked. It at last settled down precisely to the tale I have related, and not a man, woman, or child in the neighborhood but knew it by heart. Some always pretended to doubt the reality of it, and insisted that Rip had been out of his head, and that this was one point on which he always remained flighty. The old Dutch inhabitants, however, almost universally gave it full credit. Even to this day they never hear a thunder-storm of a summer afternoon about the Kaatskill, but they say Hendrick Hudson and his crew are at their game of ninepins; and it is a common wish of all hen-pecked husbands in the neighborhood, when life hangs heavy on their hands, that they might have a quieting draught out of Rip Van Winkle's flagon.

NOTE

The foregoing tale, one would suspect, had been suggested to Mr. Knickerbocker by a little German superstition about the Emperor Frederick *der Rothbart,* and the Kypphaüser Mountain: the subjoined note, however, which he had appended to the tale, shows that it is an absolute fact, narrated with his usual fidelity.

"The story of Rip Van Winkle may seem incredible to many, but nevertheless I give it my full belief, for I know the vicinity of our old Dutch settlements to have been very subject to marvellous events and appearances. Indeed, I have heard many stranger stories than this, in the villages along the Hudson; all of which were too well authenticated to admit of a doubt. I have even talked with Rip Van Winkle myself, who, when last I saw him, was a very venerable old man, and so perfectly rational and consistent on every other point, that I think no conscientious person could refuse to take this into the bargain; nay, I have seen a certificate on the subject taken before a country justice and signed with a cross, in the justice's own handwriting. The story, therefore, is beyond the possibility of doubt.

"D.K."

POSTSCRIPT

The following are travelling notes from a memorandum-book of Mr. Knickerbocker.

The Kaatsberg, or Catskill Mountains, have always been a region full of fable. The Indians considered them the abode of spirits, who influenced the weather, spreading sunshine or clouds over the landscape, and sending good or bad hunting-seasons. They were ruled by an old squaw spirit, said to be their mother. She dwelt on the highest peak of the Catskills, and had charge of the doors of day and night to open and shut them at the proper hour. She hung up the new moons in the skies, and cut up the old ones into stars. In times of drought, if properly propitiated, she would spin light summer clouds out of cobwebs and morning dew, and send them off from the crest of the mountain, flake after flake, like flakes of carded cotton, to float in the air; until, dissolved by the heat of the sun, they would fall in gentle showers, causing the grass to spring, the fruits to ripen, and the corn to grow an inch an hour. If displeased, however, she would brew up clouds black as ink, sitting in the midst of them like a bottle-bellied spider in the midst of its web; and when these clouds broke, woe betide the valleys!

In old times, say the Indian traditions, there was a kind of Manitou or Spirit, who kept about the wildest recesses of the Catskill Mountains, and took a mischievous pleasure in wreaking all kinds of evils and vexations upon the red men. Sometimes he would assume the form of a bear, a panther, or a deer, lead the bewildered hunter a weary chase through tangled forests and among ragged rocks; and then spring off with a loud ho! ho! leaving him aghast on the brink of a beetling precipice or raging torrent.

The favorite abode of this Manitou is still shown. It is a great rock or cliff on the loneliest part of the mountains, and, from the flowering vines which clamber about it, and the wild flowers which abound in its neighborhood, is known by the name of the Garden Rock. Near the foot of it is a small lake, the haunt of the solitary bittern, with water-snakes basking in the sun on the leaves of the pond-lilies which lie on the surface. This place was held in great awe by the Indians, insomuch that the boldest hunter would not pursue his game within its precincts. Once upon a time, however, a hunter who had lost his way, penetrated to the Garden Rock, where he beheld a number of gourds placed in the crotches of trees. One of these he seized and made off with it, but in the hurry of his retreat he let it fall among the rocks, when a great stream gushed forth, which washed him away and swept him down precipices, where he was dashed to pieces, and the stream made its way to the Hudson, and continues to flow to the present day; being the identical stream known by the name of the Kaaterskill.

Strange Stories by a Nervous Gentleman

I'll tell you more, there was a fish taken
A monstrous fish, with a sword by 's side, a long sword,
A pike in 's neck, and a gun in 's nose, a huge gun,
And letters of mart in 's mouth from the Duke of
    Florence.
    CLEANTHES.—This is a monstrous lie.
    TONY.—I do confess it.
Do you think I'd tell you truths?
                     —FLETCHER'S Wife for a Month

The Great Unknown

A PREFACE

T he following adventures were related to me by the same nervous gentleman who told me the romantic tale of the Stout Gentleman, published in *Bracebridge Hall*. It is very singular, that, although I expressly stated that story to have been told to me, and described the very person who told it, still it has been received as an adventure that happened to myself. Now I protest I never met with any adventure of the kind. I should not have grieved at this, had it not been intimated by the author of *Waverley*† in an introduction to his novel of *Peveril of the Peak*, that he was himself the stout gentleman alluded to. I have ever since been importuned by questions and letters from gentlemen, and particularly from ladies without number, touching what I had seen of the Great Unknown.

Now all this is extremely tantalizing. It is like being congratulated on the high prize when one has drawn a blank; for I have just as great a desire as any one of the public to penetrate the mystery of that very singular personage, whose voice fills every corner of the world, without any one being able to tell whence it comes.

My friend, the nervous gentleman, also, who is a man of very shy, retired habits, complains that he has been excessively annoyed in consequence of its getting about in his neighborhood that he is the fortunate personage. Insomuch, that he has become a character of considerable notoriety in two or three country-towns, and has been repeatedly teased to exhibit himself at blue-stocking parties, for no other reason than that of being "the gentleman who has had a glimpse of the author of *Waverley*."

†Sir Walter Scott

Indeed the poor man has grown ten times as nervous as ever since he has discovered, on such good authority, who the stout gentleman was; and will never forgive himself for not having made a more resolute effort to get a full sight of him. He has anxiously endeavored to call up a recollection of what he saw of that portly personage; and has ever since kept a curious eye on all gentlemen of more than ordinary dimensions, whom he has seen getting into stage-coaches. All in vain! The features he had caught a glimpse of seem common to the whole race of stout gentlemen, and the Great Unknown remains as great an unknown as ever.

Having premised these circumstances, I will now let the nervous gentleman proceed with his stories.

The Hunting-Dinner

I was once at a hunting-dinner, given by a worthy fox-hunting old Baronet, who kept bachelor's hall in jovial style in an ancient rook-haunted family-mansion, in one of the middle counties. He had been a devoted admirer of the fair sex in his younger days; but, having travelled much, studied the sex in various countries with distinguished success, and returned home profoundly instructed, as he supposed, in the ways of woman, and a perfect master of the art of pleasing, had the mortification of being jilted by a little boarding-school girl, who was scarcely versed in the accidence of love.

The Baronet was completely overcome by such an incredible defeat; retired from the world in disgust; put himself under the government of his housekeeper; and took to fox-hunting like a perfect Nimrod. Whatever poets may say to the contrary, a man will grow out of love as he grows old; and a pack of fox-hounds may chase out of his heart even the memory of a boarding-school goddess. The Baronet was, when I saw him, as merry and mellow an old bachelor as ever followed a hound; and the love he had once felt for one woman had spread itself over the whole sex, so that there was not a pretty face in the whole country round but came in for a share.

The dinner was prolonged till a late hour; for our host having no ladies in his household to summon us to the drawing-room, the bottle maintained its true bachelor sway, unrivalled by its potent enemy, the tea-kettle. The old hall in which we dined echoed to bursts of robustious fox-hunting merriment, that made the ancient antlers shake on the walls.

By degrees, however, the wine and the wassail of mine host began to operate upon bodies already a little jaded by the chase. The choice spirits which flashed up at the beginning of the dinner, sparkled for a time, then gradually went out one after another, or only emitted now and then a faint gleam from the socket. Some of the briskest talkers, who had given tongue so bravely at the first burst, fell fast asleep; and none kept on their way but certain of those long-winded prosers, who, like short-legged hounds, worry on unnoticed at the bottom of conversation, but are sure to be in at the death. Even these at length subsided into silence; and scarcely anything was heard but the nasal communications of two or three veteran masticators, who having been silent while awake, were indemnifying the company in their sleep.

At length the announcement of tea and coffee in the cedar-parlor roused all hands from this temporary torpor. Every one awoke marvellously renovated, and while sipping the refreshing beverage out of the Baronet's old-fashioned hereditary china, began to think of departing for their several homes. But here a sudden difficulty arose. While we had been prolonging our repast, a heavy winter storm had set in, with snow, rain, and sleet, driven by such bitter blasts of wind, that they threatened to penetrate to the very bone.

"It's all in vain," said our hospitable host, "to think of putting one's head out of doors in such weather. So, gentlemen, I hold you my guests for this night at least, and will have your quarters prepared accordingly."

The unruly weather, which became more and more tempestuous, rendered the hospitable suggestion unanswerable. The only question was, whether such an unexpected accession of company to an already crowded house would not put the housekeeper to her trumps to accommodate them.

"Pshaw," cried mine host; "did you ever know a bachelor's hall that was not elastic, and able to accommodate twice as many as it could hold?" So, out of a good-humored pique, the housekeeper was summoned to a consultation before us all. The old lady appeared in her gala suit of faded brocade, which rustled with flurry and agitation; for, in spite of our host's bravado, she was a little perplexed. But in a bachelor's house, and with bachelor guests, these matters are readily managed. There is no lady of the house to stand upon squeamish points about lodging gentlemen in odd holes and corners, and exposing the shabby parts of the establishment. A bachelor's housekeeper is used to shifts and emergencies; so, after much worrying to and fro, and divers consultations about the red-room, and the blue-room, and the chintz-room, and the damask-room, and the little room with the bow-window, the matter was finally arranged.

When all this was done, we were once more summoned to the standing rural amusement of eating. The time that had been consumed in dozing after dinner, and in the refreshment and consultation of the cedar-parlor, was sufficient, in the opinion of the rosy-faced butler, to engender a reasonable appetite for supper. A slight repast had, therefore, been tricked up from the residue of dinner, consisting of a cold sirloin of beef, hashed venison, a devilled leg of a turkey or so, and a few other of those light articles taken by country gentlemen to ensure sound sleep and heavy snoring.

The nap after dinner had brightened up every one's wit; and a great deal of excellent humor was expended upon the perplexities of mine host and his housekeeper, by certain married gentlemen of the company, who considered themselves privileged in joking with a bachelor's establishment. From this the banter turned as to what quarters each would find, on being thus suddenly billeted in so antiquated a mansion.

"By my soul," said an Irish captain of dragoons, one of the most merry and boisterous of the party, "by my soul, but I should not be surprised if some of those good-looking gentlefolks that hang along the walls should walk about the rooms of this stormy night; or if I should find the ghosts of one of those long-waisted ladies turning into my bed in mistake for her grave in the churchyard."

"Do you believe in ghosts, then?" said a thin, hatchet-faced gentleman, with projecting eyes like a lobster.

I had remarked this last personage during dinner-time for one of those incessant questioners, who have a craving, unhealthy appetite in conversation. He never seemed satisfied with the whole of a story; never laughed when others laughed; but always put the joke to the question. He never could enjoy the kernel of the nut, but pestered himself to get more out of the shell. "Do you believe in ghosts, then?" said the inquisitive gentleman.

"Faith, but I do," replied the jovial Irishman. "I was brought up in the fear and belief of them. We had a Benshee in our own family, honey."

"A Benshee, and what's that?" cried the questioner.

"Why, an old lady ghost that tends upon your real Milesian families, and waits at their window to let them know when some of them are to die."

"A mighty pleasant piece of information!" cried an elderly gentleman with a knowing look, and with a flexible nose, to which he could give a whimsical twist when he wished to be waggish.

"By my soul, but I'd have you to know it's a piece of distinction to be waited on by a Benshee. It's a proof that one has pure blood in one's veins. But i' faith, now we are talking of ghosts, there never was a house or a night better fitted than the present for a ghost adventure. Pray, Sir John, haven't you such a thing as a haunted chamber to put a guest in?"

"Perhaps," said the Baronet, smiling, "I might accommodate you even on that point."

"Oh, I should like it of all things, my jewel. Some dark oaken room, with ugly woe-begone portraits, that stare dismally at one; and about which the housekeeper has a power of delightful stories of love and murder. And then a dim lamp, a table with a rusty sword across it, and a spectre all in white, to draw aside one's curtains at midnight——"

"In truth," said an old gentleman at one end of the table, "you put me in mind of an anecdote——"

"Oh, a ghost-story! a ghost-story!" was vociferated round the board, every one edging his chair a little nearer.

The attention of the whole company was now turned upon the speaker. He was an old gentleman, one side of whose face was no match for the other. The eyelid drooped and hung down like an unhinged window-shutter. Indeed, the whole side of his head was dilapidated, and seemed like the wing of a house shut up and haunted. I'll warrant that side was well stuffed with ghost-stories.

There was a universal demand for the tale.

"Nay," said the old gentleman, "it's a mere anecdote, and a very commonplace one; but such as it is you shall have it. It is a story that I once heard my uncle tell as having happened to himself. He was a man very apt to meet with strange adventures. I have heard him tell of others much more singular."

"What kind of a man was your uncle?" said the questioning gentleman.

"Why, he was rather a dry, shrewd kind of body; a great traveller, and fond of telling his adventures."

"Pray, how old might he have been when that happened?"

"When what happened?" cried the gentleman with the flexible nose, impatiently. "Egad, you have not given anything a chance to happen. Come, never mind our uncle's age; let us have his adventures."

The inquisitive gentleman being for the moment silenced, the old gentleman with the haunted head proceeded.

The Adventure of My Uncle

M any years since, some time before the French Revolution, my uncle passed several months at Paris. The English and French were on better terms in those days than at present, and mingled cordially in society. The English went abroad to spend money then, and the French were always ready to help them: they go abroad to save money at present, and that they can do without French assistance. Perhaps the travelling English were fewer and choicer than at present, when the whole nation has broke loose and inundated the Continent. At any rate, they circulated more readily and currently in foreign society, and my uncle, during his residence in Paris, made many very intimate acquaintances among the French noblesse.

Some time afterwards, he was making a journey in the winter-time in that part of Normandy called the Pays de Caux, when, as evening was closing in, he perceived the turrets of an ancient château rising out of the trees of its walled park; each turret with its high conical roof of gray slate, like a candle with an extinguisher on it.

"To whom does the château belong, friend?" cried my uncle to a meagre but fiery postilion, who, with tremendous jack-boots and cocked hat, was floundering on before him.

"To Monseigneur the Marquis de———," said the postilion, touching his hat, partly out of respect to my uncle, and partly out of reverence to the noble name pronounced.

My uncle recollected the Marquis for a particular friend in Paris, who had often expressed a wish to see him at his paternal chateau. My uncle was an old traveller, one who knew well how to turn things to account. He revolved for a few moments in his mind, how agreeable it would be to his friend the Marquis to be surprised in this sociable way by a pop visit; and how much more agreeable to himself to get into snug quarters in a chateau, and have a relish of the Marquis's well-known kitchen, and a smack of his superior Champagne and Burgundy, rather than put up with the miserable lodgment and miserable fare of a provincial inn. In a few minutes, therefore, the meagre postilion was cracking his whip like a very devil, or like a true Frenchman, up the long, straight avenue that led to the chateau.

You have no doubt all seen French chateaus, as everybody travels in France nowadays. This was one of the oldest; standing naked and alone in the midst of a desert of gravel walks and cold stone terraces; with a cold-looking, formal garden, cut into angles and rhomboids; and a cold, leafless park, divided geometrically by straight alleys; and two or three cold-looking noseless statues; and fountains spouting cold water enough to make one's teeth chatter. At least such was the feeling they imparted on the wintry day of my uncle's visit; though, in hot summer weather, I'll warrant there was glare enough to scorch one's eyes out.

The smacking of the postilion's whip, which grew more and more intense the nearer they approached, frightened a flight of pigeons out of a dove-cot, and rooks out of the roofs, and finally a crew of servants out of the chateau, with the Marquis at their head. He was enchanted to see my uncle, for his chateau, like the house of our worthy host, had not many more guests at the time than it could accommodate. So he kissed my uncle on each cheek, after the French fashion, and ushered him into the castle.

The Marquis did the honors of the house with the urbanity of his country. In fact, he was proud of his old family chateau, for part of it was extremely old. There was a tower and chapel which had been built almost before the memory of man; but the rest was more modern, the castle having been nearly demolished during the wars of the league. The Marquis dwelt upon this event with great satisfaction, and seemed really to entertain a grateful feeling towards Henry the Fourth, for having thought his paternal mansion worth battering down. He had many stories to tell of the prowess of his ancestors; and several skull-caps, helmets, and cross-bows, and divers huge boots and buff jerkins, to show, which had been worn by the leaguers. Above all, there was a two-handed sword, which he could hardly wield, but which he displayed, as a proof that there had been giants in his family.

In truth, he was but a small descendant from such great warriors. When you looked at their bluff visages and brawny limbs, as depicted in their portraits, and then at the little Marquis, with his spindle shanks, and his sallow lantern visage, flanked with a pair of powdered ear-locks, or *aîles de pigeon,* that seemed ready to fly away with it, you could hardly believe him to be of the same race. But when you looked at the eyes that sparkled out like a beetle's from each side of his hooked nose, you saw at once that he inherited all the fiery spirit of his forefathers. In fact, a Frenchman's spirit never exhales, however his body may dwindle. It rather rarefies, and grows more inflammable, as the earthly particles diminish; and I have seen valor enough in a little fiery-hearted French dwarf to have furnished out a tolerable giant.

When once the Marquis, as was his wont, put on one of the old helmets stuck up in his hall, though his head no more filled it than a dry pea its peascod, yet his eyes flashed from the bottom of the iron cavern with the brilliancy of carbuncles; and when he poised the ponderous two-handed sword of his ancestors, you would have thought you saw the doughty little David wielding the sword of Goliath, which was unto him like a weaver's beam.

However, gentlemen, I am dwelling too long on this description of the Marquis and his château, but you must excuse me; he was an old friend of my uncle; and whenever my uncle told the story, he was always fond of talking a great deal about his host. Poor little Marquis! He was one of that handful of gallant courtiers who made such a devoted but hopeless stand in the cause of their sovereign, in the château of the Tuileries, against the irruption of the mob on the sad tenth of August. He displayed the valor of a *preux* French chevalier to the last; flourishing feebly his little court-sword with a *ça-ça!* in face of a whole legion of *sans-culottes;* but was pinned to the wall like a butterfly, by the pike of a *poissarde,* and his heroic soul was borne up to heaven on his *aîles de pigeon.*

But all this has nothing to do with my story. To the point, then. When the hour arrived for retiring for the night, my uncle was shown to his room in a venerable old tower. It was the oldest part of the chateau, and had in ancient times been the donjon or stronghold; of course the chamber was none of the best. The Marquis had put him there, however, because he knew him to be a traveller of taste, and fond of antiquities; and also because the better apartments were already occupied. Indeed, he perfectly reconciled my uncle to his quarters by mentioning the great personages who had once inhabited them, all of whom were, in some way or other, connected with the family. If you would take his word for it, John Baliol, or as he called him, Jean de Bailleul, had died of chagrin in this very chamber, on hearing of the success of his rival, Robert de Bruce, at the battle of Bannockburn. And when he added that the Duke de Guise had slept in it, my uncle was fain to felicitate himself on being honored with such distinguished quarters.

The night was shrewd and windy, and the chamber none of the warmest. An old long-faced, long-bodied servant, in quaint livery, who attended upon my uncle, threw down an armful of wood beside the fireplace, gave a queer look about the room, and then wished him *bon repos* with a grimace and a shrug that would have been suspicious from any other than an old French servant.

The chamber had indeed a wild, crazy look, enough to strike any one who had read romances with apprehension and foreboding. The windows were high and narrow, and had once been loop-holes, but had been rudely enlarged, as well as the extreme thickness of the walls would permit; and the ill-fitted casements rattled to every breeze. You would have thought, on a windy night, some of the old leaguers were tramping and clanking about the apartment in their huge boots and rattling spurs. A door which stood ajar, and, like a true French door, would stand ajar in spite of every reason and effort to the contrary, opened upon a long dark corridor, that led the Lord knows whither, and seemed just made for ghosts to air themselves in, when they turned out of their graves at midnight. The wind would spring up into a hoarse murmur through this passage, and creak the door to and fro, as if some dubious ghost were balancing in its mind whether to come in or not. In a word, it was precisely the kind of comfortless apartment that a ghost, if ghost there were in the château, would single out for its favorite lounge.

My uncle, however, though a man accustomed to meet with strange adventures, apprehended none at the time. He made several attempts to shut the door, but in vain. Not that he apprehended anything, for he was too old a traveller to be daunted by a wild-looking apartment; but the night, as I have said, was cold and gusty, and the wind howled about the old turret pretty much as it does round this old mansion at this moment, and the breeze from the long dark corridor came in as damp and as chilly as if from a dungeon. My uncle, therefore, since he could not close the door, threw a quantity of wood on the fire, which soon sent up a flame in the great wide-mouthed chimney that illumined the whole chamber; and made the shadow of the tongs on the opposite wall look like a long-legged giant. My uncle now clambered on the top of the half-score of mattresses which form a French bed, and which stood in a deep recess; then tucking himself snugly in, and burying himself up to the chin in the bedclothes, he lay looking at the fire, and listening to the wind, and thinking how knowingly he had come over his friend the Marquis for a night's lodging—and so he fell asleep.

He had not taken above half of his first nap when he was awakened by the clock of the château, in the turret over his chamber, which struck midnight. It was just such an old clock as ghosts are fond of. It had a deep, dismal tone, and struck so slowly and tediously that my uncle thought it would never have done. He counted and counted till he was confident he counted thirteen, and then it stopped.

The fire had burnt low, and the blaze of the last fagot was almost expiring, burning in small blue flames, which now and then lengthened up into little white gleams. My uncle lay with his eyes half closed, and his nightcap drawn almost down to his nose. His fancy was already wandering, and began to mingle up the present scene with the crater of Vesuvius, the French Opera, the Coliseum at Rome, Dolly's chop-house in London, and all the farrago of noted places with which the brain of a traveller is crammed—in a word, he was just falling asleep.

Suddenly he was roused by the sound of footsteps, slowly pacing along the corridor. My uncle, as I have often heard him say himself, was a man not easily frightened. So he lay quiet, supposing this some other guest, or some servant on his way to bed. The footsteps, however, approached the door; the door gently opened; whether of its own accord, or whether pushed open, my uncle could not distinguish: a figure all in white glided in. It was a female, tall and stately, and of a commanding air. Her dress was of an ancient fashion, ample in volume, and sweeping the floor. She walked up to the fireplace, without regarding my uncle, who raised his nightcap with one hand, and stared earnestly at her. She remained for some time standing by the fire, which, flashing up at intervals, cast blue and white gleams of light, that enabled my uncle to remark her appearance minutely.

Her face was ghastly pale, and perhaps rendered still more so by the bluish light of the fire. It possessed beauty, but its beauty was saddened by care and anxiety. There was the look of one accustomed to trouble, but of one whom trouble could not cast down nor subdue; for there was still the predominating air of proud, unconquerable resolution. Such at least was the opinion formed by my uncle, and he considered himself a great physiognomist.

The figure remained, as I said, for some time by the fire, putting out first one hand, then the other; then each foot alternately, as if warming itself; for your ghosts, if ghost it really was, are apt to be cold. My uncle, furthermore, remarked that it wore high-heeled shoes, after an ancient fashion, with paste or diamond buckles, that sparkled as though they were alive. At length the figure turned gently round, casting a glassy look about the apartment, which, as it passed over my uncle, made his blood run cold, and chilled the very marrow in his bones. It then stretched its arms towards heaven, clasped its hands, and wringing them in a supplicating manner, glided slowly out of the room.

My uncle lay for some time meditating on this visitation, for (as he remarked when he told me the story) though a man of firmness, he was also a man of reflection, and did not reject a thing because it was out of the regular course of events. However, being, as I have before said, a great traveller, and accustomed to strange adventures, he drew his nightcap resolutely over his eyes, turned his back to the door, hoisted the bedclothes high over his shoulders, and gradually fell asleep.

How long he slept he could not say, when he was awakened by the voice of some one at his bedside. He turned round, and beheld the old French servant, with his ear-locks in tight buckles on each side of a long lantern face, on which habit had deeply wrinkled an everlasting smile. He made a thousand grimaces, and asked a thousand pardons for disturbing Monsieur, but the morning was considerably advanced. While my uncle was dressing, he called vaguely to mind the visitor of the preceding night. He asked the ancient domestic what lady was in the habit of rambling about this part of the chateau at night. The old valet shrugged his shoulders as high as his head, laid one hand on his bosom, threw open the other with every finger extended, made a most whimsical grimace which he meant to be complimentary, and replied, that it was not for him to know anything of *les bonnes fortunes* of Monsieur.

My uncle saw there was nothing satisfactory to be learned in this quarter. After breakfast, he was walking with the Marquis through the modern apartments of the chateau, sliding over the well-waxed floors of silken saloons, amidst furniture rich in gilding and brocade, until they came to a long picture-gallery, containing many portraits, some in oil and some in chalks.

Here was an ample field for the eloquence of his host, who had all the pride of a nobleman of the *ancien régime*. There was not a grand name in Normandy, and hardly one in France, which was not, in some way or other, connected with his house. My uncle stood listening with inward impatience, resting sometimes on one leg, sometimes on the other, as the little Marquis descanted, with his usual fire and vivacity, on the achievements of his ancestors, whose portraits hung along the wall; from the martial deeds of the stern warriors in steel, to the gallantries and intrigues of the blue-eyed gentlemen, with fair smiling faces, powdered ear-locks, laced ruffles, and pink and blue silk coats and breeches;—not forgetting the conquests of the lovely shepherdesses, with hooped petticoats, and waists no thicker than an hour-glass, who appeared ruling over their sheep and their swains, with dainty crooks decorated with fluttering ribbons.

In the midst of his friend's discourse, my uncle was startled on beholding a full-length portrait, the very counterpart of his visitor of the preceding night.

"Methinks," said he, pointing to it, "I have seen the original of this portrait."

"*Pardonnez moi,*" replied the Marquis politely, "that can hardly be, as the lady has been dead more than a hundred years. That was the beautiful Duchess de Longueville, who figured during the minority of Louis the Fourteenth."

"And was there anything remarkable in her history?"

Never was question more unlucky. The little Marquis immediately threw himself into the attitude of a man about to tell a long story. In fact, my uncle had pulled upon himself the whole history of the civil war of the Fronde, in which the beautiful Duchess had played so distinguished a part. Turenne, Coligni, Mazarin, were called up from their graves to grace his narration; nor were the affairs of the Barricadoes, nor the chivalry of the Port Cochères forgotten. My uncle began to wish himself a thousand leagues off from the Marquis and his merciless memory, when suddenly the little man's recollections took a more interesting turn. He was relating the imprisonment of the Duke de Longueville with the Princes Condé and Conti in the château of Vincennes, and the ineffectual efforts of the Duchess to rouse the sturdy Normans to their rescue. He had come to that part where she was invested by the royal forces in the Castle of Dieppe.

"The spirit of the Duchess," proceeded the Marquis, "rose from her trials. It was astonishing to see so delicate and beautiful a being buffet so resolutely with hardships. She determined on a desperate means of escape. You may have seen the château in which she was mewed up— an old ragged wart of an edifice, standing on the knuckle of a hill, just above the rusty little town of Dieppe. One dark unruly night she issued secretly out of a small postern gate of the castle, which the enemy had neglected to guard. The postern gate is there to this very day; opening upon a narrow bridge over a deep fosse between the castle and the brow of the hill. She was followed by her female attendants, a few domestics, and some gallant cavaliers, who still remained faithful to her fortunes. Her object was to gain a small port about two leagues distant, where she had privately provided a vessel for her escape in case of emergency.

"The little band of fugitives were obliged to perform the distance on foot. When they arrived at the port the wind was high and stormy, the tide contrary, the vessel anchored far off in the road, and no means of getting on board but by a fishing-shallop which lay tossing like a cockle-shell on the edge of the surf. The Duchess determined to risk the attempt. The seamen endeavored to dissuade her, but the imminence of her danger on shore, and the magnanimity of her spirit, urged her on. She had to be borne to the shallop in the arms of a mariner. Such was the violence of the wind and waves that he faltered, lost his foothold, and let his precious burden fall into the sea.

"The Duchess was nearly drowned, but partly through her own struggles, partly by the exertions of the seamen, she got to land. As soon as she had a little recovered strength, she insisted on renewing the attempt. The storm, however, had by this time become so violent as to set all efforts at defiance. To delay, was to be discovered and taken prisoner. As the only resource left, she procured horses, mounted with her female attendants, *en croupe,* behind the gallant gentlemen who accompanied her, and scoured the country to seek some temporary asylum.

"While the Duchess," continued the Marquis, laying his forefinger on my uncle's breast to arouse his flagging attention, "—while the Duchess, poor lady, was wandering amid the tempest in this disconsolate manner, she arrived at this château. Her approach caused some uneasiness; for the clattering of a troop of horse at dead of night up the avenue of a lonely château, in those unsettled times, and in a troubled part of the country, was enough to occasion alarm.

"A tall, broad-shouldered chasseur, armed to the teeth, galloped ahead, and announced the name of the visitor. All uneasiness was dispelled. The household turned out with flambeaux to receive her, and never did torches gleam on a more weather-beaten, travel-stained band than came tramping into the court. Such pale, care-worn faces, such bedraggled dresses, as the poor Duchess and her females presented, each seated behind her cavalier: while the half-drenched, half-drowsy pages and attendants seemed ready to fall from their horses with sleep and fatigue.

"The Duchess was received with a hearty welcome by my ancestor. She was ushered into the hall of the château, and the fires soon crackled and blazed, to cheer herself and her train; and every spit and stew-pan was put in requisition to prepare ample refreshment for the wayfarers.

"She had a right to our hospitalities," continued the Marquis, drawing himself up with a slight degree of stateliness, "for she was related to our family. I'll tell you how it was. Her father, Henry de Bourbon, Prince of Condé——"

"But did the Duchess pass the night in the château?" said my uncle rather abruptly, terrified at the idea of getting involved in one of the Marquis's genealogical discussions.

"Oh, as to the Duchess, she was put into the very apartment you occupied last night, which at that time was a kind of state-apartment. Her followers were quartered in the chambers opening upon the neighboring corridor, and her favorite page slept in an adjoining closet. Up and down the corridor walked the great chasseur who had announced her arrival, and who acted as a kind of sentinel or guard. He was a dark, stern, powerful-looking fellow; and as the light of a lamp in the corridor fell upon his deeply marked face and sinewy form, he seemed capable of defending the castle with his single arm.

"It was a rough, rude night; about this time of the year—apropos!—now I think of it, last night was the anniversary of her visit. I may well remember the precise date, for it was a night not to be forgotten by our house. There is a singular tradition concerning it in our family." Here the Marquis hesitated, and a cloud seemed to gather about his bushy eyebrows. "There is a tradition—that a strange occurrence took place that night. A strange, mysterious, inexplicable occurrence——" Here he checked himself, and paused.

"Did it relate to that lady?" inquired my uncle, eagerly.

"It was past the hour of midnight," resumed the Marquis, "when the whole château——" Here he paused again. My uncle made a movement of anxious curiosity.

"Excuse me," said the Marquis, a slight blush streaking his sallow visage. "There are some circumstances connected with our family history which I do not like to relate. That was a rude period. A time of great crimes among great men: for you know high blood, when it runs wrong, will not run tamely, like blood of the *canaille*—poor lady!—But I have a little family pride, that—excuse me—we will change the subject, if you please——"

My uncle's curiosity was piqued. The pompous and magnificent introduction had led him to expect something wonderful in the story to which it served as a kind of avenue. He had no idea of being cheated out of it by a sudden fit of unreasonable squeamishness. Besides, being a traveller in quest of information, he considered it his duty to inquire into everything.

The Marquis, however, evaded every question.

"Well," said my uncle, a little petulantly, "whatever you may think of it, I saw that lady last night."

The Marquis stepped back and gazed at him with surprise.

"She paid me a visit in my bedchamber."

The Marquis pulled out his snuff-box with a shrug and a smile; taking this no doubt for an awkward piece of English pleasantry, which politeness required him to be charmed with.

My uncle went on gravely, however, and related the whole circumstance. The Marquis heard him through with profound attention, holding his snuff-box unopened in his hand. When the story was finished, he tapped on the lid of his box deliberately, took a long, sonorous pinch of snuff——

"Bah!" said the Marquis, and walked towards the other end of the gallery.

Here the narrator paused. The company waited for some time for him to resume his narration; but he continued silent.

"Well," said the inquisitive gentleman, "—and what did your uncle say then?"

"Nothing," replied the other.

"And what did the Marquis say farther?"

"Nothing."

"And is that all?"

"That is all," said the narrator, filling a glass of wine.

"I surmise," said the shrewd old gentleman with the waggish nose, "—I surmise the ghost must have been the old housekeeper, walking her rounds to see that all was right."

"Bah!" said the narrator. "My uncle was too much accustomed to strange sights not to know a ghost from a housekeeper."

There was a murmur round the table, half of merriment, half of disappointment. I was inclined to think the old gentleman had really an after-part of his story in reserve; but he sipped his wine and said nothing more; and there was an odd expression about his dilapidated countenance which left me in doubt whether he were in drollery or earnest.

"Egad," said the knowing gentleman, with the flexible nose, "this story of your uncle puts me in mind of one that used to be told of an aunt of mine, by the mother's side; though I don't know that it will bear a comparison, as the good lady was not so prone to meet with strange adventures. But at any rate you shall have it."

The Adventure of My Aunt

My aunt was a lady of large frame, strong mind, and great resolution: she was what might be termed a very manly woman. My uncle was a thin, puny little man, very meek and acquiescent, and no match for my aunt. It was observed that he dwindled and dwindled gradually away, from the day of his marriage. His wife's powerful mind was too much for him; it wore him out. My aunt, however, took all possible care of him: had half the doctors in town to prescribe for him; made him take all their prescriptions, and dosed him with physic enough to cure a whole hospital. All was in vain. My uncle grew worse and worse the more dosing and nursing he underwent, until in the end he added another to the long list of matrimonial victims who have been killed with kindness.

"And was it his ghost that appeared to her?" asked the inquisitive gentleman, who had questioned the former story-teller.

"You shall hear," replied the narrator.

My aunt took on mightily for the death of her poor dear husband. Perhaps she felt some compunction at having given him so much physic, and nursed him into the grave. At any rate, she did all that a widow could do to honor his memory. She spared no expense in either the quantity or quality of her mourning weeds; wore a miniature of him about her neck as large as a little sun-dial, and had a full-length portrait of him always hanging in her bed-chamber. All the world extolled her conduct to the skies; and it was determined that a woman who behaved so well to the memory of one husband deserved soon to get another.

It was not long after this that she went to take up her residence in an old country-seat in Derbyshire, which had long been in the care of merely a steward and housekeeper. She took most of her servants with her, intending to make it her principal abode. The house stood in a lonely wild part of the country, among the gray Derbyshire hills, with a murderer hanging in chains on a bleak height in full view.

The servants from town were half frightened out of their wits at the idea of living in such a dismal, pagan-looking place; especially when they got together in the servants' hall in the evening, and compared notes on all the hobgoblin stories picked up in the course of the day. They were afraid to venture alone about the gloomy, black-looking chambers. My lady's maid, who was troubled with nerves, declared she could never sleep alone in such a "gashly rummaging old building"; and the footman, who was a kind-hearted young fellow, did all in his power to cheer her up.

My aunt was struck with the lonely appearance of the house. Before going to bed, therefore, she examined well the fastnesses of the doors and windows; locked up the plate with her own hands, and carried the keys, together with a little box of money and jewels, to her own room; for she was a notable woman, and always saw to all things herself. Having put the keys under her pillow, and dismissed her maid, she sat by her toilet arranging her hair; for being, in spite of her grief for my uncle, rather a buxom widow, she was somewhat particular about her person. She sat for a little while looking at her face in the glass, first on one side, then on the other, as ladies are apt to do when they would ascertain whether they have been in good looks; for a roistering country squire of the neighborhood, with whom she had flirted when a girl, had called that day to welcome her to the country.

All of a sudden she thought she heard something move behind her. She looked hastily round, but there was nothing to be seen. Nothing but the grimly painted portrait of her poor dear man, hanging against the wall.

She gave a heavy sigh to his memory, as she was accustomed to do whenever she spoke of him in company, and then went on adjusting her night-dress, and thinking of the squire. Her sigh was re-echoed, or answered by a long-drawn breath. She looked round again, but no one was to be seen. She ascribed these sounds to the wind oozing through the rat-holes of the old mansion, and proceeded leisurely to put her hair in papers, when, all at once, she thought she perceived one of the eyes of the portrait move.

"The back of her head being towards it!" said the story-teller with the ruined head—"good!"

"Yes, sir!" replied dryly the narrator, "her back being towards the portrait, but her eyes fixed on its reflection in the glass."

Well, as I was saying, she perceived one of the eyes of the portrait move. So strange a circumstance, as you may well suppose, gave her a sudden shock. To assure herself of the fact, she put one hand to her forehead as if rubbing it; peeped through her fingers, and moved the candle with the other hand. The light of the taper gleamed on the eye, and was reflected from it. She was sure it moved. Nay, more, it seemed to give her a wink, as she had sometimes known her husband to do when living! It struck a momentary chill to her heart; for she was a lone woman, and felt herself fearfully situated.

The chill was but transient. My aunt, who was almost as resolute a personage as your uncle, sir, (turning to the old story-teller) became instantly calm and collected. She went on adjusting her dress. She even hummed an air, and did not make even a single false note. She casually overturned a dressing-box; took a candle and picked up the articles one by one from the floor; pursued a rolling pin-cushion that was making the best of its way under the bed; then opened the door; looked for an instant into the corridor, as if in doubt whether to go; and then walked quietly out.

She hastened downstairs, ordered the servants to arm themselves with the weapons first at hand, placed herself at their head, and returned almost immediately.

Her hastily levied army presented a formidable force. The steward had a rusty blunder-buss, the coachman a loaded whip, the footman a pair of horse-pistols, the cook a huge chopping-knife, and the butler a bottle in each hand. My aunt led the van with a red-hot poker, and in my opinion she was the most formidable of the party. The waiting-maid, who dreaded to stay alone in the servants' hall, brought up the rear, smelling to a broken bottle of volatile salts, and expressing her terror of the ghostesses. "Ghosts!" said my aunt, resolutely. "I'll singe their whiskers for them!"

They entered the chamber. All was still and undisturbed as when she had left it. They approached the portrait of my uncle.

"Pull down that picture!" cried my aunt. A heavy groan, and a sound like the chattering of teeth, issued from the portrait. The servants shrunk back; the maid uttered a faint shriek, and clung to the footman for support.

"Instantly!" added my aunt, with a stamp of the foot.

The picture was pulled down, and from a recess behind it, in which had formerly stood a clock, they hauled forth a round-shouldered, black-bearded varlet, with a knife as long as my arm, but trembling all over like an aspen-leaf.

"Well, and who was he? No ghost, I suppose," said the inquisitive gentleman.

"A Knight of the Post," replied the narrator, "who had been smitten with the worth of the wealthy widow; or rather a marauding Tarquin, who had stolen into her chamber to violate her purse, and rifle her strong-box, when all the house should be asleep. In plain terms," continued he, "the vagabond was a loose idle fellow of the neighborhood, who had once been a servant in the house, and had been employed to assist in arranging it for the reception of its mistress. He confessed that he had contrived this hiding-place for his nefarious purpose, and had borrowed an eye from the portrait by way of a reconnoitring-hole."

"And what did they do with him?—did they hang him?" resumed the questioner.

"Hang him!—how could they?" exclaimed a beetle-browed barrister, with a hawk's nose. "The offence was not capital. No robbery, no assault had been committed. No forcible entry or breaking into the premises——"

"My aunt," said the narrator, "was a woman of spirit, and apt to take the law in her own hands. She had her own notions of cleanliness also. She ordered the fellow to be drawn through the horse-pond, to cleanse away all offences, and then to be well rubbed down with an oaken towel."

"And what became of him afterwards?" said the inquisitive gentleman.

"I do not exactly know. I believe he was sent on a voyage of improvement to Botany Bay."

"And your aunt," said the inquisitive gentleman; "I'll warrant she took care to make her maid sleep in the room with her after that."

"No, sir, she did better; she gave her hand shortly after to the roistering squire; for she used to observe, that it was a dismal thing for a woman to sleep alone in the country."

"She was right," observed the inquisitive gentleman, nodding sagaciously; "but I am sorry they did not hang that fellow."

It was agreed on all hands that the last narrator had brought his tale to the most satisfactory conclusion, though a country clergyman present regretted that the uncle and aunt, who figured in the different stories, had not been married together; they certainly would have been well matched.

"But I don't see, after all," said the inquisitive gentleman, "that there was any ghost in this last story."

"Oh! If it's ghosts you want, honey," cried the Irish captain of dragoons, "if it's ghosts you want, you shall have a whole regiment of them. And since these gentlemen have given the adventures of their uncles and aunts, faith, and I'll even give you a chapter out of my own family-history."

The Bold Dragoon

or THE ADVENTURE OF MY GRANDFATHER

My grandfather was a bold dragoon, for it's a profession, d' ye see, that has run in the family. All my forefathers have been dragoons, and died on the field of honor, except myself, and I hope my posterity may be able to say the same; however, I don't mean to be vainglorious. Well, my grandfather, as I said, was a bold dragoon, and had served in the Low Countries. In fact, he was one of that very army, which according to my uncle Toby, swore so terribly in Flanders. He could swear a good stick himself; and moreover was the very man that introduced the doctrine Corporal Trim mentions of radical heat and radical moisture, or, in other words, the mode of keeping out the damps of ditchwater by burnt brandy. Be that as it may, it's nothing to the purport of my story. I only tell it to show you that my grandfather was a man not easily to be humbugged. He had seen service, or, according to his own phrase, he had seen the devil—and that's saying everything.

Well, gentlemen, my grandfather was on his way to England, for which he intended to embark from Ostend—bad luck to the place! for one where I was kept by storms and headwinds for three long days, and the devil of a jolly companion or pretty girl to comfort me. Well, as I was saying, my grandfather was on his way to England, or rather to Ostend—no matter which, it's all the same. So one evening, towards night-fall, he rode jollily into Bruges.—Very like you all know Bruges, gentlemen; a queer old-fashioned Flemish town, once, they say, a great place for trade and money-making in old times, when the Mynheers were in their glory; but almost as large and as empty as an Irishman's pocket at the present day.—Well, gentlemen, it was at the time of the annual fair. All Bruges was crowded; and the canals swarmed with Dutch boats, and the streets swarmed with Dutch merchants; and there was hardly any getting along for goods, wares, and merchandises, and peasants in big breeches, and women in half a score of petticoats.

My grandfather rode jollily along, in his easy, slashing way, for he was a saucy, sun-shiny fellow—staring about him at the motley crowd, the old houses with gable ends to the street, and storks' nests in the chimneys; winking at the yafrows who showed their faces at the windows and joking the women right and left in the street; all of whom laughed, and took it in amazing good part; for though he did not know a word of the language, yet he had always a knack of making himself understood among the women.

Well, gentlemen, it being the time of the annual fair, all the town was crowded, every inn and tavern full, and my grandfather applied in vain from one to the other for admittance. At length he rode up to an old rickety inn, that looked ready to fall to pieces, and which all the rats would have run away from, if they could have found room in any other house to put their heads. It was just such a queer building as you see in Dutch pictures, with a tall roof that reached up into the clouds, and as many garrets, one over the other, as the seven heavens of Mahomet. Nothing had saved it from tumbling down but a stork's nest on the chimney, which always brings good luck to a house in the Low Countries; and at the very time of my grandfather's arrival, there were two of these long-legged birds of grace standing like ghosts on the chimney-top. Faith, but they've kept the house on its legs to this very day, for you may see it any time you pass through Bruges, as it stands there yet, only it is turned into a brewery of strong Flemish beer—at least it was so when I came that way after the battle of Waterloo.

My grandfather eyed the house curiously as he approached. It might not have altogether struck his fancy, had he not seen in large letters over the door,

HEER VERKOOPT MAN GOEDEN DRANK

My grandfather had learnt enough of the language to know that the sign promised good liquor. "This is the house for me," said he, stopping short before the door.

The sudden appearance of a dashing dragoon was an event in an old inn frequented only by the peaceful sons of traffic. A rich burgher of Antwerp, a stately ample man in a broad Flemish hat, and who was the great man and great patron of the establishment, sat smoking a clean long pipe on one side of the door; a fat little distiller of Geneva, from Schiedam, sat smoking on the other; and the bottle-nosed host stood in the door, and the comely hostess, in crimped cap, beside him; and the hostess's daughter, a plump Flanders lass, with long gold pendants in her ears, was at a side-window.

"Humph!" said the rich burgher of Antwerp, with a sulky glance at the stranger.

"De duyvel!" said the fat little distiller of Schiedam.

The landlord saw, with the quick glance of a publican, that the new guest was not at all to the taste of the old ones; and, to tell the truth, he did not like my grandfather's saucy eye. He shook his head. "Not a garret in the house but was full."

"Not a garret!" echoed the landlady.

"Not a garret!" echoed the daughter.

The burgher of Antwerp, and the little distiller of Schiedam, continued to smoke their pipes sullenly, eying the enemy askance from under their broad hats, but said nothing.

My grandfather was not a man to be browbeaten. He threw the reins on his horse's neck, cocked his head on one side, stuck one arm akimbo—"Faith and troth!" said he, "but I'll sleep in this house this very night." As he said this he gave a slap on his thigh, by way of emphasis—the slap went to the landlady's heart.

He followed up the vow by jumping off his horse, and making his way past the staring Mynheers into the public room. Maybe you've been in the bar-room of an old Flemish inn—faith, but a handsome chamber it was as you'd wish to see; with a brick floor, and a great fireplace, with the whole Bible history in glazed tiles; and then the mantel-piece, pitching itself head foremost out of the wall, with a whole regiment of cracked tea-pots and earthen jugs paraded on it; not to mention half a dozen great Delft platters, hung about the room by way of pictures; and the little bar in one corner, and the bouncing bar-maid inside of it, with a red calico cap, and yellow ear-drops.

My grandfather snapped his fingers over his head, as he cast an eye round the room—"Faith, this is the very house I've been looking after," said he.

There was some further show of resistance on the part of the garrison; but my grandfather was an old soldier, and an Irishman to boot, and not easily repulsed, especially after he had got into the fortress. So he blarneyed the landlord, kissed the landlord's wife, tickled the landlord's daughter, chucked the bar-maid under the chin; and it was agreed on all hands that it would be a thousand pities, and a burning shame into the bargain, to turn such a bold dragoon into the streets. So they laid their heads together, that is to say, my grandfather and the landlady, and it was at length agreed to accommodate him with an old chamber that had been for some time shut up.

"Some say it's haunted," whispered the landlord's daughter; "but you are a bold dragoon, and I dare say don't fear ghosts."

"The devil a bit!" said my grandfather, pinching her plump cheek. "But if I should be troubled by ghosts, I've been to the Red Sea in my time, and have a pleasant way of laying them, my darling."

And then he whispered something to the girl which made her laugh, and give him a good-humored box on the ear. In short, there was nobody knew better how to make his way among the petticoats than my grandfather.

In a little while, as was his usual way, he took complete possession of the house, swaggering all over it; into the stable to look after his horse, into the kitchen to look after his supper. He had something to say or do with every one; smoked with the Dutchmen, drank with the Germans, slapped the landlord on the shoulder, romped with his daughter and the bar-maid;—never, since the days of Alley Croaker, had such a rattling blade been seen. The landlord stared at him with astonishment; the landlord's daughter hung her head and giggled whenever he came near; and as he swaggered along the corridor, with his sword trailing by his side, the maids looked after him, and whispered to one another, "What a proper man!"

At supper, my grandfather took command of the *table d'hôte* as though he had been at home; helped everybody, not forgetting himself; talked with every one, whether he understood their language or not; and made his way into the intimacy of the rich burgher of Antwerp, who had never been known to be sociable with any one during his life. In fact, he revolutionized the whole establishment, and gave it such a rouse, that the very house reeled with it. He outsat every one at table, excepting the little fat distiller of Schiedam, who sat soaking a long time before he broke forth; but when he did, he was a very devil incarnate. He took a violent affection for my grandfather; so they sat drinking and smoking, and telling stories, and singing Dutch and Irish songs, without understanding a word each other said, until the little Hollander was fairly swamped with his own gin and water, and carried off to bed, whooping and hickuping, and trolling the burden of a Low Dutch love-song.

Well, gentlemen, my grandfather was shown to his quarters up a large staircase, composed of loads of hewn timber; and through long rigmarole passages, hung with blackened paintings of fish, and fruit, and game, and country frolics, and huge kitchens, and portly burgomasters, such as you see about old-fashioned Flemish inns, till at length he arrived at his room.

An old-times chamber it was, sure enough, and crowded with all kinds of trumpery. It looked like an infirmary for decayed and superannuated furniture, where everything diseased or disabled was sent to nurse or to be forgotten. Or rather it might be taken for a general congress of old legitimate movables, where every kind and country had a representative. No two chairs were alike. Such high backs and low backs, and leather bottoms, and worsted bottoms, and straw bottoms, and no bottoms; and cracked marble tables with curiously carved legs, holding balls in their claws, as though they were going to play at ninepins.

My grandfather made a bow to the motley assemblage as he entered, and, having undressed himself, placed his light in the fireplace, asking pardon of the tongs, which seemed to be making love to the shovel in the chimney-corner, and whispering soft nonsense in its ear.

The rest of the guests were by this time sound asleep, for your Mynheers are huge sleepers. The housemaids, one by one, crept up yawning to their attics; and not a female head in the inn was laid on a pillow that night without dreaming of the bold dragoon.

My grandfather, for his part, got into bed, and drew over him one of those great bags of down, under which they smother a man in the Low

Countries; and there he lay, melting between two feather beds, like an anchovy sandwich between two slices of toast and butter. He was a warm-complexioned man, and this smothering played the very deuce with him. So, sure enough, in a little time it seemed as if a legion of imps were twitching at him, and all the blood in his veins was in a fever-heat.

He lay still, however, until all the house was quiet excepting the snoring of the Mynheers from the different chambers; who answered one another in all kinds of tones and cadences, like so many bull-frogs in a swamp. The quieter the house became, the more unquiet became my grandfather. He waxed warmer and warmer, until at length the bed became too hot to hold him.

"Maybe the maid had warmed it too much?" said the curious gentleman, inquiringly.

"I rather think the contrary," replied the Irishman. "But, be that as it may, it grew too hot for my grandfather."

" 'Faith, there's no standing this any longer,' says he. So he jumped out of bed, and went strolling about the house."

"What for?" said the inquisitive gentleman.

"Why, to cool himself, to be sure—or perhaps to find a more comfortable bed—or perhaps—But no matter what he went for—he never mentioned—and there's no use in taking up our time in conjecturing."

Well, my grandfather had been for some time absent from his room, and was returning, perfectly cool, when just as he reached the door, he heard a strange noise within. He paused and listened. It seemed as if some one were trying to hum a tune in defiance of the asthma. He recollected the report of the room being haunted; but he was no believer in ghosts, so he pushed the door gently open and peeped in.

Egad, gentlemen, there was a gambol carrying on within enough to have astonished St. Anthony himself. By the light of the fire he saw a pale weazen-faced fellow, in a long flannel gown and a tall white night-cap with a tassel to it, who sat by the fire with a bellows under his arm by way of bagpipe, from which he forced the asthmatical music that had bothered my grandfather. As he played, too, he kept twitching about with a thousand queer contortions, nodding his head, and bobbing about his tasselled night-cap.

My grandfather thought this very odd and mighty presumptuous, and was about to demand what business he had to play his wind-instrument in another gentleman's quarters, when a new cause of astonishment met his eye. From the opposite side of the room a long-backed, bandy-legged chair, covered with leather, and studded all over in a coxcombical fashion with little brass nails, got suddenly into motion, thrust out first a claw-foot, then a crooked arm, and at length, making a leg, slided gracefully up to an easy-chair of tarnished brocade, with a hole in its bottom, and led it gallantly out in a ghostly minuet about the floor.

The musician now played fiercer and fiercer, and bobbed his head and his night-cap about like mad. By degrees the dancing mania seemed to seize upon all the other pieces of furniture. The antique, long-bodied chairs paired off in couples and led down a country-dance; a three-legged stool danced a hornpipe, though horribly puzzled by its supernumerary limb; while the amorous tongs seized the shovel round the waist, and whirled it about the room in a German waltz. In short, all the movables got in motion; pirouetting hands across, right and left, like so many devils; all except a great clothes-press, which kept curtseying and curtseying in a corner, like a dowager, in exquisite time to the music; being rather too corpulent to dance, or perhaps at a loss for a partner.

My grandfather concluded the latter to be the reason; so being, like a true Irishman, devoted to the sex, and at all times ready for a frolic, he bounced into the room, called to the musician to strike up Paddy O'Rafferty, capered up to the clothes-press, and seized upon the two handles to lead her out: when—whirr!—the whole revel was at an end. The chairs, tables, tongs and shovel, slunk in an instant as quietly into their places as if nothing had happened, and the musician vanished up the chimney, leaving the bellows behind him in his hurry. My grandfather found himself seated in the middle of the floor with the clothes-press sprawling before him, and the two handles jerked off, and in his hands.

"Then, after all, this was a mere dream," said the inquisitive gentleman.

"The divil a bit of a dream!" replied the Irishman. "There never was a truer fact in this world. Faith, I should have liked to see any man tell my grandfather it was a dream."

Well, gentlemen, as the clothes-press was a mighty heavy body, and my grandfather likewise, particularly in rear, you may easily suppose that two such heavy bodies coming to the ground would make a bit of a noise. Faith, the old mansion shook as though it had mistaken it for an earthquake. The whole garrison was alarmed. The landlord, who slept below, hurried up with a candle to inquire the cause, but with all his haste his daughter had arrived at the scene of uproar before him. The landlord was followed by the landlady, who was followed by the bouncing bar-maid, who was followed by the simpering chambermaids, all holding together, as well as they could, such garments as they first laid hands on; but all in a terrible hurry to see what the deuce was to pay in the chamber of the bold dragoon.

My grandfather related the marvellous scene he had witnessed, and the broken handles of the prostrate clothes-press bore testimony to the fact. There was no contesting such evidence; particularly with a lad of my grandfather's complexion, who seemed able to make good every word either with sword or shillelah. So the landlord scratched his head and looked silly, as he was apt to do when puzzled. The landlady scratched—no, she did not scratch her head, but she knit her brow, and did not seem half pleased with the explanation. But the landlady's daughter corroborated it by recollecting that the last person who had dwelt in that chamber was a famous juggler who died of St. Vitus's dance, and had no doubt infected all the furniture.

This set all things to rights, particularly when the chambermaids declared that they had all witnessed strange carryings on in that room; and as they declared this "upon their honors," there could not remain a doubt upon this subject.

"And did your grandfather go to bed again in that room?" said the inquisitive gentleman.

"That's more than I can tell. Where he passed the rest of the night was a secret he never disclosed. In fact, though he had seen much service, he was but indifferently acquainted with geography, and apt to make blunders in his travels about inns at night, which it would have puzzled him sadly to account for in the morning."

"Was he ever apt to walk in his sleep?" said the knowing old gentleman.

"Never that I heard of."

There was a little pause after this rigmarole Irish romance, when the old gentleman with the haunted head observed, that the stories hitherto related had rather a burlesque tendency. "I recollect an adventure however," added he, "which I heard of during a residence in Paris, for the truth of which I can undertake to vouch, and which is of a very grave and singular nature."

The Adventure of the German Student

On a stormy night, in the tempestuous times of the French Revolution, a young German was returning to his lodgings, at a late hour, across the old part of Paris. The lightning gleamed, and the loud claps of thunder rattled through the lofty narrow streets— but I should first tell you something about this young German.

Gottfried Wolfgang was a young man of good family. He had studied for some time at Göttingen, but being of a visionary and enthusiastic character, he had wandered into those wild and speculative doctrines which have so often bewildered German students. His secluded life, his intense application, and the singular nature of his studies, had an effect on both mind and body. His health was impaired; his imagination diseased. He had been indulging in fanciful speculations on spiritual essences, until, like Swedenborg, he had an ideal world of his own around him. He took up a notion, I do not know from what cause, that there was an evil influence hanging over him; an evil genius or spirit seeking to ensnare him and ensure his perdition. Such an idea working on his melancholy temperament, produced the most gloomy effects. He became haggard and desponding. His friends discovered the mental malady preying upon him, and determined that the best cure was a change of scene; he was sent, therefore, to finish his studies amidst the splendors and gayeties of Paris.

Wolfgang arrived at Paris at the breaking out of the revolution. The popular delirium at first caught his enthusiastic mind, and he was captivated by the political and philosophical theories of the day: but the

204

scenes of blood which followed shocked his sensitive nature, disgusted him with society and the world, and made him more than ever a recluse. He shut himself up in a solitary apartment in the Pays Latin, the quarter of students. There, in a gloomy street not far from the monastic walls of the Sorbonne, he pursued his favorite speculations. Sometimes he spent hours together in the great libraries of Paris, those catacombs of departed authors, rummaging among their hordes of dusty and obsolete works in quest of food for his unhealthy appetite. He was, in a manner, a literary ghoul, feeding in the charnel-house of decayed literature.

Wolfgang, though solitary and recluse, was of an ardent temperament, but for a time it operated merely upon his imagination. He was too shy and ignorant of the world to make any advances to the fair, but he was a passionate admirer of female beauty, and in his lonely chamber would often lose himself in reveries on forms and faces which he had seen, and his fancy would deck out images of loveliness far surpassing the reality.

While his mind was in this excited and sublimated state, a dream produced an extraordinary effect upon him. It was of a female face of transcendent beauty. So strong was the impression made, that he dreamt of it again and again. It haunted his thoughts by day, his slumbers by night; in fine, he became passionately enamoured of this shadow of a dream. This lasted so long that it became one of those fixed ideas which haunt the minds of melancholy men, and are at times mistaken for madness.

Such was Gottfried Wolfgang, and such his situation at the time I mentioned. He was returning home late one stormy night, through some of the old and gloomy streets of the Marais, the ancient part of Paris. The loud claps of thunder rattled among the high houses of the narrow streets. He came to the Place de Grève, the square where public executions are performed. The lightning quivered about the pinnacles of the ancient Hôtel de Ville, and shed flickering gleams over the open space in front. As Wolfgang was crossing the square, he shrank back with horror at finding himself close by the guillotine. It was the height of the Reign of Terror, when this dreadful instrument of death stood ever ready, and its scaffold was continually running with the blood of the virtuous and the brave. It had that very day been actively employed in the work of carnage, and there it stood in grim array, amidst a silent and sleeping city, waiting for fresh victims.

Wolfgang's heart sickened within him, and he was turning shuddering from the horrible engine, when he beheld a shadowy form, cowering as it were at the foot of the steps which led up to the scaffold. A succession of vivid flashes of lightning revealed it more distinctly. It was a female figure, dressed in black. She was seated on one of the lower steps of the scaffold, leaning forward, her face hid in her lap; and her long dishevelled tresses hanging to the ground, streaming with the rain which fell in torrents. Wolfgang paused. There was something awful in this solitary monument of woe. The female had the appearance of being above the common order. He knew the times to be full of vicissitude, and that many a fair head, which had once been pillowed on down, now wandered houseless. Perhaps this was some poor mourner whom the dreadful axe had rendered desolate, and who sat here heart-broken on the strand of existence, from which all that was dear to her had been launched into eternity.

He approached, and addressed her in the accents of sympathy. She raised her head and gazed wildly at him. What was his astonishment at beholding, by the bright glare of the lightning, the very face which had haunted him in his dreams. It was pale and disconsolate, but ravishingly beautiful.

Trembling with violent and conflicting emotions, Wolfgang again accosted her. He spoke something of her being exposed at such an hour of the night, and to the fury of such a storm, and offered to conduct her to her friends. She pointed to the guillotine with a gesture of dreadful signification.

"I have no friend on earth!" said she.

"But you have a home," said Wolfgang.

"Yes—in the grave!"

The heart of the student melted at the words.

"If a stranger dare make an offer," said he, "without danger of being misunderstood, I would offer my humble dwelling as a shelter; myself as a devoted friend. I am friendless myself in Paris, and a stranger in the land; but if my life could be of service, it is at your disposal, and should be sacrificed before harm or indignity should come to you."

There was an honest earnestness in the young man's manner that had its effect. His foreign accent, too, was in his favor; it showed him not to be a hackneyed inhabitant of Paris. Indeed, there is an eloquence in true enthusiasm that is not to be doubted. The homeless stranger confided herself implicitly to the protection of the student.

He supported her faltering steps across the Pont Neuf, and by the place where the statue of Henry the Fourth had been overthrown by the populace. The storm had abated, and the thunder rumbled at a distance. All Paris was quiet; that great volcano of human passion slumbered for a while, to gather fresh strength for the next day's eruption. The student conducted his charge through the ancient streets of the Pays Latin, and by the dusky walls of the Sorbonne, to the great dingy hotel which he inhabited. The old portress who admitted them stared with surprise at the unusual sight of the melancholy Wolfgang with a female companion.

On entering his apartment, the student, for the first time, blushed at the scantiness and indifference of his dwelling. He had but one chamber—an old-fashioned saloon—heavily carved, and fantastically furnished with the remains of former magnificence, for it was one of those hotels in the quarter of the Luxembourg Palace, which had once belonged to nobility. It was lumbered with books and papers, and all the usual apparatus of a student, and his bed stood in a recess at one end.

When lights were brought, and Wolfgang had a better opportunity of contemplating the stranger, he was more than ever intoxicated by her beauty. Her face was pale, but of a dazzling fairness, set off by a profusion of raven hair that hung clustering about it. Her eyes were large and brilliant, with a singular expression approaching almost to wildness. As far as her black dress permitted her shape to be seen, it was of perfect symmetry. Her whole appearance was highly striking, though she was dressed in the simplest style. The only thing approaching to an ornament which she wore, was a broad black band round her neck, clasped by diamonds.

The perplexity now commenced with the student how to dispose of the helpless being thus thrown upon his protection. He thought of abandoning his chamber to her, and seeking shelter for himself elsewhere. Still he was so fascinated by her charms, there seemed to be such a spell upon his thoughts and senses, that he could not tear himself from her presence. Her manner, too, was singular and unaccountable. She spoke no more of the guillotine. Her grief had abated. The attentions of the student had first won her confidence, and then, apparently, her heart. She was evidently an enthusiast like himself, and enthusiasts soon understand each other.

In the infatuation of the moment, Wolfgang avowed his passion for her. He told her the story of his mysterious dream, and how she had possessed his heart before he had even seen her. She was strangely affected by his recital, and acknowledged to have felt an impulse towards him equally unaccountable. It was the time for wild theory and wild actions. Old prejudices and superstitions were done away; everything was under the sway of the "Goddess of Reason." Among other rubbish of the old times, the forms and ceremonies of marriage began to be considered superfluous bonds for honorable minds. Social compacts were the vogue. Wolfgang was too much of a theorist not to be tainted by the liberal doctrines of the day.

"Why should we separate?" said he; "our hearts are united; in the eye of reason and honor we are as one. What need is there of sordid forms to bind high souls together?"

The stranger listened with emotion: she had evidently received illumination at the same school.

"You have no home or family," continued he, "let me be everything to you, or rather let us be everything to one another. If form is necessary, form shall be observed—there is my hand. I pledge myself to you forever."

"Forever?" said the stranger, solemnly.

"Forever!" repeated Wolfgang.

The stranger clasped the hand extended to her: "Then I am yours," murmured she, and sank upon his bosom.

The next morning the student left his bride sleeping, and sallied forth at an early hour to seek more spacious apartments suitable to the change in his situation. When he returned, he found the stranger lying with her head hanging over the bed, and one arm thrown over it. He spoke to her, but received no reply. He advanced to awaken her from her uneasy posture. On taking her hand, it was cold—there was no pulsation—her face was pallid and ghastly. In a word, she was a corpse.

Horrified and frantic, he alarmed the house. A scene of confusion ensued. The police were summoned. As the officer of police entered the room, he started back on beholding the corpse.

"Great heaven!" cried he, "how did this woman come here?"

"Do you know anything about her?" said Wolfgang eagerly.

"Do I?" exclaimed the officer: "she was guillotined yesterday."

He stepped forward; undid the black collar round the neck of the corpse, and the head rolled on the floor!

The student burst into a frenzy. "The fiend! the fiend has gained possession of me!" shrieked he; "I am lost forever."

They tried to soothe him, but in vain. He was possessed with the frightful belief that an evil spirit had reanimated the dead body to ensnare him. He went distracted, and died in a mad-house.

Here the old gentleman with the haunted head finished his narrative.

"And is this really a fact?" said the inquisitive gentleman.

"A fact not to be doubted," replied the other. "I had it from the best authority. The student told it me himself. I saw him in a mad-house in Paris."

The Adventure of the Mysterious Picture

As one story of the kind produces another and as all the company seemed fully engrossed with the subject, and disposed to bring their relatives and ancestors upon the scene, there is no knowing how many more strange adventures we might have heard, had not a corpulent old fox-hunter, who had slept soundly through the whole, now suddenly awakened, with a loud and long-drawn yawn. The sound broke the charm: the ghosts took to flight, as though it had been cock-crowing, and there was a universal move for bed.

"And now for the haunted chamber," said the Irish captain, taking his candle.

"Ay, who's to be the hero of the night?" said the gentleman with the ruined head.

"That we shall see in the morning," said the old gentleman with the nose; "whoever looks pale and grizzly will have seen the ghost."

"Well, gentlemen," said the Baronet, "there's many a true thing said in jest—in fact, one of you will sleep in the room tonight——"

"What—a haunted room?—a haunted room—I claim the adventure—and I—and I—and I," said a dozen guests, talking and laughing at the same time.

"No, no," said mine host, "there is a secret about one of my rooms on which I feel disposed to try an experiment: so, gentlemen, none of you shall know who has the haunted chamber until circumstances reveal it. I will not even know it myself, but will leave it to chance and the allotment of the housekeeper. At the same time, if it will be any satisfaction to you, I will observe, for the honor of my paternal mansion, that there's scarcely a chamber in it but is well worthy of being haunted."

We now separated for the night, and each went to his allotted room. Mine was in one wing of the building, and I could not but smile at its resemblance in style to those eventful apartments described in the tales of the supper-table. It was spacious and gloomy, decorated with lamp-black portraits; a bed of ancient damask, with a tester sufficiently lofty to grace a couch of state, and a number of massive pieces of old-fashioned furniture. I drew a great claw-footed arm-chair before the wide fireplace; stirred up the fire; sat looking into it, and musing upon the odd stories I had heard, until, partly overcome by the fatigue of the day's hunting and partly by the wine and wassail of mine host, I fell asleep in my chair.

The uneasiness of my position made my slumber troubled, and laid me at the mercy of all kinds of wild and fearful dreams. Now it was that my perfidious dinner and supper rose in rebellion against my peace. I was hag-ridden by a fat saddle of mutton; a plum-pudding weighed like lead upon my conscience; the merry thought of a capon filled me with horrible suggestions; and a devilled leg of a turkey stalked in all kinds of diabolical shapes through my imagination. In short, I had a violent fit of the nightmare. Some strange, indefinite evil seemed hanging over me which I could not avert; something terrible and loathsome oppressed me which I could not shake off. I was conscious of being asleep, and strove to rouse myself, but every effort redoubled the evil; until gasping, struggling, almost strangling, I suddenly sprang bolt upright in my chair, and awoke.

The light on the mantel-piece had burnt low, and the wick was divided; there was a great winding-sheet made by the dripping wax on the side towards me. The disordered taper emitted a broad flaring flame, and threw a strong light on a painting over the fireplace which I had not hitherto observed. It consisted merely of a head, or rather a face, staring full upon me, with an expression that was startling. It was without a frame, and at the first glance I could hardly persuade myself that it was not a real face thrusting itself out of the dark oaken panel. I sat in my chair gazing at it, and the more I gazed, the more it disquieted me. I had never before been affected in the same way by any painting. The emotions it caused were strange and indefinite. They were something like what I have heard ascribed to the eyes of the basilisk, or like that mysterious influence in reptiles termed fascination. I passed my hand over my eyes several times, as if seeking instinctively to brush away the illusion—in vain. They instantly reverted to the picture, and its chilling, creeping influence over my flesh and blood was redoubled. I looked round the room on other pictures, either to divert my attention, or to see whether the same effect would be produced by them. Some of them were grim enough to produce the effect, if the mere grimness of the painting produced it. No such thing—my eye passed over them all with perfect indifference, but the moment it reverted to this visage over the fireplace, it was as if an electric shock darted through me. The other pictures were dim and faded, but this one protruded from a plain background in the strongest relief, and with wonderful truth of coloring. The expression was that of agony—the agony of intense bodily pain; but a menace scowled upon the brow, and a few sprinklings of blood added to its ghastliness. Yet it was not all these characteristics; it was some horror of the mind, some inscrutable antipathy awakened by this picture, which harrowed up my feelings.

I tried to persuade myself that this was chimerical, that my brain was confused by the fumes of mine host's good cheer, and in some measure by the odd stories about paintings which had been told at supper. I determined to shake off these vapors of the mind; rose from my chair; walked about the room; snapped my fingers; rallied myself; laughed aloud—it was a forced laugh, and the echo of it in the old chamber jarred upon my ear. I walked to the window, and tried to discern the landscape through the glass. It was pitch darkness, and a howling storm without; and as I heard the wind moan among the trees, I caught a reflection of this accursed visage in the pane of glass, as though it were staring through the window at me. Even the reflection of it was thrilling.

How was this vile nervous fit, for such I now persuaded myself it was, to be conquered? I determined to force myself not to look at the painting, but to undress quickly and get into bed. I began to undress, but in spite of every effort I could not keep myself from stealing a glance every now and then at the picture; and a glance was sufficient to distress me. Even when my back was turned to it, the idea of this strange face behind me, peeping over my shoulder, was insupportable. I threw off my clothes and hurried into bed, but still this visage gazed upon me. I had a full view of it in my bed, and for some time could not take my eyes from it. I had grown nervous to a dismal degree. I put out the light, and tried to force myself to sleep—all in vain. The fire gleaming up a little, threw an uncertain light about the room, leaving, however, the region of the picture in deep shadow. What, thought I, if this be the chamber about which mine host spoke as having a mystery reigning over it? I had taken his words merely as spoken in jest; might they have a real import? I looked around. The faintly lighted apartment had all the qualifications requisite for a haunted chamber. It began in my infected imagination to assume strange appearances—the old portraits turned paler and paler, and blacker and blacker; the streaks of light and shadow thrown among the quaint articles of furniture gave them more singular shapes and characters. There was a huge dark clothes-press of antique form, gorgeous in brass and lustrous with wax, that began to grow oppressive to me.

"Am I then," thought I, "indeed the hero of the haunted room? Is there really a spell laid upon me, or is this all some contrivance of mine host to raise a laugh at my expense?" The idea of being hag-ridden by my own fancy all night, and then bantered on my haggard looks the next day, was intolerable; but the very idea was sufficient to produce the effect, and to render me still more nervous. "Pish," said I, "it can be no such thing. How could my worthy host imagine that I, or any man, would be so worried by a mere picture? It is my own diseased imagination that torments me."

I turned in bed, and shifted from side to side, to try to fall asleep; but all in vain; when one cannot get asleep by lying quiet, it is seldom that tossing about will effect the purpose. The fire gradually went out, and left the room in total darkness. Still I had the idea of that inexplicable countenance gazing and keeping watch upon me through the gloom— nay, what was worse, the very darkness seemed to magnify its terrors. It was like having an unseen enemy hanging about one in the night. Instead of having one picture now to worry me, I had a hundred. I fancied it in every direction—"There it is," thought I, "and there! and there! with its horrible and mysterious expression still gazing and gazing on me! No—if I must suffer the strange and dismal influence, it were better face a single foe than thus be haunted by a thousand images of it."

Whoever has been in a state of nervous agitation, must know that the longer it continues the more uncontrollable it grows. The very air of the chamber seemed at length infected by the baleful presence of this picture. I fancied it hovering over me. I almost felt the fearful visage from the wall approaching my face—it seemed breathing upon me. "This is not to be borne," said I, at length, springing out of bed: "I can stand this no longer—I shall only tumble and toss about here all night; make a very spectre of myself, and become the hero of the haunted chamber in good earnest. Whatever be the ill consequences, I'll quit this cursed room and seek a night's rest elsewhere—they can but laugh at me, at all events, and they'll be sure to have the laugh upon me if I pass a sleepless night, and show them a haggard and woe-begone visage in the morning."

All this was half-muttered to myself as I hastily slipped on my clothes, which having done, I groped my way out of the room and downstairs to the drawing-room. Here, after tumbling over two or three pieces of furniture, I made out to reach a sofa, and stretching myself upon it, determined to bivouac there for the night. The moment I found myself out of the neighborhood of that strange picture, it seemed as if the charm were broken. All its influence was at an end. I felt assured that it was confined to its own dreary chamber, for I had, with a sort of instinctive caution, turned the key when I closed the door. I soon calmed down, therefore, into a state of tranquillity; from that into a drowsiness, and finally into a deep sleep; out of which I did not awake until the housemaid, with her besom and her matin-song, came to put the room in order. She stared at finding me stretched upon the sofa, but I presume circumstances of the kind were not uncommon after hunting-dinners in her master's bachelor establishment, for she went on with her song and her work, and took no further heed of me.

I had an unconquerable repugnance to return to my chamber; so I found my way to the butler's quarters, made my toilet in the best way circumstances would permit, and was among the first to appear at the breakfast-table. Our breakfast was a substantial fox-hunter's repast, and the company generally assembled at it. When ample justice had been done to the tea, coffee, cold meats, and humming ale, for all these were furnished in abundance, according to the tastes of the different guests, the conversation began to break out with all the liveliness and freshness of morning mirth.

"But who is the hero of the haunted chamber—who has seen the ghost last night?" said the inquisitive gentleman, rolling his lobster-eyes about the table.

The question set every tongue in motion; a vast deal of bantering, criticising of countenances, of mutual accusation and retort took place. Some had drunk deep, and some were unshaven, so that there were suspicious faces enough in the assembly. I alone could not enter with ease and vivacity into the joke—I felt tongue-tied, embarrassed. A recollection of what I had seen and felt the preceding night still haunted my mind. It seemed as if the mysterious picture still held a thrall upon me. I thought also that our host's eye was turned on me with an air of curiosity. In short, I was conscious that I was the hero of the night, and felt as if every one might read it in my looks. The joke, however, passed over, and no suspicion seemed to attach to me. I was just congratulating myself on my escape, when a servant came in, saying, that the gentleman who had slept on the sofa in the drawing-room had left his watch under one of the pillows. My repeater was in his hand.

"What!" said the inquisitive gentleman, "did any gentleman sleep on the sofa?"

"Soho! Soho! a hare—a hare!" cried the old gentleman with the flexible nose.

I could not avoid acknowledging the watch, and was rising in great confusion, when a boisterous old squire who sat beside me exclaimed, slapping me on the shoulder, " 'Sblood, lad, thou art the man as has seen the ghost!"

The attention of the company was immediately turned on me: if my face had been pale the moment before, it now glowed almost to burning. I tried to laugh, but could only make a grimace, and found the muscles of my face twitching at sixes and sevens, and totally out of all control.

It takes but little to raise a laugh among a set of fox-hunters; there was a world of merriment and joking on the subject, and as I never relished a joke overmuch when it was at my own expense, I began to feel a little nettled. I tried to look cool and calm, and to restrain my pique; but the coolness and calmness of a man in a passion are confounded treacherous.

"Gentlemen," said I, with a slight cocking of the chin and a bad attempt at a smile, "this is all very pleasant—ha! ha!—very pleasant—

but I'd have you know, I am as little superstitious as any of you—ha! ha!—and as to anything like timidity—you may smile, gentlemen, but I trust there's no one here means to insinuate that—as to a room's being haunted—I repeat, gentlemen (growing a little warm at seeing a cursed grin breaking out round me), as to a room being haunted, I have as little faith in such silly stories as any one. But, since you put the matter home to me, I will say that I have met with something in my room strange and inexplicable to me. (A shout of laughter.) Gentlemen, I am serious; I know well what I am saying; I am calm, gentlemen (striking my fist upon the table), by Heaven, I am calm. I am neither trifling, nor do I wish to be trifled with. (The laughter of the company suppressed, and with ludicrous attempts at gravity.) There is a picture in the room in which I was put last night, that has had an effect upon me the most singular and incomprehensible."

"A picture?" said the old gentleman with the haunted head. "A picture!" cried the narrator with the nose. "A picture! a picture!" echoed several voices. Here there was an ungovernable peal of laughter. I could not contain myself. I started up from my seat; looked round on the company with fiery indignation; thrust both of my hands into my pockets, and strode up to one of the windows as though I would have walked through it. I stopped short, looked out upon the landscape without distinguishing a feature of it, and felt my gorge rising almost to suffocation.

Mine host saw it was time to interfere. He had maintained an air of gravity through the whole of the scene; and now stepped forth, as if to shelter me from the overwhelming merriment of my companions.

"Gentlemen," said he, "I dislike to spoil sport, but you have had your laugh, and the joke of the haunted chamber has been enjoyed. I must now take the part of my guest. I must not only vindicate him from your pleasantries, but I must reconcile him to himself, for I suspect he is a little out of humor with his own feelings; and, above all, I must crave his pardon for having made him the subject of a kind of experiment. Yes, gentlemen, there is something strange and peculiar in the chamber to which our friend was shown last night; there is a picture in my house which possesses a singular and mysterious influence, and with which there is connected a very curious story. It is a picture to which I attach a value from a variety of circumstances; and though I have often been tempted to destroy it, from the odd and uncomfortable sensations which it produces in every one that beholds it, yet I have never been able to prevail upon myself to make the sacrifice. It is a picture I never like to look upon myself, and which is held in awe by all my servants. I have therefore banished it to a room but rarely used, and should have had it covered last night, had not the nature of our conversation, and the whimsical talk about a haunted chamber, tempted me to let it remain, by way of experiment, to see whether a stranger, totally unacquainted with its story, would be affected by it."

The words of the Baronet had turned every thought into a different channel. All were anxious to hear the story of the mysterious picture; and, for myself, so strangely were my feelings interested, that I forgot to feel piqued at the experiment mine host had made upon my nerves, and joined eagerly in the general entreaty. As the morning was stormy, and denied all egress, mine host was glad of any means of entertaining his company; so, drawing his arm-chair towards the fire, he began.

The Adventure of the Mysterious Stranger

Many years since, when I was a young man, and had just left Oxford, I was sent on the grand tour to finish my education. I believe my parents had tried in vain to inoculate me with wisdom; so they sent me to mingle with society, in hopes that I might take it the natural way. Such, at least, appears the reason for which nine tenths of our youngsters are sent abroad. In the course of my tour I remained some time at Venice. The romantic character of that place delighted me; I was very much amused by the air of adventure and intrigue prevalent in this region of masks and gondolas; and I was exceedingly smitten by a pair of languishing black eyes, that played upon my heart from under an Italian mantle; so I persuaded myself that I was lingering at Venice to study men and manners; at least I persuaded my friends so, and that answered all my purposes.

I was a little prone to be struck by peculiarities in character and conduct, and my imagination was so full of romantic associations with Italy that I was always on the look-out for adventure. Everything chimed in with such a humor in this old mermaid of a city. My suite of apartments was in a proud, melancholy palace on the Grand Canal, formerly the residence of a magnifico, and sumptuous with the traces of decayed grandeur. My gondolier was one of the shrewdest of his class, active, merry, intelligent, and, like his brethren, secret as the grave; that is to say, secret to all the world except his master. I had not had him a week before he put me behind all the curtains in Venice. I liked the silence and the mystery of the place, and when I sometimes saw from my window a black gondola gliding mysteriously along in the dusk of the evening, with nothing visible but its little glimmering lantern, I would jump into my own *zendeletta*, and give a signal for pursuit. ("But I am running away from my subject with the recollection of youthful follies," said the Baronet, checking himself. "Let us come to the point.")

Among my familiar resorts was a casino under the arcades on one side of the grand square of St. Mark. Here I used frequently to lounge and take my ice, on those warm summer-nights, when in Italy everybody lives abroad until morning. I was seated here one evening, when a group of Italians took their seat at a table on the opposite side of the saloon. Their conversation was gay and animated, and carried on with Italian vivacity and gesticulation. I remarked among them one young man, however, who appeared to take no share, and to find no enjoyment in the conversation, though he seemed to force himself to attend to it. He was tall and slender, and of extremely prepossessing appearance. His features were fine, though emaciated. He had a profusion of black glossy hair, that curled lightly about his head, and contrasted with the extreme paleness of his countenance. His brow was haggard; deep furrows seemed to have been ploughed into his visage by care, not by age, for he was evidently in the prime of youth. His eye was full of expression and fire, but wild and unsteady. He seemed to be tormented by some strange fancy or apprehension. In spite of every effort to fix his attention on the conversation of his companions, I noticed that every now and then he would turn his head slowly round, give a glance over his shoulder, and then withdraw it with a sudden jerk, as if something painful met his eye. This was repeated at intervals of about a minute, and he appeared hardly to have recovered from one shock, before I saw him slowly preparing to encounter another.

After sitting some time in the casino, the party paid for the refreshment they had taken, and departed. The young man was the last to leave the saloon, and I remarked him glancing behind him in the same way, just as he passed out of the door. I could not resist the impulse to rise and follow him; for I was at an age when a romantic feeling of curiosity is easily awakened. The party walked slowly down the arcades, talking and laughing as they went. They crossed the *piazzetta,* but paused in the middle of it to enjoy the scene. It was one of those moonlit nights, so brilliant and clear in the pure atmosphere of Italy. The moonbeams streamed on the tall tower of St. Mark, and lighted up the magnificent front and swelling domes of the cathedral. The party expressed their delight in animated terms. I kept my eye upon the young man. He alone seemed abstracted and self-occupied. I noticed the same singular and, as it were, furtive glance over the shoulder, which had attracted my attention in the casino. The party moved on, and I followed; they passed along the walk called the Broglio, turned the corner of the Ducal Palace, and getting into the gondola, glided swiftly away.

The countenance and conduct of this young man dwelt upon my mind, and interested me exceedingly. I met him a day or two afterwards in a gallery of paintings. He was evidently a connoisseur, for he always singled out the most masterly productions, and a few remarks drawn from him by his companions showed an intimate acquaintance with the art. His own taste, however, ran on singular extremes. On Salvator Rosa, in his most savage and solitary scenes; or Raphael, Titian, and Correggio, in their softest delineations of female beauty; on these he would occasionally gaze with transient enthusiasm. But this seemed only a momentary forgetfulness. Still would recur that cautious glance behind, and always quickly withdrawn, as though something terrible met his view.

I encountered him frequently afterwards at the theatre, at balls, at concerts; at promenades in the gardens of San Giorgio; at the grotesque exhibitions in the square of St. Mark; among the throng of merchants on the exchange by the Rialto. He seemed, in fact, to seek crowds; to hunt after bustle and amusement; yet never to take any interest in either the business or the gayety of the scene. Ever an air of painful thought, of wretched abstraction; and ever that strange and recurring movement of glancing fearfully over the shoulder. I did not know at first but this might be caused by apprehension of arrest; or, perhaps, from dread of assassination. But if so, why should he go thus continually abroad? Why expose himself at all times and in all places?

I became anxious to know this stranger. I was drawn to him by that romantic sympathy which sometimes draws young men towards each other. His melancholy threw a charm about him, no doubt heightened by the touching expression of his countenance, and the manly graces of his person; for manly beauty has its effect even upon men. I had an

Englishman's habitual diffidence and awkwardness to contend with; but from frequently meeting him in the casinos, I gradually edged myself into his acquaintance. I had no reserve on his part to contend with. He seemed, on the contrary, to court society; and, in fact, to seek anything rather than be alone.

When he found that I really took an interest in him, he threw himself entirely on my friendship. He clung to me like a drowning man. He would walk with me for hours up and down the place of St. Mark—or would sit, until night was far advanced, in my apartments. He took rooms under the same roof with me; and his constant request was that I would permit him, when it did not incommode me, to sit by me in my saloon. It was not that he seemed to take a particular delight in my conversation, but rather that he craved the vicinity of a human being; and, above all, of a being that sympathized with him. "I have often heard," said he, "of the sincerity of Englishmen—thank God I have one at length for a friend!"

Yet he never seemed disposed to avail himself of my sympathy other than by mere companionship. He never sought to unbosom himself to me: there appeared to be a settled, corroding anguish in his bosom that neither could be soothed "by silence nor by speaking."

A devouring melancholy preyed upon his heart, and seemed to be drying up the very blood in his veins. It was not a soft melancholy, the disease of the affections, but a parching, withering agony. I could see at times that his mouth was dry and feverish; he panted rather than breathed; his eyes were bloodshot; his cheeks pale and livid; with now and then faint streaks of red athwart them, baleful gleams of the fire that was consuming his heart. As my arm was within his, I felt him press it at times with a convulsive motion to his side; his hands would clinch themselves involuntarily, and a kind of shudder would run through his frame.

I reasoned with him about his melancholy, sought to draw from him the cause; he shrunk from all confiding: "Do not seek to know it," said he, "you could not relieve it if you knew it; you would not even seek to relieve it. On the contrary, I should lose your sympathy, and that," said he, pressing my hand convulsively, "that I feel has become too dear to me to risk."

I endeavored to awaken hope within him. He was young; life had a thousand pleasures in store for him; there was a healthy reaction in the youthful heart; it medicines all its own wounds; "Come, come," said I, "there is no grief so great that youth cannot outgrow it."—"No! no!" said he, clinching his teeth, and striking repeatedly, with the energy of despair, on his bosom—"it is here! here! deep-rooted; draining my heart's blood. It grows and grows, while my heart withers and withers. I have a dreadful monitor that gives me no repose—that follows me step by step—and will follow me step by step, until it pushes me into my grave!"

As he said this he involuntarily gave one of those fearful glances over his shoulder, and shrunk back with more than usual horror. I could not resist the temptation to allude to this movement, which I supposed to be some mere malady of the nerves. The moment I mentioned it, his face became crimsoned and convulsed; he grasped me by both hands—

"For God's sake," exclaimed he, with a piercing voice, "never allude to that again. Let us avoid this subject, my friend; you cannot relieve me, indeed you cannot relieve me, but you may add to the torments I suffer. At some future day you shall know all."

I never resumed the subject; for however much my curiosity might be roused, I felt too true a compassion for his sufferings to increase them by my intrusion. I sought various ways to divert his mind, and to arouse him from the constant meditations in which he was plunged. He saw my efforts, and seconded them as far as in his power, for there was nothing moody or wayward in his nature. On the contrary, there was something frank, generous, unassuming, in his whole deportment. All the senti-ments he uttered were noble and lofty. He claimed no indulgence, asked no toleration, but seemed content to carry his load of misery in silence, and only sought to carry it by my side. There was a mute beseeching manner about him, as if he craved companionship as a charitable boon; and a tacit thankfulness in his looks, as if he felt grateful to me for not repulsing him.

I felt this melancholy to be infectious. It stole over my spirits; interfered with all my gay pursuits, and gradually saddened my life; yet I could not prevail upon myself to shake off a being who seemed to hang upon me for support. In truth, the generous traits of character which beamed through all his gloom penetrated to my heart. His bounty was lavish and open-handed; his charity melting and spontaneous; not confined to mere donations, which humiliate as much as they relieve. The tone of his voice, the beam of his eye, enhanced every gift, and surprised the poor suppliant with that rarest and sweetest of charities, the charity not merely of the hand, but of the heart. Indeed his liberality seemed to have something in it of self-abasement and expiation. He, in a manner, humbled himself before the mendicant. "What right have I to ease and affluence"—would he murmur to himself—"when innocence wanders in misery and rags?"

The carnival-time arrived. I hoped the gay scenes then presented might have some cheering effect. I mingled with him in the motley throng that crowded the place of St. Mark. We frequented operas, masquerades, balls—all in vain. The evil kept growing on him. He became more and more haggard and agitated. Often, after we had returned from one of these scenes of revelry, I entered his room and found him lying on his face on the sofa; his hands clinched in his fine hair, and his whole countenance bearing traces of the convulsions of his mind.

The carnival passed away; the time of Lent succeeded; passion-week arrived; we attended one evening a solemn service in one of the churches, in the course of which a grand piece of vocal and instrumental music was performed relating to the death of our Saviour.

I had remarked that he was always powerfully affected by music; on this occasion he was so in an extraordinary degree. As the pealing notes swelled through the lofty aisles, he seemed to kindle with fervor; his eyes rolled upwards, until nothing but the whites were visible; his hands were clasped together, until the fingers were deeply imprinted in the flesh. When the music expressed the dying agony, his face gradually sank upon his knees; and at the touching words resounding through the church, "*Jesu mori*," sobs burst from him uncontrolled—I had never seen him weep before. His had always been agony rather than sorrow. I augered well from the circumstance, and let him weep on uninterrupted. When the service was ended, we left the church. He hung on my arm as we walked homewards with something of a softer and more subdued manner, instead of that nervous agitation I had been accustomed to witness. He alluded to the service we had heard. "Music," said he, "is indeed the voice of heaven; never before have I felt more impressed by the story of the atonement of our Saviour. Yes, my friend," said he, clasping his hands with a kind of transport, "I know that my Redeemer liveth!"

We parted for the night. His room was not far from mine, and I heard him for some time busied in it. I fell asleep, but was awakened before daylight. The young man stood by my bedside, dressed for travelling. He held a sealed packet and a large parcel in his hand, which he laid on the table.

"Farewell, my friend," said he, "I am about to set forth on a long journey; but, before I go, I leave with you these remembrances. In this packet you will find the particulars of my story. When you read them I shall be far away; do not remember me with aversion. You have been indeed a friend to me. You have poured oil into a broken heart, but you could not heal it. Farewell! let me kiss your hand—I am unworthy to embrace you." He sank on his knees, seized my hand in despite of my efforts to the contrary, and covered it with kisses. I was so surprised by all the scene, that I had not been able to say a word—"But we shall meet again," said I, hastily, as I saw him hurrying towards the door. "Never, never, in this world!" said he solemnly. He sprang once more to my bedside—seized my hand, pressed it to his heart and to his lips, and rushed out of the room.

Here the Baronet paused. He seemed lost in thought, and sat looking upon the floor, and drumming with his fingers on the arm of his chair.

"And did this mysterious personage return?" said the inquisitive gentleman.

"Never!" replied the Baronet, with a pensive shake of the head—"I never saw him again."

"And pray what has all this to do with the picture?" inquired the old gentleman with the nose.

"True," said the questioner; "is it the portrait of that crack-brained Italian?"

"No," said the Baronet, dryly, not half liking the appellation given to his hero; "but this picture was enclosed in the parcel he left with me. The sealed packet contained its explanation. There was a request on the outside that I would not open it until six months had elapsed. I kept my promise in spite of my curiosity. I have a translation of it by me, and had meant to read it by way of accounting for the mystery of the chamber; but I fear I have already detained the company too long."

Here there was a general wish expressed to have the manuscript read, particularly on the part of the inquisitive gentleman; so the worthy Baronet drew out a fairly-written manuscript, and, wiping his spectacles, read aloud the following story.

The Story of the Young Italian

I was born at Naples. My parents, though of noble rank, were limited, in fortune, or rather, my father was ostentatious beyond his means, and expended so much on his palace, his equipage, and his retinue, that he was continually straitened in his pecuniary circumstances. I was a younger son, and looked upon with indifference by my father, who, from a principle of family pride, wished to leave all his property to my elder brother. I showed, when quite a child, an extreme sensibility. Everything affected me violently. While yet an infant in my mother's arms, and before I had learned to talk, I could be wrought upon to a wonderful degree of anguish or delight by the power of music. As I grew older, my feelings remained equally acute, and I was easily transported into paroxysms of pleasure or rage. It was the amusement of my relations and of the domestics to play upon this irritable temperament. I was moved to tears, tickled to laughter, provoked to fury, for the entertainment of company, who were amused by such a tempest of mighty passion in a pigmy frame;—they little thought, or perhaps little heeded the dangerous sensibilities they were fostering. I thus became a little creature of passion before reason was developed. In a short time I grew too old to be a plaything, and then I became a torment. The tricks and passions I had been teased into became irksome, and I was disliked by my teachers for the very lessons they had taught me. My mother died; and my power as a spoiled child was at an end. There was no longer any necessity to humor or tolerate me, for there was nothing to be gained by it, as I was no favorite of my father. I therefore experienced the fate of a spoiled child in such a situation, and was neglected, or noticed only to be crossed and contradicted. Such was the early treatment of a heart which, if I can judge of it at all, was naturally disposed to the extremes of tenderness and affection.

My father, as I have already said, never liked me—in fact, he never understood me; he looked upon me as wilful and wayward, as deficient in natural affection. It was the stateliness of his own manner, the loftiness and grandeur of his own look, which had repelled me from his arms. I always pictured him to myself as I had seen him, clad in his senatorial robes, rustling with pomp and pride. The magnificence of his person daunted my young imagination. I could never approach him with the confiding affection of a child.

My father's feelings were wrapt up in my elder brother. He was to be the inheritor of the family title and the family dignity, and everything was sacrificed to him—I, as well as everything else. It was determined to devote me to the Church, that so my humors and myself might be removed out of the way, either of tasking my father's time and trouble, or interfering with the interests of my brother. At an early age, therefore, before my mind had dawned upon the world and its delights, or known anything of it beyond the precincts of my father's palace, I was sent to a convent, the superior of which was my uncle, and was confided entirely to his care.

My uncle was a man totally estranged from the world: he had never relished, for he had never tasted, its pleasures; and he regarded rigid self-denial as the great basis of Christian virtue. He considered every one's temperament like his own; or at least he made them conform to it. His character and habits had an influence over the fraternity of which he was superior: a more gloomy, saturnine set of beings were never assembled together. The convent, too, was calculated to awaken sad and solitary thoughts. It was situated in a gloomy gorge of those mountains away south of Vesuvius. All distant views were shut out by sterile volcanic heights. A mountain-stream raved beneath its walls, and eagles screamed about its turrets.

I had been sent to this place at so tender an age as soon to lose all distinct recollection of the scenes I had left behind. As my mind expanded, therefore, it formed its idea of the world from the convent and its vicinity, and a dreary world it appeared to me. An early tinge of melancholy was thus infused into my character; and the dismal stories of the monks, about devils and evil spirits, with which they affrighted my young imagination, gave me a tendency to superstition which I could never effectually shake off. They took the same delight to work upon my ardent feelings, that had been so mischievously executed by my father's household. I can recollect the horrors with which they fed my heated fancy during an eruption of Vesuvius. We were distant from that volcano, with mountains between us; but its convulsive throes shook the solid foundations of nature. Earthquakes threatened to topple down our convent-towers. A lurid, baleful light hung in the heavens at night, and showers of ashes, borne by the wind, fell in our narrow valley. The monks talked of the earth being honey-combed beneath us; of streams of molten lava raging through its veins; of caverns of sulphurous flames roaring in the centre, the abodes of demons and the damned; of fiery gulfs ready to yawn beneath our feet. All these tales were told to the doleful accompaniment of the mountain's thunders, whose low bellowing made the walls of our convent vibrate.

One of the monks had been a painter, but had retired from the world, and embraced this dismal life in expiation of some crime. He was a melancholy man, who pursued his art in the solitude of his cell, but made it a source of penance to him. His employment was to portray, either on canvas or in waxen models, the human face and human form, in the agonies of death, and in all the stages of dissolution and decay. The fearful mysteries of the charnel-house were unfolded in his labors; the loathsome banquet of the beetle and the worm. I turn with shuddering even from the recollection of his works; yet, at the time, my strong but ill-directed imagination seized with ardor upon his instructions in his art. Anything was a variety from the dry studies and monotonous duties of the cloister. In a little while I became expert with my pencil, and my gloomy productions were thought worthy of decorating some of the altars of the chapel.

In this dismal way was a creature of feeling and fancy brought up. Everything genial and amiable in my nature was repressed, and nothing brought out but what was unprofitable and ungracious. I was ardent in my temperament; quick, mercurial, impetuous, formed to be a creature all love and adoration; but a leaden hand was laid on all my finer qualities. I was taught nothing but fear and hatred. I hated my uncle. I hated the monks. I hated the convent in which I was immured. I hated the world; and I almost hated myself for being, as I supposed, so hating and hateful an animal.

When I had nearly attained the age of sixteen, I was suffered, on one occasion, to accompany one of the brethren on a mission to a distant part of the country. We soon left behind us the gloomy valley in which I had been pent up for so many years, and after a short journey among the mountains, emerged upon the voluptuous landscape that spreads itself about the Bay of Naples. Heavens! how transported was I, when I stretched my gaze over a vast reach of delicious sunny country, gay with groves and vineyards; with Vesuvius rearing its forked summit to my right; the blue Mediterranean to my left, with its enchanting coast, studded with shining towns and sumptuous villas; and Naples, my native Naples, gleaming far, far in the distance.

Good God! was this the lovely world from which I had been excluded! I had reached that age when the sensibilities are in all their bloom and freshness. Mine had been checked and chilled. They now burst forth with the suddenness of a retarded spring-time. My heart, hitherto unnaturally shrunk up, expanded into a riot of vague but delicious emotions. The beauty of nature intoxicated—bewildered me. The song of the peasants, their cheerful looks, their happy avocations, the pictur-esque gayety of their dresses, their rustic music, their dances, all broke upon me like witchcraft. My soul responded to the music, my heart danced in my bosom. All the men appeared amiable, all the women lovely.

I returned to the convent; that is to say, my body returned, but my heart and soul never entered there again. I could not forget this glimpse of a beautiful and happy world—a world so suited to my natural character. I had felt so happy while in it; so different a being from what I felt myself when in the convent—that tomb of the living. I contrasted the countenances of the beings I had seen, full of fire and freshness and enjoyment, with the pallid, leaden, lack-lustre visages of the monks: the dance with the droning chant of the chapel. I had before found the exercises of the cloister wearisome—they now became intolerable.

The dull round of duties wore away my spirit; my nerves became irritated by the fretful tinkling of the convent-bell, evermore dinging among the mountain-echoes, evermore calling me from my repose at night, my pencil by day, to attend to some tedious and mechanical ceremony of devotion.

I was not of a nature to meditate long without putting my thoughts into action. My spirit had been suddenly aroused, and was now all awake within me. I watched an opportunity, fled from the convent, and made my way on foot to Naples. As I entered its gay and crowded streets, and beheld the variety and stir of life around me, the luxury of palaces, the splendor of equipages, and the pantomimic animation of the motley populace, I seemed as if awakened to a world of enchantment, and solemnly vowed that nothing should force me back to the monotony of the cloister.

I had to inquire my way to my father's palace, for I had been so young on leaving it that I knew not its situation. I found some difficulty in getting admitted to my father's presence; for the domestics scarcely knew that there was such a being as myself in existence, and my monastic dress did not operate in my favor. Even my father entertained no recollection of my person. I told him my name, threw myself at his feet, implored his forgiveness, and entreated that I might not be sent back to the convent.

He received me with the condescension of a patron, rather than the fondness of a parent; listened patiently, but coldly, to my tale of monastic grievances and disgusts, and promised to think what else could be done for me. This coldness blighted and drove back all the frank affection of my nature, that was ready to spring forth at the least warmth of parental kindness. All my early feelings towards my father revived. I again looked up to him as the stately, magnificent being that had daunted my childish imagination, and felt as if I had no pretensions to his sympathies. My brother engrossed all his care and love; he inherited his nature, and carried himself towards me with a protecting rather than a fraternal air. It wounded my pride, which was great. I could brook condescension from my father, for I looked up to him with awe, as a superior being; but I could not brook patronage from a brother, who I felt was intellectually my inferior. The servants perceived that I was an unwelcome intruder in the paternal mansion, and, menial-like, they treated me with neglect. Thus baffled at every point, my affections outraged wherever they would attach themselves, I became sullen, silent, and desponding. My feelings, driven back upon myself, entered and preyed upon my own heart. I remained for some days an unwelcome guest rather than a restored son in my father's house. I was doomed never to be properly known there. I was made, by wrong treatment, strange even to myself, and they judged of me from my strangeness.

I was startled one day at the sight of one of the monks of my convent gliding out of my father's room. He saw me, but pretended not to notice me, and this very hypocrisy made me suspect something. I had become sore and susceptible in my feelings—everything inflicted a wound on them. In this state of mind, I was treated with marked disrespect by a pampered minion, the favorite servant of my father. All the pride and passion of my nature rose in an instant, and I struck him to the earth. My father was passing by; he stopped not to inquire the reason, nor indeed could he read the long course of mental sufferings which were the real cause. He rebuked me with anger and scorn; summoning all the haughtiness of his nature and grandeur of his look to give weight to the contumely with which he treated me. I felt that I had not deserved it. I felt that I was not appreciated. I felt that I had that within me which merited better treatment. My heart swelled against a father's injustice. I broke through my habitual awe of him—I replied to him with impatience. My hot spirit flushed in my cheek and kindled in my eye; but my sensitive heart swelled as quickly, and before I had half vented my passion, I felt it suffocated and quenched in my tears. My father was astonished and incensed at this turning of the worm, and ordered me to my chamber. I retired in silence, choking with contending emotions.

I had not been long there when I overheard voices in an adjoining apartment. It was a consultation between my father and the monk about the means of getting me back quietly to the convent. My resolution was taken. I had no longer a home nor a father. That very night I left the paternal roof. I got on board a vessel about making sail from the harbor, and abandoned myself to the wide world. No matter to what port she steered; any part of so beautiful a world was better than my convent. No matter where I was cast by fortune; any place would be more a home to me than the home I had left behind. The vessel was bound to Genoa. We arrived there after a voyage of a few days.

As I entered the harbor between the moles which embrace it, and beheld the amphitheatre of palaces and churches and splendid gardens rising one above another, I felt at once its title to the appellation of Genoa the Superb. I landed on the mole an utter stranger, without knowing what to do, or whither to direct my steps. No matter: I was released from the thraldom of the convent and the humiliations of home. When I traversed the Strada Balbi and the Strada Nuova, those streets of palaces, and gazed at the wonders of architecture around me; when I wandered at close of day amid a gay throng of the brilliant and the beautiful, through the green alleys of the Aqua Verde, or among the colonnades and terraces of the magnificent Doria Gardens; I thought it impossible to be ever otherwise than happy in Genoa. A few days sufficed to show me my mistake. My scanty purse was exhausted, and for the first time in my life I experienced the sordid distress of penury. I had never known the want of money, and had never adverted to the possibility of such an evil. I was ignorant of the world and all its ways; and when first the idea of destitution came over my mind, its effect was withering. I was wandering penniless through the streets which no longer delighted my eyes, when chance led my steps into the magnificent Church of the Annunciata.

A celebrated painter of the day was at that moment superintending the placing of one of his pictures over an altar. The proficiency which I had acquired in his art during my residence in the convent, had made me an enthusiastic amateur. I was struck, at the first glance, with the painting. It was the face of a Madonna. So innocent, so lovely, such a divine expression of maternal tenderness! I lost, for the moment, all recollection of myself in the enthusiasm of my art. I clasped my hands together, and uttered an ejaculation of delight. The painter perceived my emotion. He was flattered and gratified by it. My air and manner pleased him, and he accosted me. I felt too much the want of friendship to repel the advances of a stranger; and there was something in this one so benevolent and winning that in a moment he gained my confidence.

I told him my story and my situation, concealing only my name and rank. He appeared strongly interested by my recital, invited me to his house, and from that time I became his favorite pupil. He thought he perceived in me extraordinary talents for the art, and his encomiums awakened all my ardor. What a blissful period of my existence was it that I passed beneath his roof! Another being seemed created within me; or rather, all that was amiable and excellent was drawn out. I was as recluse as ever I had been at the convent, but how different was my seclusion! My time was spent in storing my mind with lofty and poetical ideas; in meditating on all that was striking and noble in history and fiction; in studying and tracing all that was sublime and beautiful in nature. I was always a visionary, imaginative being, but now my reveries and imaginings all elevated me to rapture. I looked up to my master as to a benevolent genius that had opened to me a region of enchantment. He was not a native of Genoa, but had been drawn thither by the solicitations of several of the nobility, and had resided there but a few years for the completion of certain works. His health was delicate, and he had to confide much of the filling up of his designs to the pencils of his scholars. He considered me as particularly happy in delineating the human countenance; in seizing upon characteristic though fleeting expressions, and fixing them powerfully upon my canvas. I was employed continually, therefore, in sketching faces, and often, when some particular grace or beauty of expression was wanted in a countenance, it was intrusted to my pencil. My benefactor was fond of bringing me forward; and partly, perhaps, through my actual skill, and partly through his partial praises, I began to be noted for the expressions of my countenances.

Among the various works which he had undertaken was an historical piece for one of the palaces of Genoa, in which were to be introduced the likenesses of several of the family. Among these was one intrusted to my pencil. It was that of a young girl, as yet in a convent for her education. She came out for the purpose of sitting for the picture. I first saw her in an apartment of one of the sumptuous palaces of Genoa. She stood before a casement that looked out upon the bay; a stream of vernal sunshine fell upon her, and shed a kind of glory round her, as it lit up the rich crimson chamber. She was but sixteen years of age—and oh, how lovely! The scene broke upon me like a mere vision of spring and youth and beauty. I could have fallen down and worshipped her. She was like one of those fictions of poets and painters, when they would express the *beau ideal* that haunts their minds with shapes of indescribable perfection. I was permitted to watch her countenance in various positions, and I fondly protracted the study that was undoing me. The more I gazed on her, the more I became enamoured; there was something almost painful in my intense admiration. I was but nineteen years of age, shy, diffident, and inexperienced. I was treated with attention by her mother; for my youth and my enthusiasm in my art had won favor for me; and I am inclined to think something in my air and manner inspired interest and respect. Still the kindness with which I was treated could not dispel the embarrassment into which my own imagination threw me when in the presence of this lovely being. It elevated her into something almost more than mortal. She seemed too exquisite for earthly use; too delicate and exalted for human attainment. As I sat tracing her charms on my canvas, with my eyes occasionally riveted on her features, I drank in delicious poison that made me giddy. My heart alternately gushed with tenderness and ached with despair. Now I became more than ever sensible of the violent fires that had lain dormant at the bottom of my soul. You who were born in a more temperate climate, and under a cooler sky, have little idea of the violence of passion in southern bosoms.

A few days finished my task. Bianca returned to her convent, but sensible of the violent fires that had lain dormant at the bottom of my imagination; it became my pervading idea of beauty. It had an effect even upon my pencil. I became noted for my felicity in depicting female loveliness: it was but because I multiplied the image of Bianca. I soothed and yet fed my fancy by introducing her in all the productions of my master. I have stood, with delight, in one of the chapels of the Annunciata, and heard the crowd extol the seraphic beauty of a saint which I had painted. I have seen them bow down in adoration before the painting; they were bowing before the loveliness of Bianca.

I existed in this kind of dream, I might almost say delirium, for upwards of a year. Such is the tenacity of my imagination, that the image formed in it continued in all its power and freshness. Indeed, I was a solitary, meditative being, much given to reverie, and apt to foster ideas which had once taken strong possession of me. I was roused from this fond, melancholy, delicious dream by the death of my worthy benefactor. I cannot describe the pangs his death occasioned me. It left me alone, and almost broken-hearted. He bequeathed to me his little property, which, from the liberality of his disposition, and his expensive style of living, was indeed but small; and he most particularly recommended me, in dying, to the protection of a nobleman who had been his patron.

The latter was a man who passed for munificent. He was a lover and an encourager of the arts, and evidently wished to be thought so. He fancied he saw in me indications of future excellence; my pencil had already attracted attention; he took me at once under his protection. Seeing that I was overwhelmed with grief, and incapable of exerting myself in the mansion of my late benefactor, he invited me to sojourn for a time at a villa which he possessed on the border of the sea, in the picturesque neighborhood of Sestri di Ponente.

I found at the villa the Count's only son, Filippo. He was nearly of my age; prepossessing in his appearance and fascinating in his manners, he attached himself to me, and seemed to court my good opinion. I thought there was something of profession in his kindness, and of caprice in his disposition; but I had nothing else near me to attach myself to, and my heart felt the need of something to repose upon. His education had been neglected; he looked upon me as his superior in mental powers and acquirements, and tacitly acknowledged my superiority. I felt that I was his equal in birth, and that gave independence to my manners, which had its effect. The caprice and tyranny I saw sometimes exercised on others, over whom he had power, were never manifested towards me. We became intimate friends and frequent companions. Still I loved to be alone, and to indulge in the reveries of my own imagination among the scenery by which I was surrounded. The villa commanded a wide view of the Mediterranean, and of the picturesque Ligurian coast. It stood alone in the midst of ornamented grounds, finely decorated with statues and fountains, and laid out in groves and alleys and shady lawns. Everything was assembled here that could gratify the taste or agreeably occupy the mind. Soothed by the tranquillity of this elegant retreat, the turbulence of my feelings gradually subsided, and blending with the romantic spell which still reigned over my imagination, produced a soft, voluptuous melancholy.

I had not been long under the roof of the Count, when our solitude was enlivened by another inhabitant. It was a daughter of a relative of the Count, who had lately died in reduced circumstances, bequeathing this only child to his protection. I had heard much of her beauty from Filippo, but my fancy had become so engrossed by one idea of beauty, as not to admit of any other. We were in the central saloon of the villa when she arrived. She was still in mourning, and approached, leaning on the Count's arm. As they ascended the marble portico, I was struck by the grace with which the *mezzaro*, the bewitching veil of Genoa, was folded about her slender form. They entered. Heavens! what was my surprise when I beheld Bianca before me! It was herself; pale with grief, but still more matured in loveliness than when I had last beheld her. The time that had elapsed had developed the graces of her person, and the sorrow she had undergone had diffused over her countenance an irresistible tenderness.

She blushed and trembled at seeing me, and tears rushed into her eyes, for she remembered in whose company she had been accustomed to behold me. For my part, I cannot express what were my emotions. By degrees I overcame the extreme shyness that had formerly paralyzed me in her presence. We were drawn together by sympathy of situation. We had each lost our best friend in the world; we were each, in some measure, thrown upon the kindness of others. When I came to know her intellectually all my ideal picturings of her were confirmed. Her newness to the world, her delightful susceptibility to everything beautiful and agreeable in nature, reminded me of my own emotions when first I escaped from the convent. Her rectitude of thinking delighted my judgment; the sweetness of her nature wrapped itself round my heart; and then her young, and tender, and budding loveliness, lent a delicious madness to my brain.

I gazed upon her with a kind of idolatry, as something more than mortal; and I felt humiliated at the idea of my comparative unworthiness. Yet she was mortal; and one of mortality's most susceptible and loving compounds—for she loved me!

How first I discovered the transporting truth I cannot recollect. I believe it stole upon me by degrees as a wonder past hope or belief. We were both at such a tender and loving age; in constant intercourse with each other; mingling in the same elegant pursuits—for music, poetry, and painting were our mutual delights, and we were almost separated from society among lovely and romantic scenery. Is it strange that two young hearts, thus brought together, should readily twine round each other?

Oh, gods! what a dream—a transient dream of unalloyed delight—then passed over my soul! Then it was that the world around me was indeed a paradise; for I had woman—lovely, delicious woman, to share it with me! How often have I rambled along the picturesque shores of Sestri, or climbed its wild mountains, with the coast gemmed with villas, and the blue sea far below me, and the slender Faro of Genoa on its romantic promontory in the distance; and as I sustained the faltering steps of Bianca, have thought there could no unhappiness enter into so beautiful a world! How often have we listened together to the nightingale, as it poured forth its rich notes among the moonlit bowers of the garden, and have wondered that poets could ever have fancied anything melancholy in its song! Why, oh why is this budding season of life and tenderness so transient! why is this rosy cloud of love, that sheds such a glow over the morning of our days, so prone to brew up into the whirlwind and storm!

I was the first to awaken from this blissful delirium of the affections. I had gained Bianca's heart, what was I to do with it? I had no wealth nor prospect to entitle me to her hand; was I to take advantage of her ignorance of the world, of her confiding affection, and draw her down to my own poverty? Was this requiting the hospitality of the Count? Was this requiting the love of Bianca?

Now first I began to feel that even successful love may have its bitterness. A corroding care gathered about my heart. I moved about the palace like a guilty being. I felt as if I had abused its hospitality, as if I were a thief within its walls. I could no longer look with unembarrassed mien in the countenance of the Count. I accused myself of perfidy to him, and I thought he read it in my looks, and began to distrust and despise me. His manner had always been ostentatious and condescending; it now appeared cold and haughty. Filippo, too, became reserved and distant; or at least I suspected him to be so. Heavens! was this the mere coinage of my brain? Was I to become suspicious of all the world? a poor, surmising wretch; watching looks and gestures; and torturing myself with misconstructions? Or, if true, was I to remain beneath a roof where I was merely tolerated, and linger there on sufferance? "This is not to be endured!" exclaimed I: "I will tear myself from this state of self-abasement—I will break through this fascination, and fly—fly!—Whither? from the world? for where is the world when I leave Bianca behind me?"

My spirit was naturally proud, and swelled within me at the idea of being looked upon with contumely. Many times I was on the point of declaring my family and rank, and asserting my equality in the presence of Bianca, when I thought her relations assumed an air of superiority. But the feeling was transient. I considered myself discarded and condemned by my family; and had solemnly vowed never to own relationship to them until they themselves should claim it.

The struggle of my mind preyed upon my happiness and my health. It seemed as if the uncertainty of being loved would be less intolerable than thus to be assured of it, and yet not dare to enjoy the conviction. I was no longer the enraptured admirer of Bianca; I no longer hung in ecstasy on the tones of her voice, nor drank in with insatiate gaze the beauty of her countenance. Her very smiles ceased to delight me, for I felt culpable in having won them.

She could not but be sensible of the change in me, and inquired the cause with her usual frankness and simplicity. I could not evade the inquiry, for my heart was full to aching. I told her all the conflict of my soul; my devouring passion, my bitter self-upbraiding. "Yes," said I, "I am unworthy of you. I am an offcast from my family—a wanderer—a nameless, homeless wanderer—with nothing but poverty for my portion; and yet I have dared to love you—have dared to aspire to your love."

My agitation moved her to tears, but she saw nothing in my situation so hopeless as I had depicted it. Brought up in a convent, she knew nothing of the world—its wants—its cares: and indeed what woman is a worldly casuist in the matters of the heart? Nay, more, she kindled into sweet enthusiasm when she spoke of my fortunes and myself. We had dwelt together on the works of the famous masters. I related to her their histories, the high reputation, the influence, the magnificence to which they had attained. The companions of princes, the favorites of kings, the pride and boast of nations. All this she applied to me. Her love saw nothing in all their great productions that I was not able to achieve; and when I beheld the lovely creature glow with fervor, and her whole countenance radiant with visions of my glory, I was snatched up for the moment into the heaven of her own imagination.

I am dwelling too long upon this part of my story; yet I cannot help lingering over a period of my life on which, with all its cares and conflicts, I look back with fondness, for as yet my soul was unstained by a crime. I do not know what might have been the result of this struggle between pride, delicacy, and passion, had I not read in a Neapolitan gazette an account of the sudden death of my brother. It was accompanied by an earnest inquiry for intelligence concerning me, and a prayer, should this meet my eye, that I would hasten to Naples to comfort an infirm and afflicted father.

I was naturally of an affectionate disposition, but my brother had never been as a brother to me. I had long considered myself as disconnected from him, and his death caused me but little emotion. The thoughts of my father, infirm and suffering, touched me, however, to the quick; and when I thought of him, that lofty, magnificent being, now bowed down and desolate, and suing to me for comfort, all my resentment for past neglect was subdued, and a glow of filial affection was awakened within me.

The predominant feeling, however, that overpowered all others, was transport at the sudden change in my whole fortunes. A home, a name, rank, wealth, awaited me; and love painted a still more rapturous prospect in the distance. I hastened to Bianca, and threw myself at her feet. "Oh, Bianca!" exclaimed I, "at length I can claim you for my own. I am no longer a nameless adventurer, a neglected, rejected outcast. Look—read—behold the tidings that restore me to my name and to myself!"

I will not dwell on the scene that ensued. Bianca rejoiced in the reverse of my situation because she saw it lightened my heart of a load of care; for her own part, she had loved me for myself, and had never doubted that my own merits would command both fame and fortune.

I now felt all my native pride buoyant within me. I no longer walked with my eyes bent to the dust; hope elevated them to the skies—my soul was lit up with fresh fires, and beamed from my countenance.

I wished to impart the change in my circumstances to the Count; to let him know who and what I was—and to make formal proposals for the hand of Bianca; but he was absent on a distant estate. I opened my whole soul to Filippo. Now first I told him of my passion, of the doubts and fears that had distracted me, and of the tidings that had suddenly dispelled them. He overwhelmed me with congratulations, and with the warmest expressions of sympathy; I embraced him in the fulness of my heart—I felt compunctions for having suspected him of coldness, and asked his forgiveness for ever having doubted his friendship.

Nothing is so warm and enthusiastic as a sudden expansion of the heart between young men. Filippo entered into our concerns with the most eager interest. He was our confidant and counsellor. It was determined that I should hasten at once to Naples, to re-establish myself in my father's affections and my paternal home; and the moment the reconciliation was effected, and my father's consent insured, I should return and demand Bianca of the Count. Filippo engaged to secure his father's acquiescence; indeed, he undertook to watch over our interest, and to be the channel through which we might correspond.

My parting with Bianca was tender—delicious—agonizing. It was in a little pavilion of the garden which had been one of our favorite resorts. How often and often did I return to have one more adieu, to have her look once more on me in speechless emotion; to enjoy once more the rapturous sight of those tears streaming down her lovely cheeks; to seize once more on that delicate hand, the frankly accorded pledge of love, and cover it with tears and kisses! Heavens! there is a delight even in the parting agony of two lovers, worth a thousand tame pleasures of the world. I have her at this moment before my eyes, at the window of the pavilion, putting aside the vines which clustered about the casement, her form beaming forth in virgin light, her countenance all tears and smiles, sending a thousand and a thousand adieus after me, as hesitating, in a delirium of fondness and agitation, I faltered my way down the avenue.

As the bark bore me out of the harbor of Genoa, how eagerly my eye stretched along the coast of Sestri till it discovered the villa gleaming from among the trees at the foot of the mountain. As long as day lasted I gazed and gazed upon it, till it lessened and lessened to a mere white speck in the distance; and still my intense and fixed gaze discerned it, when all other objects of the coast had blended into indistinct confusion, or were lost in the evening gloom.

On arriving at Naples, I hastened to my paternal home. My heart yearned for the long-withheld blessing of a father's love. As I entered the proud portal of the ancestral palace, my emotions were so great that I could not speak. No one knew me—the servants gazed at me with curiosity and surprise. A few years of intellectual elevation and development had made a prodigious change in the poor fugitive stripling from the convent. Still, that no one should know me in my rightful home was overpowering. I felt like the prodigal son returned. I was a stranger in the house of my father. I burst into tears and wept aloud. When I made myself known, however, all was changed. I, who had once been almost repulsed from its walls, and forced to fly as an exile, was welcomed back with acclamation, with servility. One of the servants hastened to prepare my father for my reception; my eagerness to receive the paternal embrace was so great that I could not await his return, but hurried after him. What a spectacle met my eyes as I entered the chamber! My father, whom I had left in the pride of vigorous age, whose noble and majestic bearing had so awed my young imagination, was bowed down and withered into decrepitude. A paralysis had ravaged his stately form, and left it a shaking ruin. He sat propped up in his chair, with pale, relaxed visage, and glassy, wandering eye. His intellects had evidently shared in the ravages of his frame. The servant was endeavoring to make him comprehend that a visitor was at hand. I tottered up to him, and sank at his feet. All his past coldness and neglect were forgotten in his present sufferings. I remembered only that he was my parent, and that I had deserted him. I clasped his knee; my voice was almost filled with convulsive sobs.

"Pardon! oh! my father!" was all that I could utter. His apprehension seemed slowly to return to him. He gazed at me for some moments with a vague, inquiring look; a convulsive tremor quivered about his lips: he feebly extended a shaking hand; laid it upon my head, and burst into an infantine flow of tears.

From that moment he would scarcely spare me from his sight. I appeared the only object that his heart responded to in the world; all else was as a blank to him. He had almost lost the power of speech, and the reasoning faculty seemed at an end. He was mute and passive, excepting that fits of childlike weeping would sometimes come over him without any immediate cause. If I left the room at any time, his eye was incessantly fixed on the door till my return, and on my entrance there was another gush of tears.

To talk with him of all my concerns, in this ruined state of mind, would have been worse than useless; to have left him for ever so short a time would have been cruel, unnatural. Here, then, was a new trial for my affections. I wrote to Bianca an account of my return, and of my actual situation, painting in colors vivid, for they were true, the torments I suffered at our being thus separated; for the youthful lover every day of absence is an age of love lost. I enclosed the letter in one to Filippo, who was the channel of our correspondence. I received a reply from him full of friendship and sympathy; from Bianca, full of assurances of affection and constancy. Week after week, and month after month elapsed, without making any change in my circumstances. The vital flame which had seemed nearly extinct when first I met my father, kept fluttering on without any apparent diminution. I watched him constantly, faithfully—I had almost said patiently. I knew that his death alone would set me free—yet I never at any moment wished it. I felt too glad to be able to make any atonement for past disobedience; and denied, as I had been, all endearments of relationship in my early days, my heart yearned towards a father, who, in his age and helplessness, had thrown himself entirely on me for comfort.

My passion for Bianca gained daily more force from absence: by constant meditation it wore itself a deeper and deeper channel. I made no new friends nor acquaintances; sought none of the pleasures of Naples, which my rank and fortune threw open to me. Mine was a heart that confined itself to few objects, but dwelt upon them with the intenser passion. To sit by my father, administer to his wants, and to meditate on Bianca in the silence of his chamber, was my constant habit. Sometimes I amused myself with my pencil, in portraying the image ever present to my imagination. I transferred to canvas every look and smile of hers that dwelt in my heart. I showed them to my father, in hopes of awakening an interest in his bosom for the mere shadow of my love; but he was too far sunk in intellect to take any notice of them. When I received a letter from Bianca, it was a new source of solitary luxury. Her letters, it is true, were less and less frequent, but they were always full of assurances of unabated affection. They breathed not the frank and innocent warmth with which she expressed herself in conversation, but I accounted for it from the embarrassment which inexperienced minds have often to express themselves upon paper. Filippo assured me of her unaltered constancy. They both lamented, in the strongest terms, our continued separation, though they did justice to the filial piety that kept me by my father's side.

Nearly two years elapsed in this protracted exile. To me they were so many ages. Ardent and impetuous by nature, I scarcely know how I should have supported so long an absence, had I not felt assured that the faith of Bianca was equal to my own. At length my father died. Life went out from him almost imperceptibly. I hung over him in mute affliction, and watched the expiring spasms of nature. His last faltering accents whispered repeatedly a blessing on me. Alas! how has it been fulfilled!

When I had paid due honors to his remains and laid them in the tomb of our ancestors, I arranged briefly my affairs, put them in a posture to be easily at my command from a distance, and embarked once more with a bounding heart for Genoa.

Our voyage was propitious, and oh! what was my rapture, when first, in the dawn of morning I saw the shadowy summits of the Apennines rising almost like clouds above the horizon! The sweet breath of summer just moved us over the long wavering billows that were rolling us on towards Genoa. By degrees the coast of Sestri rose like a creation of enchantment from the silver bosom of the deep. I beheld the line of villages and palaces studding its borders. My eye reverted to a well-known point, and at length, from the confusion of distant objects, it singled out the villa which contained Bianca. It was a mere speck in the landscape, but glimmering from afar, the polar star of my heart.

Again I gazed at it for a livelong summer's day, but oh! how different the emotion between departure and return. It now kept growing and growing, instead of lessening and lessening on my sight. My heart seemed to dilate with it. I looked at it through a telescope. I gradually defined one feature after another. The balconies of the central saloon where first I met Bianca beneath its roof; the terrace where we so often had passed the delightful summer evenings; the awning which shaded her chamber-window; I almost fancied I saw her beneath it. Could she but know her lover was in the bark whose white sail now gleamed on the sunny bosom of the sea! My fond impatience increased as we neared the coast; the ship seemed to lag lazily over the billows; I could almost have sprang into the sea, and swam to the desired shore.

The shadows of evening gradually shrouded the scene; but the moon arose in all her fulness and beauty, and shed the tender light, so dear to lovers, over the romantic coast of Sestri. My soul was bathed in unutterable tenderness. I anticipated the heavenly evenings I should pass in once more wandering with Bianca by the light of that blessed moon.

It was late at night before we entered the harbor. As early next morning as I could get released from the formalities of landing, I threw myself on horseback, and hastened to the villa. As I galloped round the rocky promontory on which stands the Faro, and saw the coast of Sestri opening upon me, a thousand anxieties and doubts suddenly sprang up in my bosom. There is something fearful in returning to those we love, while yet uncertain what ills or changes absence may have effected. The turbulence of my agitation shook my very frame. I spurred my horse to redoubled speed; he was covered with foam when we both arrived panting at the gateway that opened to the grounds around the villa. I left my horse at a cottage, and walked through the grounds, that I might regain tranquillity for the approaching interview. I chid myself for having suffered mere doubts and surmises thus suddenly to overcome me; but I was always prone to be carried away by gusts of the feelings.

On entering the garden, everything bore the same look as when I had left it; and this unchanged aspect of things reassured me. There were the alleys in which I had so often walked with Bianca, as we listened to the song of the nightingale; the same shades under which we had so often sat during the noontide heat. There were the same flowers of which she was so fond; and which appeared still to be under the ministry of her hand. Everything looked and breathed of Bianca; hope and joy flushed in my bosom at every step. I passed a little arbor, in which we had often sat and read together;—a book and glove lay on the bench—it was Bianca's glove; it was a volume of the *Metastasio* I had given her. The glove lay in my favorite passage. I clasped them to my heart with rapture. "All is safe!" exclaimed I; "she loves me, she is still my own!"

I bounded lightly along the avenue, down which I had faltered at my departure. I beheld her favorite pavilion, which had witnessed our parting scene. The window was open, with the same vine clambering about it, precisely as when she waved and wept me an adieu. Oh how transporting was the contrast in my situation! As I passed near the pavilion, I heard the tones of a female voice: they thrilled through me with an appeal to my heart not to be mistaken. Before I could think I *felt* they were Bianca's. For an instant I paused, overpowered with agitation. I feared to break so suddenly upon her. I softly ascended the steps of the pavilion. The door was open. I saw Bianca seated at a table; her back was towards me; she was warbling a soft melancholy air, and was occupied in drawing. A glance sufficed to show me that she was copying one of my own paintings. I gazed on her for a moment in a delicious tumult of emotions. She paused in her singing: a heavy sigh, almost a sob, followed. I could no longer contain myself. "Bianca!" exclaimed I, in a half-smothered voice. She started at the sound, brushed back the ringlets that hung clustering about her face, darted a glance at me, uttered a piercing shriek, and would have fallen to the earth, had I not caught her in my arms.

"Bianca! my own Bianca!" exclaimed I, folding her to my bosom, my voice stifled in sobs of convulsive joy. She lay in my arms without sense or motion. Alarmed at the effects of my precipitation, I scarce knew what to do. I tried by a thousand endearing words to call her back to consciousness. She slowly recovered, and half opened her eyes.— "Where am I?" murmured she faintly. "Here!" exclaimed I, pressing her close to my bosom, "close to the heart that adores you—in the arms of your faithful Ottavio!" "Oh, no! no! no!" shrieked she, starting into sudden life and terror—"away! away! leave me! leave me!"

She tore herself from my arms; rushed to a corner of the saloon and covered her face with her hands, as if the very sight of me were baleful. I was thunderstruck. I could not believe my senses. I followed her, trembling—confounded. I endeavored to take her hand; but she shrunk from my very touch with horror.

"Good heavens, Bianca!" exclaimed I, "what is the meaning of this? Is this my reception after so long an absence? Is this the love you professed for me?"

At the mention of love, a shuddering ran through her. She turned to me a face wild with anguish: "No more of that—no more of that!" gasped she; "talk not of love—I—I—am married!"

I reeled as if I had received a mortal blow—a sickness struck to my very heart. I caught at a window-frame for support. For a moment or two everything was chaos around me. When I recovered, I beheld Bianca lying on a sofa, her face buried in the pillow, and sobbing convulsively. Indignation for her fickleness for a moment overpowered every other feeling.

"Faithless! perjured!" cried I, striding across the room. But another glance at that beautiful being in distress checked all my wrath. Anger could not dwell together with her idea in my soul.

"Oh! Bianca," exclaimed I, in anguish, "could I have dreamt of this? Could I have suspected you would have been false to me?"

She raised her face all streaming with tears, all disordered with emotion, and gave me one appealing look. "False to you? They told me you were dead!"

"What," said I, "in spite of our constant correspondence?"

She gazed wildly at me; "Correspondence? What correspondence?"

"Have you not repeatedly received and replied to my letters?"

She clasped her hands with solemnity and fervor. "As I hope for mercy—never!"

A horrible surmise shot through my brain. "Who told you I was dead?"

"It was reported that the ship in which you embarked for Naples perished at sea."

"But who told you the report?"

She paused for an instant, and trembled;—"Filippo!"

"May the God of heaven curse him!" cried I, extending my clinched fists aloft.

"Oh, do not curse him, do not curse him!" exclaimed she; "he is—he is—my husband!"

This was all that was wanting to unfold the perfidy that had been practised upon me. My blood boiled like liquid fire in my veins. I gasped with rage too great for utterance—I remained for a time bewildered by the whirl of horrible thoughts that rushed through my mind. The poor victim of deception before me thought it was with her I was incensed. She faintly murmured forth her exculpation. I will not dwell upon it. I saw in it more than she meant to reveal. I saw with a glance how both of us had been betrayed.

" 'Tis well," muttered I to myself in smothered accents of concentrated fury. "He shall render an account of all this."

Bianca overheard me. New terror flashed in her countenance. "For mercy's sake, do not meet him!—say nothing of what has passed—for my sake say nothing to him—I only shall be the sufferer!"

A new suspicion darted across my mind—"What!" exclaimed I, "do you then *fear* him? Is he *unkind* to you? Tell me," reiterated I, grasping her hand and looking her eagerly in the face, "tell me—*dares* he to use you harshly?"

"No! no! no!" cried she, faltering and embarrassed; but the glance at her face had told volumes. I saw in her pallid and wasted features, in the prompt terror and subdued agony of her eye, a whole history of a mind broken down by tyranny. Great God! and was this beauteous flower snatched from me to be thus trampled upon? The idea roused me to madness. I clinched my teeth and hands; I foamed at the mouth; every passion seemed to have resolved itself into the fury that like a lava boiled within my heart. Bianca shrunk from me in speechless affright. As I strode by the window, my eye darted down the alley. Fatal moment! I beheld Filippo at a distance! My brain was in delirium—I sprang from the pavilion, and was before him with the quickness of lightning. He saw me as I came rushing upon him—he turned pale, looked wildly to right and left, as if he would have fled, and trembling, drew his sword.

"Wretch!" cried I, "well may you draw your weapon!"

I spoke not another word—I snatched forth a stiletto, put by the sword which trembled in his hand, and buried my poniard in his bosom. He fell with the blow, but my rage was unsated. I sprang upon him with the blood-thirsting feeling of a tiger; redoubled my blows; mangled him in my frenzy, grasped him by the throat until, with reiterated wounds and strangling convulsions, he expired in my grasp. I remained glaring on the countenance, horrible in death, that seemed to stare back with its protruded eyes upon me. Piercing shrieks roused me from my delirium. I looked round and beheld Bianca flying distractedly towards us. My brain whirled—I waited not to meet her; but fled from the scene of horror. I fled forth from the garden like another Cain—a hell within my bosom, and a curse upon my head. I fled without knowing whither, almost without knowing why. My only idea was to get farther and farther from the horrors I had left behind; as if I could throw space between myself and my conscience. I fled to the Apennines, and wandered for days and days among their savage heights. How I existed, I cannot tell; what rocks and precipices I braved, and how I braved them, I know not. I kept on and on, trying to out-travel the curse that clung to me. Alas! the shrieks of Bianca rung forever in my ears. The horrible countenance of my victim was forever before my eyes. The blood of Filippo cried to me from the ground. Rocks, trees, and torrents, all resounded with my crime. Then it was I felt how much more insupport-able is the anguish of remorse than every other mental pang. Oh! could I but have cast off this crime that festered in my heart—could I but have regained the innocence that reigned in my breast as I entered the garden at Sestri—could I have but restored my victim to life, I felt as if I could look on with transport, even though Bianca were in his arms.

By degrees this frenzied fever of remorse settled into a permanent malady of the mind—into one of the most horrible that ever poor wretch was cursed with. Wherever I went, the countenance of him I had slain appeared to follow me. Whenever I turned my head, I beheld it behind me, hideous with the contortions of the dying moment. I have tried in every way to escape from this horrible phantom, but in vain. I know not whether it be an illusion of the mind, the consequence of my dismal education at the convent, or whether a phantom really sent by Heaven to punish me, but there it ever is—at all times—in all places. Nor has time nor habit had any effect in familiarizing me with its terrors. I have travelled from place to place—plunged into amuse-ments—tried dissipation and distraction of every kind—all—all in vain. I once had recourse to my pencil, as a desperate experiment. I painted an exact resemblance of this phantom-face. I placed it before me, in hopes that by constantly contemplating the copy I might dimin-ish the effect of the original. But I only doubled instead of diminishing the misery. Such is the curse that has clung to my footsteps—that has made my life a burden, but the thought of death terrible. God knows what I have suffered—what days and days, and nights and nights of sleepless torment—what a never-dying worm has preyed upon my heart—what an unquenchable fire has burned within my brain! He knows the wrongs that wrought upon my poor weak nature; that converted the tenderest of affections into the deadliest of fury. He knows best whether a frail erring creature has expiated by long-enduring torture and measureless remorse the crime of a moment of madness. Often, often have I prostrated myself in the dust, and implored that He would give me a sign of His forgiveness, and let me die—

Thus far had I written some time since. I had meant to leave this record of misery and crime with you, to be read when I should be no more.

My prayer to Heaven has at length been heard. You were witness to my emotions last evening at the church, when the vaulted temple resounded with the words of atonement and redemption. I heard a voice speaking to me from the midst of the music; I heard it rising above the pealing of the organ and the voices of the choir—it spoke to me in tones of celestial melody—it promised mercy and forgiveness, but demanded from me full expiation. I go to make it. Tomorrow I shall be on my way to Genoa to surrender myself to justice. You who have pitied my sufferings, who have poured the balm of sympathy into my wounds, do not shrink from my memory with abhorrence now that you know my story. Recollect, that when you read of my crime I shall have atoned for it with my blood!

When the Baronet had finished, there was a universal desire expressed to see the painting of this frightful visage. After much entreaty the Baronet consented, on condition that they should only visit it one by one. He called his housekeeper, and gave her charge to conduct the gentlemen, singly, to the chamber. They all returned varying in their stories: some affected in one way, some in another; some more, some less; but all agreeing that there was a certain something about the painting that had a very odd effect upon the feelings.

I stood in a deep bow-window with the Baronet, and could not help but express my wonder. "After all," said I, "there are certain mysteries in our nature, certain inscrutable impulses and influences, which warrant one in being superstitious. Who can account for so many persons of different characters being thus strangely affected by a mere painting?"

"And especially when not one of them has seen it?" said the Baronet, with a smile.

"How!" exclaimed I, "not seen it?"

"Not one of them!" replied he, laying his finger on his lips, in sign of secrecy. "I saw that some of them were in a bantering vein, and did not choose that the memento of the poor Italian should be made a jest of. So I gave the housekeeper a hint to show them all to a different chamber!"

Thus ends the stories of the Nervous Gentleman.

Afterword

by HASKELL SPRINGER

R ip Van Winkle" and "The Legend of Sleepy Hollow," Washington Irving's most widely loved and respected stories, appeared in
1819–20 in *The Sketch Book of Geoffrey Crayon, Gent.,* the first
book by an American author to win international acclaim. From the time
of its publication Irving became a celebrity; and by 1848, when G. P.
Putnam began issuing the volumes of the Author's Revised Edition of
Irving's complete works, the titles of these tales were such a familiar part
of American life that reviewers assumed that anyone who could read at
all had read them. Now, more than one hundred fifty years after the
appearance of *The Sketch Book,* "Rip" and "The Legend" seem so
basically American that it is hard to realize that Irving borrowed the
ideas from German sources. He so successfully transformed them that
they fit their American dress better than he could have imagined.

Anyone who has driven around the United States, and seen, in state
after state, Rip Van Winkle Motels and Sleepy Hollow Motor Inns,
realizes that the stories have become, in that superficial way at least, part
of modern America. But their great popularity and enduring appeal to
all ages, and to students of literature as well as to motel keepers, is not
explained merely by the sleepiness and dreaminess of Irving's narrations.
The stories reveal as well Irving's special ability to entertain and delight
by means of his remarkable control of the English language, combined
with his witty, perceptive insight into human nature and the American
scene.

Irving's light, genial humor has always been highly admired and imitated, and these two tales are perhaps the finest illustrations of his skill. In "The Legend of Sleepy Hollow," for example, we hear the well-modulated, kindly yet ironic voice of Irving's narrator saying, "In this by-place of nature, there abode, in a remote period of American history, that is to say, some thirty years since, a worthy wight of the name of Ichabod Crane . . ." and we smile, both at the diction and the American self-awareness. Ichabod, "though lank, had the dilating powers of an anaconda," and Balt Van Tassel "loved his daughter better even than his pipe." In such perfectly phrased comments Irving excels. And his longer passages, commenting on human quirks and eccentricities, building subtly colored word pictures of scenes and characters (such as Rip's old town and dream-haunted Catskill Mountains or the pedagogical Ichabod, whose vision is clouded by dollar signs and who dwells not in wonder but in fearful superstition) are so gracefully created that there is not the slightest strain or stumble in their wit, wisdom, and affection.

Just as engaging, and in addition a key to the timeless excellence of both stories, is what might be called Irving's technique of deliberate contradiction. Irving insists on the absolute reality of the unreal in one story, while in the other he treats perfectly rational, realistic events as mysterious and legendary. "Rip Van Winkle," whose central events (a meeting with Henry Hudson and a twenty-year sleep) are, of course, tolerantly disbelieved by the reader, is full of assertions of truthfulness. From the bland lie in the headnote about the "unquestionable authority" of Diedrich Knickerbocker's *A History of New York,* through the epigraph which asserts that "Truth is a thing that ever I will keep," until the endnote which supports Mr. Knickerbocker's tale as "an absolute fact, narrated with his usual fidelity," the story declares its literal factuality. Of course (tongue in cheek), we know we can believe these assertions because Knickerbocker himself saw an affidavit on the matter, "taken before a country justice and signed with a cross, in the justice's own handwriting. The story, therefore, is beyond the possibility of doubt" [!].

Complementing the strategy in "Rip Van Winkle" is the narrative ploy of "The Legend of Sleepy Hollow," which is to call the key events of the tale mysterious, even though the story clearly intends us to understand that Brom Bones (not the Hessian) threw the pumpkin (not his head) at Ichabod Crane. Here Irving is intentionally calling legendary something which he himself has made clear and rational. He even has his narrator, when questioned by the literal-minded doubter, state that he does not "believe one-half" of the story himself. In both stories the result of this deliberate self-contradiction is to leave the reader somewhere between the real and the imaginary. But where, and why?

When the anonymous narrator of "The Legend of Sleepy Hollow" confounds the doubting old gentleman with a false syllogism supposedly explaining his tale, or when the self-important, disbelieving man in the three-cornered hat in "Rip Van Winkle" is utterly defeated, we are all on the side of the narrator and Rip. We enjoy the skeptic's discomfort and laugh at it. But the two stories do not tell us to replace logic with fantasy. Rather, Irving's method is to mingle the two, to let one humorously contradict the other, until a sort of imaginative middle ground is established, in which we need neither search irritably for the "truth" of the matter nor relinquish completely our hold on reality for the sake of fantasy.

What Irving does is show us the value of imagination in bringing wonder and enjoyment into our logic-bound lives. The excitement and wonder in the lives of the Sleepy Hollow folk are created by that "visionary propensity" of theirs, and we ourselves should have, Irving suggests, a similar ability. For just as Rip's mountaintop encounter and long sleep do not remove him from reality forever, we all come back from excursions into imagination, and if we can, like Rip, bring back with us the fruits of that experience, or like Irving, find where reality and fantasy mix and mingle, perhaps we can supply ourselves and our rationalistic, skeptical society with an imaginative freedom it needs and enjoys.

So it has been through classic American literature, as Irving, Edgar Allan Poe, Nathaniel Hawthorne, and other fine writers have created their own imaginative borderlands and have shown Americans the creative use of their imaginations. These realms conceived by some of our best writers are really not very far from our ordinary mental geography; and these authors of ours, including Irving, have a great deal to tell us about life as we know it. Now, in fact, in the last third of the twentieth century, Washington Irving's two fine stories have a special meaning for us. The main clue to that meaning is in the return scene in "Rip Van Winkle."

After twenty years of sleep on the mountain, Rip comes home to find everything changed. The absence of his shrewish wife does not, to be sure, disturb him very much, but the whole character of the place has been altered; and to Rip as well as to the narrator (Diedrich Knickerbocker, alias Geoffrey Crayon, alias Washington Irving) this change is very disturbing. What has happened? The village has expanded and strangers abound; the old drowsy tranquillity has disappeared and the people have become "busy, bustling, disputatious"; the sedentary, patriarchal Nicholas Vedder and his small "junto" have been replaced by a "self-important," browbeating, cowardly old man who controls the opinions of the *crowd*.

Irving's whole description of the village clearly implies that the community has lost rather than gained by the transformation; and in this changed world Rip has also lost something—his very identity. Not only is he out of his time, but his son, whom we saw earlier as a little boy tagging along behind his mother, has now grown into a perfect model of Rip in his younger days, and is to the town their Rip Van Winkle. To use a term from our own day, old Rip suffers from "future shock"; the suddenness of the change has made the world incomprehensible. In his own home town Rip is a stranger in a strange land. But what has really occurred to that village in the Catskills? It has merely experienced what virtually all of America from before Irving's day to ours has known: immigration, population boom, building boom, constantly accelerating change—in a word, *progress*.

In recent times we have come to be a bit dubious about the benefits of material progress, because we have seen its frequently catalogued ill effects, from alienation to pollution. And in response to the pressures created by these results of progress, more and more we try to escape. We go to the woods and to the few small towns that somehow have managed to retain the peace and charm of an earlier day, or have been restored to give at least the semblance of a simpler, quieter life. In this we are very much like the villagers in that bustling Catskills town. To them Rip is a valuable asset: he is a storytelling link with the past, with a slower, simpler way of life. And that is one reason why Washington Irving himself is our own valuable asset. He is *our* storyteller, preserving for us the ambience of an earlier way of life in America, one we cherish more dearly the more remote and irreclaimable that past simplicity becomes.

A related scenario is played out in "The Legend of Sleepy Hollow." This time Diedrich Knickerbocker tells us the story of a would-be Yankee entrepreneur, not a Dutch dreamer. Ichabod Crane is certainly associated with "progress," and this story takes a similarly dim view of its implication. Ichabod, whose name means "inglorious," is a Connecticut Yankee who falls in love with the beautiful Katrina Van Tassel, not under the spell of her loveliness, but because of her father's wealth. He views the pewter, the china and silver, the mahogany furniture, and the other riches of the Van Tassel house, and "from the moment [he] laid his eyes upon these regions of delight, the peace of his mind was at an end, and his only study was how to gain the affections of the peerless daughter of Van Tassel." In fact, Ichabod's mind even confuses love and marriage with consumption of goods; as he sees the abundance of the Van Tassel farmyard, he conjures up mental pictures: ". . . the pigeons were snugly put to bed in a comfortable pie, and tucked in with a coverlet of crust . . . and the ducks pairing cosily in dishes, like snug married couples, with a decent competency of onion-sauce."

Irving writes one especially significant paragraph in which Ichabod is made to embody a particularly American, entrepreneurial idea of progress:

> As the enraptured Ichabod fancied all this, and he rolled his great green eyes over the fat meadow-lands, the rich fields of wheat, of rye, of buckwheat, and Indian corn, and the orchard burdened with ruddy fruit, which surrounded the warm tenement of Van Tassel, his heart yearned after the damsel who was to inherit these domains, and his imagination expanded with the idea how they might be readily turned into cash, and the money invested in immense tracts of wild land, and shingle palaces in the wilderness. Nay, his busy fancy already realized his hopes, and presented to him the blooming Katrina, with a whole family of children, mounted on the top of a wagon loaded with household trumpery, with pots and kettles dangling beneath; and he beheld himself bestriding a pacing mare, with a colt at her heels, setting out for Kentucky, Tennessee, or the Lord knows where.

Here is prefigured Daniel Boone, and a whole host of succeeding pioneers, settlers, land speculators, developers, and others with a particular kind of vision, who, like Ichabod, wanted to turn beautiful abundance into cash in order to buy more of nature's bounty and do the same once again. A sad version of the American Dream! But Irving shows us how, in fiction at least, that exploitive dream is frustrated, as Brom Bones, who values Katrina for herself, drives his rival from the scene.

Irving greatly values such victories made possible by literature, and makes them the focus of a number of his writings. Other themes and interests also recur in Irving's sketches. His preference for the "shadowy grandeurs of the past" over the "commonplace realities of the present," central to "Rip Van Winkle," is one of the most persistent. Other such prominent, repeated concerns are the delights of romance; the love of home, hearth, marriage, and children; the trials of bachelorhood; the superiority of rural to city life, and of the natural to the artificial; and the close relationship between literature and life.

Most pervasive, though, is the idea of mutability: All things must succumb to inexorable, destructive time; the familiar present will give way to the strange future; life and love are governed by the inevitability of change. With both sadness and humor Irving pursues this theme in his *Sketch Book,* and, in "Rip Van Winkle" at least, the problem is resolved happily. In light of the idea that perpetual change is the order of the world, we might reflect on the stability and security supplied us by our literature—by works such as "Rip Van Winkle" and "The Legend of Sleepy Hollow"—and writers such as Irving, whose perennial freshness and relevance permit us to communicate with the past and better understand the present. That service to the future has not been rendered by many. Washington Irving, as one of the few, deserves our respect, admiration, and gratitude.